Murder at Old St. Thomas's

Lisa M. Lane

Grousable Books

Murder at Old St. Thomas's

A Tommy Jones Mystery

© Lisa M. Lane 2022

Published by Grousable Books
ISBN: 979-8-9853027-2-1 (print)
ISBN: 979-8-9853027-3-8 (e-book)
Library of Congress Control Number: 2022901917

Cover illustration: Charles Thomas Cracklow, St. Thomas's Church, S.E. Southwark, *Views of the churches and chapels of ease in the county of Surry*, 1827. Digital image provided courtesy of Pitts Theology Library, Candler School of Theology, Emory University. Cover design: Sarah Lane Daymude. Cover font: Baskervville by Atelier national de recherche typographique, France. Map based on Reynold's Pocket Map of 1862, map font PT Serif by Alexandra Korolkova, Olga Umpeleva and Vladimir Yefimov.

Map of London, 1862

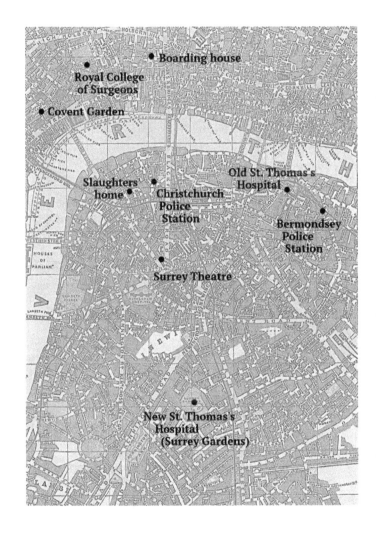

- Boarding house
- Royal College of Surgeons
- Covent Garden
- Slaughters' home
- Christchurch Police Station
- Old St. Thomas's Hospital
- Bermondsey Police Station
- Surrey Theatre
- New St. Thomas's Hospital (Surrey Gardens)

Dramatis Personae

Detective Inspector Cuthbert Slaughter
Ellie Slaughter: Cuthbert's wife, guardian of Tommy Jones
Tommy Jones: boy who lives with the Slaughters
Prudence Henderson: day maid at Slaughter household
Sir Henry Featherstone: St. Thomas's Hospital administrator
Hannah Featherstone: Sir Henry's wife, formerly Hannah Fairchild
John Addo: Sir Henry's footman
John Locke*: Liberal Member of Parliament for Southwark
Sarah Parker Redmon*: American abolitionist
Dr. William Guy*: medical superintendent, Millbank Prison
Ebenezer Farrington*: editor of magazines
Frederick Evans*: publisher of magazines
Catherine Dickens*: estranged wife of Charles Dickens
Charles Edward Pollock*: judge, Baron of Court of the Exchequer
Septimus Carver: head librarian at the Hunterian Museum
Thaddeus Morton: surgeon at St. Thomas's Hospital
Charles Woodsmith: surgeon at St. Thomas's Hospital
Sam Wetherby: dresser (surgery assistant) at St. Thomas's Hospital
Mary Simmons: nurse probationer at St. Thomas's Hospital
Felix Tapper: apothecary at St. Thomas's Hospital
Sarah Wardroper*: matron at St. Thomas's Hospital
Alfred Morris: watchman at Old St. Thomas's
Cyril Price: actor/manager of the Surrey Theatre
Geraldine Orson: star actress at the Surrey Theatre
Anthony Edwards: director at Surrey Theatre
Agnes Cook: costume designer at the Surrey Theatre
Jo Harris: magazine illustrator, friend of Ellie and Bridget
Bridget Williams: friend and housemate of Jo Harris

*historical figures

The milky glass skylight illuminated the room, casting an afternoon glow over the quiet operating theatre. Dust motes floated in the air. The room was large, with a horseshoe-shaped wooden seating area three rows deep, each row elevated above the one in front so medical students could have a perfect view of the surgery below. This made the back row high above the floor, near the skylight that comprised the ceiling.

Rails in front of each section provided not only assistance in standing and getting to one's seat on the steep rows, but also something to grip for those who might feel faint during the procedure. Eager students, thirsty for blood or angling for the clearest possible view, always occupied the front row. More squeamish students would sit higher up. But now the old hospital was closed up forever. There would be no more surgeries, no more terrified patients. Below, the double doors from the ward were closed, as was the door at the top of the back row, where students usually entered. The muted sounds of builders, hammering and carting bricks along St. Thomas's Street, could just be heard. Otherwise, it was silent.

The body sat upright in the second row of seats, staring downward. Inside the horseshoe, sawdust usually covered a slotted floor, so that blood and fluids could be collected. Now it was bare. In the middle of this area, a rectangular table was situated. Here patients would be strapped for the procedure.

It was this table on which the dead man's gaze was fixed.

1

The streets were wet, and Detective Inspector Cuthbert Slaughter moved slowly through the darkness. Gas lamps, he thought, were supposed to help this. Ahead he could see a pool of yellow light illuminating the next portion of pavement. Keeping London safe will require more than a few feeble flames, he mused. But at this hour, it was certainly better than relying on the light from people's windows.

His new overcoat felt heavy but smelled pleasantly of wet wool. He had enjoyed the evening's lecture on the criminal mind. It was important to understand how these people thought, and it was much more scientific than the phrenology lectures he'd attended as a young constable. But he'd been embarrassed, quietly, because although he had several questions to ask of the professor, shyness had prevented him. Others were happy to raise a hand, speak loudly and clearly, and not worry about looking foolish. Perhaps someone could offer a lecture on shy police inspectors, their mentality and behaviors.

He turned in to Palmer Street, toward Number 14. A nice, new house, just as he'd promised Ellie she would have when he reached the rank of Detective Inspector. The area was clean and safe, and the houses, with their steep roofs, were built in an odd northern style that appealed to him. The parlor had been kept warm because she knew it was where he removed his shoes. He didn't like wearing shoes in the house. Young Prudence had cleaned that day too, it seemed. The faded Turkish carpet was neat and squared in front of the grate. The potted plant had shiny leaves. He never could remember what kind of plant it was. Even the cushion on his wing chair had been plumped up. He hung his damp overcoat in the hall just outside the parlor door.

More tired than he should be since the lecture had come at the end of a long day, he climbed upstairs as quietly as possible. At the top of the landing, near one of his new shelves full of books, he noticed a copy of the *Penny Illustrated Paper*. Oh, dear, not again. Tommy must have brought it home from the gasworks. Ellie shouldn't read these things; they would only upset her. The lurid pictures, the breathless reporting. Tommy should know better, but he was just a lad, and Ellie treasured him. It had been Tommy's case that made him a full inspector, the trouble at the gasworks. It was lucky the boy had survived.

Slaughter undressed carefully, since Ellie was asleep, and put his clothes in the airing cupboard. Tomorrow should be easier, he thought. Honeycutt will arrive from America.

༉

"He's here, Inspector Slaughter," Constable Jones whispered. Slaughter looked up from the latest *On and Off Duty*. These days, the doings of Christian police organizations had begun to interest him.

"Why are you whispering?" he asked, suppressing a smile. Constable Jones, with his lively imagination, always added a little drama to the proceedings. He'd propped the office door open, and suddenly a very tall man appeared behind him. Jones stepped back to let him enter.

"Detective Sergeant Honeycutt," Jones announced, and in one grand movement stepped out and went about his business.

The man who entered looked even younger than Slaughter had expected. His paperwork said he was twenty-seven years old, but he looked more like twenty. And his height bordered on the ridiculous. But it wouldn't do to comment. Slaughter rose and moved from behind the desk to shake hands.

"Honeycutt," he said formally. "Nice to have you aboard. Did you have a good voyage?"

"Fairly good, sir," replied the young man.

"I hear the Great Eastern is quite a ship," said Slaughter, motioning Honeycutt to have a seat. "Seems like Brunel outdid himself before he died. Ten days from New York to Liverpool, I heard?"

"Yes, sir," said Honeycutt. "But I must say for such a huge vessel it rolled quite a bit. Lost a few pounds, I think." The man didn't look like he had much to lose.

"Well, I'm glad you're here." Slaughter realized it might take a while to get accustomed to the young man's accent. It sounded very brash, and he had an open, honest, American face, the kind that might give things away. But he knew Honeycutt was a good man.

"I have Mayor Swann's letter about you here," he said. "He recommended you highly now that the Baltimore force will return to civilian control. He said you distinguished yourself last year in the riots."

"Just doing my duty, sir." Honeycutt's gaze shifted to his shoes.

"You'll find London a bit different, I think," said Slaughter. He didn't want to ask the young man directly why he had applied to come over. The war must be causing many dislocations in America, and Baltimore was a border city between the two sides. Policing there could not have been easy. But there was a big difference between an American city of 200,000 people and London with several million. On the other hand, Lambeth and Southwark, the area covered by Christchurch station, was not that large.

Honeycutt smiled, showing straight, even teeth. Slaughter felt somewhat envious.

"I assume you'll need a day or two to get your dwelling in order, open an account at a bank, get yourself situated. I believe Constable Pearson found you good accommodations?"

"Yes, sir. I'm in Brunswick Street. Near the Rose and Crown. But sir," he said eagerly, "I don't need any time to get established. I'd be happy to start work straight away."

∽

Sir Henry Featherstone tested his new wheels first at home. He did not want to appear infirm or not in control of his chair when opening the new hospital. James Wright had done a fine job making the wheels easy to turn, even on carpet. The edge of the rug was tricky, though. He didn't want Hannah worried that any of the furnishings would be damaged.

She came sweeping into the parlor from the garden, with her hat askew and her basket full of fresh flowers.

"There you are, Henry." She leaned down and touched her cheek to his. "Is this the new chair?"

"It is indeed. What do you think?"

She stepped back, swinging the basket to her side. "I like the wide seat," said Hannah. "Might be easier for when John needs to lift you out. And the padded arm rests. Is it comfortable?"

"Not bad at all." He looked into Hannah's lovely face, flushed by the sun. So many years, and he still found her beautiful.

"I'll take it to the hospital today," he said. "I want to see how the rebuilding is progressing. They should have all the burnt material taken away by now and be almost finished with the floors and the moulding."

"Shall I go with you?" She touched her auburn hair, which was pulling out of its pins.

"No need, my dear. I know you have your callers this afternoon."

Hannah delighted in having people call. She had arranged the chairs just so. Hers was slightly taller, but the smaller chairs and settee were more comfortable. She could generously take the least comfortable seat but sit just a little bit above her visitors.

"Yes, I had hoped some ladies from the Nightingale Fund would join me, but they might be at Surrey Gardens with you."

"Not today, I think," said Henry, rolling over to the settee. He backed the chair and began the slow process of maneuvering himself over. "There is still a lot of building going on, and no one to lead a tour through."

Hannah began to arrange the flowers in the waiting vase by the window. She did not turn as Henry situated himself. He watched the sunlight catch her hair, remembering how its color had startled him when he first met her. The lovely actress, Hannah Fairchild. Never the star, but always the ingenue, the virgin, the magic princess. He'd come back to the theatre again and again, watching whatever play she was in. But no one need know her background, since now she was Lady Featherstone.

Sir Henry was in no way ashamed of his wife. Perhaps she did not always know, even now, the way a born aristocrat looks one softly in the eye. Perhaps she still used some words that were more common in Soho than here in Kensington. Her clothes, he knew, were never quite right, even though she shopped at the most fashionable places. But she was so kind, so charming to everyone they knew. And she'd pleased him in so many ways over the years.

"You look so lovely today," he said. "I do enjoy it when I'm just home with you."

She laughed. "Oh, you say that, but I know perfectly well how you love running the hospital. I don't think anyone could even think of the place without you. The Charing Cross Railway is still on people's minds, you know."

She began placing the unused stems in her basket, and fluffed up the edges of the flowers in the vase. "Your presence creates continuity at St. Thomas's, Henry, especially now the hospital has moved. You couldn't just stay home."

He smiled. It was perfectly true, but at sixty-two years old, he had thought of retiring. Even Hannah, in her early forties, would be aging. He wanted more time together with her. Taking a sip from the glass of water that was always there for him, he took a deep breath.

"I'll be off, then," he grunted, pushing himself upward and back into the chair, then wheeling toward the door. He pulled the bell on the way.

"I must make sure all three floors of the hospital are ready for the new beds. And we still need to set up the nursing school offices. See you this evening, my dear."

John, looking burly and capable, appeared at the door to help him into the carriage.

༄

"No, no, no!" shouted Anthony Edwards, slamming his script into the fifth-row seat. "You're not a petulant child. You're a royal personage who knows her husband is about to kill her."

"But I'm *distressed*, aren't I?" shouted Geraldine Orson across the gap. "Don't you want me to express that? Or is my womanly despair just too powerful for your tiny stage?"

Anthony shook his head and looked over at Cyril Price.

"Look, darling," said Cyril, easing his way down the aisle. "What you're doing is marvelous, truly marvelous. But we need to see more of that beautiful face. Try the line again, but tip your head up. Deliver to the balcony. All the way to the balcony."

"Can I be distressed, darling?" said Geraldine.

"Of course. Just be distressed to the balcony."

Geraldine tipped her head. Her face was that of a woman mourning her lost self. He'd seen the expression before, when she'd played Medea last year.

> "For never yet one hour in his bed
> Have I enjoy'd the golden dew of sleep,
> But have been waked by his timorous dreams.
> Besides, he hates me for my father Warwick;
> And will, no doubt, shortly be rid of me."

"So much better," called Anthony to the stage, then quietly, "thank you, Cyril."

"Don't despair," said Cyril. "We don't open for another fortnight. We have plenty of time. I'm going back to manage the costumes. Have Tommy get me when I'm on?"

Anthony nodded.

This will work, thought Cyril as he moved out of the aisle to the side door. We have time, and I am, after all, the greatest actor-manager in London. We will achieve this through the sheer force of my considerable talent. He brushed a thick lock of blond hair from his eyes.

Backstage there was chaos. Agnes Cook caught sight of him, her steely blue eyes peering from under heavy lashes. Pins stuck out from the band on her wrist, and her red hair fuzzed out like a halo.

"I cannot work with these people," she growled at Cyril. "They deliver the wrong fabric, charge me the wrong amount. How can I finish these on time?"

"But you will, because you are a wonderful designer and seamstress," soothed Cyril. "Every play that you have done has shined because of your work. This one will be your best ever."

"Even with the wrong fabric?" She crinkled her eyes, but there was the tiniest smile underneath.

"Even with the wrong fabric, the wrong ribbons, the wrong flowers," Cyril assured her. "No one compares to you." He leaned down and kissed her cheek. She inhaled his scent, always a bit like musk, a bit like roses.

"All right," she sighed. "For you, love. Only for you."

"And I'll check on the prices. We cannot afford much more on this one."

He entered his dressing room, pausing, as he always did, to gaze at the etching of Edmund Kean as Richard III. Cyril had been eleven when he first saw him on the stage, carried away by the powerful voice that rose fiercely in anger only to drop softly in words of love. Kean had been a magnificent actor, calculating and shrewd. He was a man with the courage to revive the tragic ending of King Lear. He was the ideal role model. But of course, he'd never managed a theatre.

✑

Jo Harris looked up from her sketch of the courtroom. Oh goodness, it was almost four o'clock. She'd never make it across town to the Women's Reform Club if she didn't hurry. Grabbing her blue cloak, the one she hoped didn't have ink stains on it, she looked around for note paper. It wouldn't do to join the meeting without both sketchbook and notepad. Snatching her hat from the bedpost, she glanced in the mirror. Wide eyes, dark hair askew, her thin lips dry from missing tea. I'm a working woman, she thought. I don't have time for this. But she remembered to lock her room and tuck the key into her bag.

It was wet outside, and she'd forgotten her umbrella. The hood of her cloak would have to do. Thank goodness her bag was sturdy leather. Her father had given it to her when she left home, and it had kept rain and dirt off her drawings for years. Jo kept her head down as she tapped quickly down the street to the omnibus stop at Holborn. It was only a mile or so to the meeting house at Red Lion Square, but the streets were muddy and the bus was faster than walking. She took a seat near the door despite the rain.

The meetings had been well-attended and inspiring lately, she thought. Must have been the speech we heard at the Exhibition in June. Sarah Parker Remond had dazzled not only the few members of the Women's Reform Club, but the entire International Congress of Charities, Correction, and Philanthropy. She'd come from America two years before and had been studying at the University of London. Her speech on slavery in America had been short and surprising. Jo had assumed that since the slave trade was outlawed, black slavery was on the decline. But she learned that in America, the war being fought was in many ways about the people still enslaved in the southern states. Miss Remond had made their misery clear enough.

In response to her speech, the Women's Reform Club had sprung into action, petitioning members of Parliament to support the Union blockade of the South. The women knew it was an uphill battle. Many M.P.s and men of business had investments connected to America. Cotton came from those southern states, produced by slaves. The war had cut off supplies to the cotton mills. Families in Lancashire were starving with the factories closing down. How could a group of women fighting to combat the evils of slavery and injustice possibly have a chance?

The subject for today, however, was the situation at Millbank Penitentiary and the frequency of insanity in the prisoner population. The club would hear a lecture by William Guy, who had conducted his census in March and would share preliminary findings. Jo was particularly interested in hearing the physical descriptions of the prisoners.

As Dr. Guy talked, she half-listened from her seat at the side. She had pulled the sketchbook from her bag quietly, and a pencil. The woman next to her shifted to give her more space as she sketched the speaker, noting the flattened patch of dark hair, the thinning whiskers, and the broad nose. He would be, she thought, in his fifties.

"I conclude," said Dr. Guy, "that the proportion of insanity among prisoners at Millbank far exceeds the proportion in the general population. Although we can assume that the criminal mind is more inclined to lunacy, there may be other factors to explain its prevalence at Millbank in particular."

Polite applause ensued, and Ellie Slaughter rose from her seat. She adjusted her skirt and turned to the audience.

"I'm sure we'd all like to thank Dr. Guy for his time and such an interesting report. We have agreed that he'll be happy to answer a few questions."

A young woman with eyeglasses raised a gloved hand and stood.

"I'd like to ask Dr. Guy whether he thinks the poor siting of the penitentiary, on marshy land, might be in any way related to the levels of lunacy?"

Dr. Guy gave a slight smile, and his mutton-chop whiskers twitched.

"An excellent question," he said. "As you know, Millbank has struggled with the cholera for exactly this reason. Our consultations with Dr. Snow indicated a problem for the prisoners' physical health, and we hope to be addressing that issue. However, we have as yet found no connection between the site of the prison and the amount of insanity."

An older woman rose.

"Dr. Guy, we have heard that the prison may resume transportation to Australia for some prisoners. Is that being anticipated?"

Guy shook his head. "No, we are hoping to avoid that, except in the most extreme cases."

Another hand. "Dr. Guy, thank you for such an interesting talk. We have heard that you are doing some work on diet and hygiene at

Millbank. Do you think this might have an effect on prisoner comfort? And might that help with behaviors one would consider aberrant?"

Dr. Guy looked pleased to be speaking to such a well-informed audience. As he launched into a discussion of his plans for hygienic practices and proper food, and the effect of these on the mind, Jo was restless in her seat. Her question was unusual. This man appeared knowledgeable, but not particularly kind. His widely set eyes gave him a look of somewhat exaggerated patience, which she had tried to capture in her drawing. She raised her hand anyway.

"Dr. Guy, we have heard that you have allowed no artists to come and draw the prisoners since you began your tenure as Medical Superintendent. Do you intend to change that rule any time soon?"

Some of the women glanced back at her. As was typical, a question about drawing from Miss Harris.

"I'm sorry to disappoint you, but no. It is my feeling that the wrong kind of visitor can be disturbing to both the prisoners and those running the system. As you know, the penitentiary was designed according to Bentham's idea of a Panopticon. The prisoners are closely watched as it is, and don't take kindly to being gazed at for long periods of time."

It's a shame, thought Jo. They would have made excellent subjects for pictures to sell to the *Illustrated London News*. At least at St. Thomas's I can draw enough to earn my keep.

2

The opening of the new hospital was a quiet affair, but Hannah Featherstone was nevertheless pleased. Sir Henry Featherstone was wheeling his way among the dozens of people on the lawn, shaking hands and smiling. She had invited all the right people from the medical community. Joseph Bazalgette, mustachioed and cheerful, was happy to attend. People kept stopping him as he walked around the grounds, asking about the new sewer system that would save the city from more cholera outbreaks. Dr. William Guy was there from Millbank Prison. John Locke, Member of Parliament for Southwark, had graciously agreed to give a short speech.

The timing had been an issue, however. Originally the opening had been scheduled for July 16th, but the complexity of preparing the wards, the nursing school, and the operating theatres all at the same time had overwhelmed the planning. Guy's Hospital, just across the street from the old St. Thomas's, had graciously agreed to Sir Henry's request that they house the patients in the interim. The old hospital would be boarded up on schedule. Hannah had hastily worked on reprinting the invitations and the notes to the press.

But now everything was ready. The wards were opened, the patients transferred. Operating equipment had been procured. Staffing was complete, with experienced Nightingale nurses on each ward, and more being trained at the school. The medical students had learned the omnibus routes and would begin attending the following week.

Locke stood at the top of the steps to the main entrance to address the group, which included the matron, several of the lecturers from the medical school, some wealthy patrons, and even a few porters. Hannah was pleased to see, from her vantage point in a seat near Locke, the surgeons. Dr. Morton, gruff as always and smoking his cigar, was shifting his weight from one foot to another. He seemed to be working his fingers in his pockets, as if practicing for something. He was the best surgeon at the hospital, but Hannah did not care for him. She preferred Dr. Woodsmith, who was standing humbly under a tree with his young wife on his arm.

Hannah rose from her chair to perform the introduction. Rather like old times, she thought, except that I am playing the wife of the director of a hospital, rather than Ophelia.

"Good day, everyone." Her voice projected beautifully across the lawn. "Thank you so much for coming. I am Hannah Featherstone, president of the Ladies' Committee of St. Thomas's Hospital. I would like to present Mr. John Locke, Liberal Member of Parliament for Southwark, always an enthusiastic supporter of the hospital." She sat gracefully to a smattering of applause.

"Thank you, Lady Featherstone." Locke bowed, then turned to face the group. His wide mouth smiled over his graying beard. "I have the honor to welcome everyone to the opening of the temporary St. Thomas's Hospital," he intoned. "It has been quite a journey to get to this point, as all of you know. I voted against the Charing Cross Railway scheme, but it may have proved to be a blessing in disguise." Several of the old staff stole glances at each other.

"A new site will soon be found, we hope nearby in Lambeth, or in the countryside. I'm sure everyone will have feelings on which they would prefer. Today, however, we celebrate the extraordinary achievement of converting Surrey Gardens to the hospital's temporary location." He gestured behind him. "What was once a large and ornate music hall, damaged by fire, is now a series of wards with hundreds of beds." He waved his hand outward. "Various other buildings have been refitted to support the fine medical and nursing schools that St. Thomas's has always boasted."

I'm so glad he agreed to do this, thought Hannah. He adds just the right note of authority and pride. Should have been on the stage.

"The matron and staff stand ready to tour you through the excellent facilities, including the operating theatres, dissection room, nursing school, hospital museum, and medical student library."

A chill wind had begun to pick up. The attendees, beginning to get restless, looked more than ready to step inside. "So, thank you again to our wonderful patrons, and to all those whose hard work has gone into preparing this excellent new hospital. May it serve our community, particularly those with lesser means, with the expertise and compassion for which St. Thomas's has always been known."

Hannah looked up at Locke gratefully and led the round of applause.

∽

Surgery dresser Sam Wetherby arrived early at the new hospital, as he always did. It was Monday morning, and the sun was peeking out from behind the clouds. He strolled past the old elephant house, under the trees, and up the steps of the old music hall. He sniffed the air as he entered through the double doors. The air smelled of floor soap, a refreshing change after the odor of char. His new shoes snapped smartly on the floor as he came into the surgeons' dressing room. His surgery coat was on its usual peg. Sam examined it closely. Yes, still clean and tidy. No need to take it to be cleaned yet.

This was not true of the other coats. Dr. Woodsmith's had only a few small dark stains on the sleeve, but Dr. Morton's had dried bloodstains on the hem and soot on the pocket. Probably from his cigars, thought Sam. It was disgusting. Had none of them read Nightingale's work? Did they think she was simply an ordinary nurse, after what she'd achieved in the Crimea? He often reminded the physicians and surgeons to wash their hands. They usually glowered at him in return. Sam's own hands were reddened from frequent washing. He put on his coat and went into the operating theatre to make sure all the equipment was ready.

The morning was occupied by tending to two surgeries, both in the same theatre, both with Dr. Woodsmith. The operations were successful, although Sam was aware you didn't know for sure until several days afterward. The twenty or so students all had a good view and took many notes. It had taken several weeks for the students to work out that anyone standing or leaning too far forward blocked the light, for themselves as observers and for the surgeons. They were accustomed to the old operating theatre, which was flooded with light from above. It was taking some time to get used to the new conditions. The space had not been built to be a hospital, after all.

Sam met Jo for tea that afternoon and immediately launched into a speech about the lack of hygiene at the hospital.

"I realize these ideas are new," said Sam, "but they do make sense, don't they?"

"They do to me," said Jo. She was sitting across the table, doodling in her sketchbook as they talked. Dear Sam, with his curl of uncontrollable hair on the very top of his head, his aquiline nose, and piercing blue eyes. He looked more like an aristocrat than most of the surgeons he worked with.

"I read the medical papers, and the journals. They must be aware of what Pasteur is doing."

"Perhaps they're not interested in putrefaction," said Jo absently. The line of his jaw was so difficult to get right.

"I've even heard that a doctor named Lister, in Glasgow, is experimenting with clean dressings for wounds. He's soaking the dressings in phenol. If it works, perhaps our surgeons will understand."

"Why," said Jo, still drawing, "can you not be a full surgeon? You read more than they do, and your hands are steadier than theirs."

Sam frowned. "For the same reason you sketch for the magazines instead of showing your work at the National Gallery," he grumbled, and stirred a third sugar into his tea.

"You're a woman?" laughed Jo.

"Not funny," said Sam, but he laughed too. He seemed to think better of his own selfishness. "On a different topic," he said, "you never showed me the sketches from last week's surgery."

Jo took her larger book from her bag and flipped to the last page. "I wasn't really close enough, sitting up there with the students. I shall need to do more work to draw their clothing and tools correctly, but I think I captured the attitudes and postures of the surgeons, and the dresser."

"That's very good! I like how the patient's head looks noble, like in a classical painting. I'm pleased I was able to talk Dr. Woodsmith into allowing you in." He smiled.

"Me too, and thank you. I could hardly have passed as a medical student," she smirked.

"Must find yourself a frock coat sometime."

"Not bloody likely."

"Will you sell this one to the *Illustrated London News*?" he asked, reaching for another sugar.

"Finish your sandwich," said Jo, slapping his wrist away.

The dressing room was untidy, with various props and costume pieces scattered about. Not for the first time did the great Geraldine Orson wonder why she was still spending her time in places like this. Not that the Surrey Theatre was bad. It wasn't. The house was a sweeping, glittering horseshoe of avid theatre goers. It was a gem of the area south of the river. The lighting had been updated, the seats reupholstered, the lobby spruced up to match anything in Soho. Cyril had done wonders.

The audience, of course, was hardly Soho quality. Here it was mostly sailors and dock workers, navvies, tanners, and publicans. The style of drama they preferred had even been given a name: transpontine. Those south of the river liked their stories intense, gory, and overblown. Melodrama of the most melodramatic kind. Heroes as noble as they came, and villains as dark as the bottom of the river. Audiences enjoyed booing and hissing, joining in the performance. And poor Cyril was trying to bring them Shakespeare. On the other hand, Shakespeare had catered to the same sort of crowd, and not far from here.

Geraldine sat at her dressing table and looked in the mirror. She was aging, certainly, but those bones! Beautiful structure, caught by the footlights, wide cheekbones framed by cascading red hair. The eyes had a little too much fire, and behind them was a weariness that cried for help. Help was there, she knew. There was even a bottle of pills in her reticule. But Felix had been cagier lately about selling her the opium. The move to the new hospital had meant a dislocation of supply, and might even lead to a firmer tallying of drugs and herbs.

The best thing would be to find him this evening as he was finishing clearing out the herb garret. She wasn't needed here. The dancers would be practicing tonight and would take over the stage to work on the funeral procession. No one would wonder where she was. Wrapping her thick cloak around her against the chill autumn evening, she stepped out the backstage door and walked around to the front of the theatre. There the carts and buggies were still clogging Blackfriars Road, right round St. George's Circus. A cab came by with lanterns lit, and she waved from under a lamp-post so he would see her.

"Where to, Miss?"

"The old St. Thomas's Hospital, please." Her voice sounded posh, and he didn't comment on the destination.

Most of the light had already faded, but she stared out the window anyway as the cab jostled around the circle and headed up Borough Road. The cabbie turned left up the causeway, then up Borough High Street, then right down St. Thomas's Street. She wondered whether it would still be called that in ten years' time. He stopped in front of the hospital church. She counted her coins before she stepped out, and reached up to pay the driver.

"Thank you, Miss," he said, tipping his hat.

Entering through the side door of the tower, she climbed the dark and narrow spiral stairs to the herb garret. Felix was there as she'd hoped, alone, carefully packing the last dried herbs into crates. He was a small man, with a fuzz of graying hair making a tonsure around the bald circle of his head. Spectacles perched on his prominent nose, he always reminded her of a startled owl. But she knew he could be devious, scheming, and unethical. It was what she liked most about him. That and the supplies he obtained for her.

"Good evening, Felix," she said in her most soothing, enticing voice.

Felix peered into the shadows until he saw her.

"Ah, Miss Orson."

The light through the garret windows was almost gone, and he'd lit a single lamp to finish his work. The pool of light under the eaves created shadows in all the corners. An interesting setting for ghosts, or a murder, thought Geraldine.

"Is the move almost completed?" She settled herself gently on one of the tall stools.

"Yes, almost." He was packing a large paper packet of an herb she didn't recognize.

"What is that?"

"Meadowsweet," he said. "Very popular. Excellent for stomach and for diarrhea."

"Oh, lovely," said Geraldine, "and knowing you, it has uses the doctors don't know about yet?"

Felix smiled, obviously flattered. "As a matter of fact," he said confidentially, "I've been prescribing it for body pain. My patients tell me it is quite helpful."

"Not as helpful as opium, I don't suppose?"

His expression changed. The look on his face was almost one of pity. But perhaps it was just the light.

"I haven't got any for you," Felix said, shaking his head. "Perhaps after the move is finished and I can tell how the books will have to be managed."

Geraldine strove to look surprised rather than despairing. "Oh? I thought the new location was already open."

"It is."

She considered making a scene where she was angry and powerful, somehow shocking him into obtaining what she needed as quickly as possible. But perhaps a more wheedling, gentle tone was needed? After all, she wasn't completely out yet, and she had a small bottle of laudanum in reserve.

"With your extraordinary intelligence, I'm sure you will find a way," she said, lowering her eyes and trying to summon a becoming blush. "I understand, of course, that the new difficulties will mean a higher price."

Felix looked at her expression and knew he was being managed. He really didn't mind. Geraldine was one of the very few people he supplied, because he genuinely admired her artistry. Many geniuses required a little extra help from the herbal world. It enhanced their creativity and added an edge to their work. But as the senior apothecary at St. Thomas's, he had to be very careful. The new conditions might cause his dispensing to be observed more closely. He was still confident that his experience and knowledge would hold sway over the younger staff, and he and Matron had an arrangement. But the surgeons had a great deal of authority.

"Yes, I'm afraid a higher price will be necessary. But you, Miss Orson, are always first on my list."

"Thank you. I know the concentration I need is inconvenient for you to make."

"Yes, but I think I can manage the thirty percent tincture, so long as I'm the one doing the measuring. Please don't worry too much. I might even be able to supply you with an actual order if you'd allow me to diagnose your ailment officially." He reached for a bowl of lavender flowers, avoiding her gaze.

"That would never do," said Geraldine, with a wave of her hand, "but I appreciate the offer." There was nothing to diagnose, she thought, and he knows that. I think I've done all I can.

"Best of luck on finishing the move," she said. "From this point, I assume I should contact you through messages to Surrey Gardens?"

"That would be best." He tried to give her a reassuring smile, but she was already rising to leave. "I hear the new play should be a success," he said. "Best of luck with it. You'll be wonderful, I know."

"Thank you, Felix," she said, as she headed for the stairs.

Young Tommy Jones had to hurry if he was going to get to the new hospital in time to help Sam set up for surgery, but he couldn't find his boots. Had Mrs. Slaughter put them somewhere to clean? He started looking under the kitchen table, but there they were, near the door. He'd left them there with mud on them from the night before, far enough from his corner bed that he didn't trip over them if he got up in the night. Strapping them on and tying the laces, he grabbed his cap and coat and ran out the back. It was a long way to

Surrey Gardens from Palmer Street, but he knew the man who drove morning deliveries. Seeing the van heading south on Blackfriars Road, he managed to jump on the back before it really got going.

Half an hour later he arrived at the hospital. Holding his cap on his head, he ran. There was no time for a detour past the elephant house. He loved it there. They did dissections there now, and sometimes he peeped through the window to watch. No one ever stopped him.

He ran around to the side door of the surgery wing, hoping, as always, that anyone who saw him would assume he was bringing a message. He did bring messages around town, in his spare time, for the gasworks or the baker on Stamford Street. He also took his broom out to sweep the Blackfriars Road crossings for ladies, so they needn't soil their skirts. Now and then he sold newspapers, and once even remedies from the apothecary's, until Mrs. Slaughter had found out they were stolen.

The side door to the surgery area was open, and Tommy was careful to wipe his boots on the scraper before he went in. Sam Wetherby didn't hold with any dirt in the surgery room unless it was tracked in by the doctors themselves. But it was too early for them to be here yet. Sam was here, though, preparing to lay out the instruments for today's surgery. It was an amputation. Tommy quietly approached.

"Good morning, Mr. Wetherby."

Sam looked up with a smile. "Ah, Mr. Jones. You're nice and early today. Bakery delivery van on time then?"

"Yes." Tommy leapt over to the sink and washed his hands. "Can I help?"

"You can indeed." Sam consulted his list. "I need a saw, the medium one with the teeth on one side."

Tommy went over to the cabinet and looked at the shelves. "I have it." He wanted to say "sir" but he knew Sam didn't like that. He even preferred "Sam" to "Mr. Wetherby," but Tommy was having trouble getting used to that idea. Sam was a surgeon's dresser, an important job, and he was at least twenty years older, Tommy figured. Informality seemed inappropriate.

"Ah," said Sam, "we're doing ether with this one. Lucky man. But it will mean a slower surgery, since it's Dr. Morton. He always takes his time when the patient's anesthetized." He put the saw on a large tray.

"Well, he can, can't he? The patient doesn't feel a thing. And the students get a closer look."

"That's true." Sam went over to the equipment drawers to find the cloths for the ether. "Trouble is, there are risks to a slower surgery. Post-operation suppuration happens more often."

Tommy was always amazed at the depth of Sam's knowledge. "What's a-supp-eration?" he asked.

"That's where the pus begins to form a few days after the surgery. Some of the doctors think that's natural and good because it brings the pyemia, the blood poison, to the surface. But often the patient dies."

"Oh!" said Tommy. He so admired Sam. "Have you been reading about this?"

"I have." Sam looked pleased. "Last month in *The Medical Times and Gazette*. A Dr. Paget, talking about treatment after surgery." He looked at his list again. "He gave a speech about shock after surgery, and how anesthesia was helping reduce shock. But the blood poison causes death. He proposed that quinine might help, but said the best influence was fresh air."

"Miss Nightingale has made sure we have that!" boasted Tommy. Sam smiled at his use of "we." Tommy was a good lad, just twelve years old, and they'd met by chance when he saw the boy looking into the dissection room before the hospital had opened. He recognized a sharp mind and ambition not unlike his own. Sam was in no position to help him in his life circumstances, but he could certainly provide information and a way to be useful.

"Now two scalpels, please, the big knife, the strap for compression, sutures, and a stack of cloths for blood." These were placed alongside the saw. "We're ready," said Sam.

"What about the ether?"

"Dr. Morton does that himself. He has the key to the cabinet."

"Why can't we do it?"

"Ether is highly explosive," explained Sam. "They only let the surgeons handle it." He admired the arrangement on the tray. "Now we just wait for Dr. High and Mighty to arrive." Tommy grinned.

3

He knew where to meet Morton, because they'd done this before. But only twice. They had first met at the gala for St. Thomas's Hospital, held at the Surrey Theatre. It had been an elegant affair, crammed into the lobby of the theatre. Jo Harris had been his companion for the evening as usual, but she had gone home early. Sir Henry had been there, of course. He'd introduced them.

"Dr. Morton, may I present our host, Cyril Price?"

"Pleased to meet you, Mr. Price," growled Morton. He didn't look pleased to meet anyone.

But he had taken his cigar from between his full lips and held out his hand. Cyril felt his power hit like a body blow. His hand was enclosed in a hot embrace, but the piercing brown eyes didn't indicate anything amiss.

"Excuse me," said Sir Henry. "I've just spotted Baroness Horton, one of our most important patrons." He turned and wheeled off across the lobby carpet, leaving them alone.

"Firm grip," said Cyril, trying not to sound breathless. "Is that so you don't lose your scalpel during surgery?"

Morton looked up into Cyril's blue eyes with some interest.

"Indeed," he said. Realizing he still held Cyril's hand, he dropped it, but continued to hold his gaze.

"Yours are too soft," said Morton more quietly. When he dropped his voice, it took on a low, sonorous quality. Cyril felt himself slipping. A wave of erotic need washed through him. He felt profoundly foolish as he resisted an impulse to drop to his knees. Surely this gruff man wasn't . . . ?

He is, Cyril thought, and he may not even know it. He pushed back a lock of hair from his forehead and tossed his scarf more fully over his left shoulder. Regaining his trained acting voice, he said, "How long have you taken an interest in the theatre?"

"I haven't," said Morton. "Still don't. I'm here because Henry wanted me to be here, to support the hospital move." He placed his cigar between his lips and looked at Cyril, noting his hair, his scarf, the cleft of his chin. Healthy, he thought. Good surgical risk. And such smooth skin. Powerless, he thought. Easy to humiliate. He liked that.

Morton realized he was staring and lowered his gaze. "Have you been to the new hospital grounds in Surrey Gardens, Mr. Price?"

"No," said Cyril, wondering whether this could be an invitation. "No, but I used to frequent the place when it was a pleasure garden," he volunteered. Everyone knew what happened in the dark corners of the pleasure garden. The term was appropriate. At least I've let him know, Cyril thought.

Morton looked surprised. He lifted a bushy eyebrow, and his eyes darkened. Excellent subject for dramatic study, thought Cyril. He's gone suddenly mercenary. He knows his own power. Cyril felt weak in the knees again.

"The hospital will open in a few weeks," Morton said. "I could give you a tour of the place, if you like. Shall I send for you?"

Oh please, Cyril thought. Please send for me. "That would be delightful, when you have the time," he said.

Morton had sent for him, just two days later. The hospital was not yet open, the note said. But let's meet in the gardens. After your Saturday performance, at the elephant house. It was more like a command than an invitation. Cyril had trouble keeping his mind on the performance that Saturday.

"What do you say, duckie," said Agnes as he had changed into his street clothes, "to drinks over at the Three Georges? It's only midnight." Her heavy lashes batted at him.

"Not tonight, my love. I'm off to an appointment." He had put on his blue paisley scarf, looked in the mirror, yanked it off, and switched to the red silk.

"Oh, I see. A hot one, eh? Well, tell her she's the lucky one." Agnes grinned.

Cyril twinkled his eyes at her. "Can't fool you, can I, love? You're right. Wish me luck."

"You don't need luck with a new girl," she said, pecking his cheek. "Everyone wants a kiss from the hero."

Much too edgy to walk, he had taken a hansom to Surrey Gardens. It was an unexpected luxury, but he had been feeling luxurious. He'd been let off at the gate and had walked to the elephant house. It was dark and quiet, a warm August night. Dissections were done in this building now, but no one was there at this hour. Old trees gently swayed above him. The stone marker was still there from the old gardens, but it was hard to read in the dark. He had seen some light from the old music hall, but this area of the grounds was in almost complete darkness. Cyril had looked around, trying to adjust his eyes. He leaned forward onto the stone marker, feeling the raised words with his palms and trying to quiet his rapid heartbeat.

"Perfect," a growl had come from behind him. "Quite perfect." Cyril had started to turn, but a hard, experienced hand had taken hold of the hair near the back of his neck. "No need to turn round." Morton's hands had been hot as he reached round to unbutton Cyril's trousers and began to stroke his hips. "So smooth," he had murmured, as he pushed Cyril forward onto the stone. Oh my God, Cyril had thought. Oh my God.

That had been six weeks ago. Now Cyril approached the marker again. He had walked this time from the theatre, his mind in tumult from the combination of need and humiliation. The chill October breeze was picking up, and he passed a few workers going to and from the hospital. Why had he answered the summons again? He was the greatest actor in London, the envy of many men with hungry wives. He could not even say he liked this man, this brilliant surgeon. Indeed, he suspected that Morton's intense power came from a certain brutality. And he felt sure that he was only wanted after particularly difficult or dangerous surgeries. Morton celebrated by reveling in his own genius and needed Cyril as an outlet for it. But Cyril was an artist, and emotion was food for the artist. The feelings of horror, and desire, and powerlessness were divine, deep, and sincere. He wanted to feel them again, and again. He stepped into the quiet shadows next to the elephant house, rested his hands on the marker, listened to the cool wind blow through the trees, and waited.

"Perfect," came a low voice, "quite perfect."

"I heard," said Ellie Slaughter, "that Elizabeth Garrett got admitted into the Worshipful Society of Apothecaries."

She, Jo, and Bridget were enjoying a sunny mid-day repast in Red Lion Square's garden, near the Women's Reform Club.

"That doesn't sound likely," said Bridget, taking the sandwiches out of the basket.

"The whole thing is so sad," said Jo. "Here she studied so hard for the medical qualification, then London University refused to allow her to sit for the examination."

"I heard," said Ellie, "that it was the chancellor's own vote that decided it."

"That's disgraceful," said Jo, as Bridget handed her a bottle of beer. She looked around. No one in the square would notice, she was sure.

"So what makes you think she was admitted to the Apothecaries?" asked Bridget, squinting a little against the sun. She'd removed her hat.

"Tommy told me," she said. Jo and Bridget looked at each other. Ellie certainly had a soft spot for the lad. "He keeps up on the medical gossip."

"Did he give any details?" Jo took a bite. Ham and pickle. Very good. Bridget knew food, and everything she made was delicious. Jo had been very lucky they'd become friends at the boarding house.

"He did," said Ellie, digging in the basket for a serviette. "Apparently there was a problem with their rules. There was nothing in there about women being prohibited, or even the word 'man' in the standards and regulations. She claimed they could not keep her out, and they had to let her in."

"I'm so glad," said Jo. "If that's true, there's hope for women as doctors."

"She'd be the first one!" said Bridget happily.

"Well . . . maybe," said Jo.

"Whatever do you mean?" said Ellie. "We would know if there'd been another woman doctor in this country."

Jo took a sip of beer, then removed her hat to get some sun on her face. She smiled enigmatically.

"You may know my cousin was a nurse in the Crimea, with Florence Nightingale?"

The other women nodded.

"She witnessed one of the doctors, James Barry, having an argument with Miss Nightingale. She wasn't sure what it was about, but at one point Dr. Barry was getting very forceful, yelling at her in his squeaky voice. She said it was quite hard to listen to. He was such a famous figure, Inspector General of all the military hospitals. Miss Nightingale had no choice but to back down. But my cousin, she has a gift for seeing the truth about people. She thinks Dr. Barry is really a woman."

"That's not possible," said Bridget with a cry. "He's known to everyone! He made more difference to improving conditions for soldiers than even Miss Nightingale."

"Besides," said Ellie, "he's retired now, respectably. And he's over seventy!"

"Well, he wasn't then," said Jo. "Mabel says he never dressed with the other doctors, even when they were all in tents in the Crimea. And he was so small, and all those pretty blond curls . . ." She left the sentence hanging.

"I'll never," said Bridget. The day was getting warmer and the traffic near the square was getting louder.

"I'm glad about Elizabeth Garrett, though," said Jo, as she put on her hat and wrapped up the remaining half of her sandwich. "We should have her come and speak at the Club, shouldn't we?"

"Excellent idea," said Ellie, as Bridget packed up the basket.

"Off to work," said Bridget. "Mr. Pratchett, World Famous Photographer, All Subjects, does not like to be kept waiting." She'd freckled a bit in the sun.

"Me too," said Jo, dusting off her skirt as she stood. "I'm due at the Old Bailey. A woman stands accused of murdering her husband with poison. I do hope she's not too pretty to make a good subject."

❧

Tommy bounced through the stage door just before lunch time. Opening night was tonight, and he knew his skills would be needed. Only yesterday he'd spent the afternoon north of the river, handing out printed flyers to passers-by in Covent Garden. He was careful not to be spotted by anyone from the Theatre Royal. Although it had been a decade since the Theatre Act, the old patent theatres didn't like competition. And he was, after all, trying to pull their audience southward.

Today he knew he should work closer to St. George's Circle, and northward along Blackfriars Road. He wanted to stop in at as many public houses as he could and pass among the workers on their lunch time. He knocked on the door of the dressing room marked "Cyril Price."

"Ah, there you are, Tommy," said Cyril. He was a little frantic, but was trying hard to exude calm in the presence of his young volunteer. "The flyers are in that box. Would you mind coming back after lunch and getting out the glue pot? Some of the posters in front are already peeling off at the corners."

"Of course, Mr. Price—happy to," said Tommy. He paused for a moment, watching Cyril jot a few notes in his script. "You're going to be wonderful tonight, Mr. Price. Just like Edmund Kean!" He ran off with the flyers, banging the door behind him.

"Just like," murmured Cyril, as he readjusted the jostled mirror.

The afternoon passed at enormous speed. Despite weeks of rehearsal, it was as if someone had rung a bell. Every last-minute thing had to be done now. Agnes had completed the funereal flowers and veils for the first scene with Lady Anne. Cyril's hunchback had been sewn securely again into his doublet, after the crisis of yesterday. Richard III simply could not have his hump fall off in mid-speech. "My kingdom for a hump," mumbled Cyril to himself.

The set workers were waxing the tracks for the walls to be pushed on and off stage. Another disaster there had narrowly been averted when the top string broke on one of the segments, and it had leaned dangerously downstage. One of the more alert actors playing a courtier had managed to sidle upstage and hold it up bodily until the scene was finished. Oh, that's right, thought Cyril, I must check on George, who was playing Buckingham, and make sure he's gotten over that bad oyster from last night. Cyril headed off, just avoiding a cart of props coming across to the other wing.

The crowd seemed quite well-behaved, considering it was Friday night and more than a few of them had spent the last hour in the pub up the road. They filled the large semi-circle, admiring the enormous chandeliers and the dramatic gas lighting. Critics of transpontine theatre noted with disdain the roughness of the attendees, but Cyril loved them. They entered the theatre in awe, and it was the acting and the story that stirred them into participation. He hoped *Richard III* was a good choice for patrons accustomed to melodrama. Richard was a perfect villain, but there wasn't really a hero. Cyril had tried to boost Buckingham's role, and directed George to deliver his lines in a way that might engender a cheer or two. The ghosts would help near the end, and the crew were ready with the trapdoors and the smoke to make them especially spooky. Geraldine could certainly be horrifically ghostly when she wanted to.

Cyril knew his lines, had known them since he'd been Tommy's age. He gave his eyebrows a last smudge of kohl and shrugged into the lumpy jerkin.

෴

It was the first anniversary of Nan's death, and Jo was feeling it deep inside herself. She'd lit a candle in her room and laid beside it the old book of poetry. It was a volume of Eliza Cook's *Melaia and Other Poems*. Jo wanted to read and remember, especially their favorite, "A Love Song":

I do not promise that our life
       Shall know no shade on heart or brow;
For human lot and mortal strife
       Would mock the falsehood of such vow.
But when the clouds of pain and care
       Shall teach us we are not divine,
My deepest sorrows thou shalt share,
       And I will strive to lighten thine.

Nan was no longer here to lighten Jo's sorrow. Jo reached under the bed and took out last year's sketchbook to look at her drawing, the one she'd done last October, a week before Nan died. Nan looked back from the page. She'd been wearing her nursing school pinafore, dressed as one of Miss Nightingale's troops against the demons of poor hygiene and slovenly patient care. Jo had worked to capture the expression on her face. The day had been cool, and the light subtle. She remembered asking her to look toward the window, but Nan had refused.

"Jo, I'd so much rather look at you. I love the look of concentration when you draw."

She had given that lovely smile, the one that twisted Jo's heart. It was a look of such love and sympathy that it would be hard to describe, yet Jo had captured it in her drawing. Most of the time, she couldn't bear to look at it. The old sketchbook lived under her bed. But now and then she wanted to see her, to remember how much they'd meant to each other. To recall the days when their doors to the corridor had been kept open and they lived in each other's rooms. Days of work and school, evenings in the parlor downstairs, nights sometimes together in Jo's bed. No one in the boarding house seemed to notice, or care.

Sam hadn't noticed either. He'd liked them both but was in love with Nan. She'd come back to the boarding house with stories of how Sam had taken her to lunch, or how they'd chatted sitting outside the nursing school. For her 25th birthday, he'd even bought her a small pin with an ouroboros, a snake eating its own tail. It had been an electroplated version of the ring Albert had given to the Queen, a symbol of both health and endless love. Jo, who was more experienced, knew it was only a matter of time before he asked Nan to marry him. She knew her time with Nan would end, that Nan would move on to become both an official nurse and the wife of a surgeon's dresser who might someday be a surgeon himself. She'd been ready to cry about that. She was prepared for years of pretending to be just a friend, so she could share in Nan's life. She was not prepared for her death.

"Oh, Nan," she said to the smiling picture. "I wish your foot hadn't been hurt. I wish you hadn't wanted to be a test patient. I wish Sam had taken you away before that happened."

There had been only one family member to contact, a cousin, so Jo had been spared spreading the news as her closest friend. But Sam had grieved so deeply, and it was natural to share the grief with him. A year later their friendship was, she felt, natural, almost like brother and sister. He would understand the candle, if not the drawing. He must be feeling the pain as well tonight. Jo hugged the sketchbook to her chest, and began to cry.

4

Alfred Morris mopped the floor slowly and contentedly. It was Monday morning. The builders had left on Friday, finished with boarding up the attic areas and the main door to the street. With no need for the charwomen to come and clean anymore, Alfred could be on his own, just tidying the space. He liked that there was no one looking over his shoulder, especially now that his painful hip made him so slow. And he had Saturdays off for a change. It didn't really matter. He'd keep the floors clean enough so the builders could finish closing the place down. The dust and dirt from the railway construction wouldn't be able to get in. Maybe someday this space would be used again for something.

He was happy to have a job, although he was sad that the hospital had to close. St. Thomas's Hospital had been here, just off the Borough High Street, for centuries. Innumerable patients, many of them poor and treated with charity, had been helped or cured, or had died here. Lives had been saved, especially in those butchering rooms they called "operating theatres." Doctors had been trained; nurses had been schooled.

Alfred couldn't begrudge the trains, though. He felt they were the future, the progress of mankind. And if a few old buildings had to be torn down in their wake, so be it. Such things were for others to think about, people with an education. All he knew was that the railway had bought the land, right up to the side wall of the ward. You couldn't have trains running past the windows of people who were ill, could you? So the hospital administrators, they'd considered dozens of possible sites, including the old Bethlehem Hospital, or building a permanent new hospital from the ground up. Whatever they decided wouldn't be ready for years. The music hall and the zoological buildings at Surrey Gardens would do for now. The patients had all been moved. It was strange to think of them lying where all those animals had been. He'd heard the cholera ward was in the old giraffe house.

A pile of lumber had been left in front of the lower door to the operating theatre, right outside the women's ward. Alfred carefully stacked it neatly by the side wall. He noticed light coming through the crack between the big double doors to the theatre. Surely that should be closed? They would be boarding up the entire theatre next week.

Alfred opened the big doors slowly, spooked as always by the theatre. It was very bright in the mornings because the ceiling was made of windows. Frosting on the windows meant the light came in evenly and steadily. Students and young doctors sitting in the theatre seats could clearly see the surgery from above. No artificial light, with its flickering and shadows, was ever needed. He gingerly entered the space where patients had been wheeled in, looking down at the floor. It was spooky too, with the boards still in place and the thick sawdust underneath. The sawdust collected the water when the floor was mopped, but by the end of a surgery it was already saturated with blood. Alfred did not like theatre cleaning duty, but he never had to do it himself. Working in the hospital for over twenty-five years had some privileges.

He didn't see the man right away, as his eyes adjusted to the brightness. But there he was, sitting upright on the second row of seats. He was dressed like a gentleman and seemed to be staring downward at the operating arena. But he wasn't moving at all. Alfred gulped, and blinked.

"Sir?" he said. His voice echoed in the large space. There was no answer. Alfred had seen a lot of death in his time at the hospital. There was no question this gentleman was dead.

❧

"I'm not sure I understand, sir." Honeycutt had grabbed his coat and was following a fast-moving Inspector Slaughter out the door. "I know I've only been here a week, but wouldn't this be a case for the Bermondsey Police Station?"

"Yes, normally," said Slaughter, as he hailed a cab. "But not in the case of murder."

It had been a busy week for Mark Honeycutt. He had unpacked his trunk and his few cases at the flat, then stopped by the Rose and Crown to acquaint himself with the area. He had not quite been expecting the amount of traffic in London compared to Baltimore and was glad he'd chosen lodgings so close to Christchurch station. Detective Inspector Slaughter had been friendly, if a bit distant. The station was large, and it seemed that everyone was always asking the inspector for approvals. The hierarchy seemed a bit firmer here. As the only Detective Sergeant, Honeycutt was assigned directly to Slaughter, and he had already learned to field questions, access the correct forms, and direct inquiries to the appropriate offices. So far, he'd only handled robberies, which seemed to be uncommonly frequent in the area. He'd made sure to lock certain items inside his trunk at the flat.

The cab stopped. "Old St. Thomas's Hospital, please, quick as you can."

The two men got in, Honeycutt awkwardly folding his body into the enclosed space and struggling with the door. He looked at the latch. The latch should be to the right, he thought.

"Bermondsey is the nearest station," the inspector explained, "but they don't have a Detective Inspector on staff. Christchurch does. Me."

Honeycutt shifted in his seat. In the last week, he had become accustomed to the plain clothes he wore as a Detective Sergeant. But he had not yet adjusted to not having a gun; his jacket felt awkwardly weighted somehow. He pulled the note out of his pocket.

"The message just says, 'suspected felonious homicide, Old St. Thomas's Hospital,'" said Honeycutt. "It's signed Sergeant Cummings. Do you know him?"

Slaughter sighed. "Yes, I do. He's been asking for a Detective Inspector for over a year. He tried to get promoted himself, but it didn't work out. Something about French."

"French, sir?"

"Yes, the Superintendent wants educated men for the rank of Detective. At least one foreign language." Honeycutt wondered whether "American" counted.

The cab swayed suddenly, and the two men looked out as they passed a cart stopped in the middle of Union Street. The horse lay expired as three men argued with each other in at least two languages.

Ellie wasn't going to like this, thought Slaughter. Murder investigations can take quite some time. But he could feel his heart beating faster. A murder. A challenge, and some real detection work. But then, there might be important people to interview. Talk to. In person.

Sergeant Cummings of Bermondsey Police Station was standing in front of the church tower at Old St. Thomas's, an impatient expression on his face. Slaughter and Honeycutt alighted from the cab. Honeycutt turned to pay the cabbie.

"How much?" he asked.

"That'll be sixpence, guv'n'r. Just like the rule says." He gave a gappy smile.

Honeycutt took a handful of coins from his pocket. Sixpence. Sixpence. Smaller than a shilling . . . oh, good, it said six pence on the back.

Slaughter approached Cummings near the door and held out his hand.

"Bonjour," said Cummings wryly. Slaughter responded with a weak smile.

"We have a good one for you this time," Cummings said, as he waved Slaughter ahead of him to the spiral stairs. "You'll find this faster than going around to the other side."

Slaughter ascended, hoping the trailing Honeycutt would know to duck his head.

"This way," said Cummings, walking across the herb garret. His steps echoed on the wooden floor. A constable, standing guard at the top, nodded to the inspector.

Cummings pointed to a door on his left as he passed it. "This would be the way into the operating theatre for the medical students. But I think you'll want to see it first from here." A ramp led down to the bottom, where the patients were wheeled in. An older man with a broom stood near the door.

"This is Alfred Morris, the watchman. He found the body. Morris, this is Detective Inspector Slaughter. He'll have some questions for you shortly."

"Good afternoon, Detective Inspector." Morris followed the two men into the operating space.

The light was clear and bright in the empty theatre. Slaughter immediately saw the body seated in the second row up from the surgery floor. The dead man's head was tipped downward slightly, as if he were looking at the spot where they stood. The inspector glanced around. They were right where the surgery table would be, if it were still there. Now it was just a table the builders were using.

Slaughter frowned. "What's holding him to the seat?" he asked Cummings.

"A board that's firmly nailed to the bench. It's pushed up the back of his waistcoat to hold him upright."

Slaughter nodded, then turned to Alfred.

"I have heard you're the watchman? Does that mean you keep watch, like a guard?"

"Not really, sir," said Alfred. "It means I keep the space clean. Like watching out for everyone, if you know what I mean."

"The place looks almost empty."

"Yes, sir." Alfred leaned slightly on the broom. "We're closing up, you see. The hospital's up and moved to Surrey Gardens."

"Oh, yes. I heard about that. They're all removed, then?"

Alfred shifted his weight. "Almost, sir."

"I'm sorry, Mr. Morris," said Slaughter. "Would you like to sit down? You look a little pale."

The older man looked grateful and shuffled over to the bench near the double doors.

"Thank you, sir. It's all been a bit of a shock."

"I understand. So tell me what happened."

"Well, sir, I was here tidying the space. I was going to move that stack of wood there." He pointed to the lumber just outside the doors. "The builders will be coming back to board up the theatre soon, so the doors should have been closed. But when I came round, I saw the doors were open. Then I looked in, and there he was."

"Did you know he was dead?"

"Oh, yes, sir. I've seen quite a bit of death in my time."

"I'm sure you have," said Slaughter. "What time did you arrive this morning?"

"Nine-thirty, sir. I don't have to come in so early now that we're moving."

"And about what time did you open the doors and see the body?"

"About a quarter of an hour after that, sir."

"Then what did you do after you saw him?"

"I knew better than to touch him, sir. I thought it would be wise to put a piece of lumber to hold the doors closed, and then I went out to find a constable at the station."

"Excellent." He then asked the obvious question, preparing himself for the mystery of identifying the victim. "Do you know who the dead man is, Mr. Morris?"

"Oh, yes, sir." Alfred perked up considerably. "It's Dr. Morton, sir. The famous surgeon."

⤳

Since the Southwark Coroner's office had jurisdiction over both St. Thomas's and Christchurch, the body would be taken just a few hundred yards to London Bridge.

"I think my boys can manage that," said Sergeant Cummings in an undertone. He sent a constable back to the station to arrange things, and asked Detective Inspector Slaughter if he was ready to go downstairs.

"Not just yet," said Slaughter. Walking out the double doors, he went up the ramp to the medical student entrance at the top of the theatre. Steps connected the different levels, so students could all see the surgeries. Approaching the body from behind, he could see the wooden stake holding it upright. Lifting Morton's jacket slightly, he noted it was just an ordinary piece of lumber, rather like the pieces he had seen out near the patient entrance. The nails had been firmly driven in, by a sure hand. The body did not seem stiff, so either rigor mortis had not set in, or it had already passed. He felt along the jacket and trouser edges for contents in the pockets, but didn't feel anything. He reached inside the pockets to be sure. In one of the jacket pockets his fingernail snagged on something, a small paper caught in the edge of the seam inside. Slaughter tugged it out gently. It looked like a handmade ticket or pass of some sort, blue with a tear across it. The date was smudged but legible: 28th of August, 6:00 PM.

"Is it all right to collect the body, sir?" asked a constable.

"Yes, that's fine. I've seen all I need to here."

He stood and watched as the constables removed the plank, wrapped the body in a clean sheet, and struggled to carry it across the aisle and down the theatre steps. Honeycutt was behind him. Slaughter had forgotten he was there.

Handing him the ticket, he asked, "What do you make of that?"

"Not sure, sir," said Honeycutt, "but I'll ask Mr. Morris if he recognizes it."

Outside in the inner courtyard, the corpse was placed on the cart as they watched. Morris had come out with them. He shook his head at the blue paper. "Nothing I've ever seen," he said.

"I may need to look around the site a bit more later," Slaughter said to Morris. "I don't want you to clean anything in the garret or in the whole theatre area. Does that cause you any problems?"

"Not at all, sir," said Morris. "There's plenty else to do. Shall you be talking to Sir Henry about the builders? That they're not to come next week?"

"Yes, we'll take care of that. You have the keys, though?"

"Oh, yes, sir. You can reach me here or at home. I don't live far." He gave Slaughter an address in Maze Pond.

"I'll go back to the station," said Sergeant Cummings, "if you don't need anything else. Very busy there, we are. Even without an Inspector."

"I'm sure," said Slaughter. "Thank you for all your help." He turned to Honeycutt. "I'd like to walk back, if you don't mind," he said, looking up at the sky. It was only a bit cloudy, not at all bad for October.

"Of course, sir. Shall I accompany you?"

They walked across the courtyard, coming out at Borough High Street.

"It's a shame St. Thomas's had to move," said Slaughter. "It's been here for over a hundred years, serving those in need. They weren't able to negotiate a large payment from the railway, either. Just over 250,000 pounds. Not enough to even refurbish Surrey Gardens, much less build a new hospital."

Honeycutt nodded.

"But Surrey Gardens will give them a chance to modernize, won't it, sir?"

"Modernizing isn't always a good thing," said Slaughter. "Things advance, but other things get lost."

"A bit old-fashioned of you, sir, if I may say so." He looked over at Slaughter, but there was no sign of consternation on his face, just attention, so Honeycutt continued. "In America, people are always looking for new ways to do things. They're building tracks connecting the railroad across the whole country, with telegraph lines alongside. Soon people will be able contact each other between the east and west coasts, do business, and expand. It could take the place of posted letters, which take weeks."

"I wonder," said Slaughter, "whether the speed of communication will change what people say to each other. How much can they say in a telegraph message?"

"Not as much as in a letter," Honeycutt conceded. "At least not yet, while it costs so much. But who knows what else is coming?"

They were walking past a bookshop, and Slaughter's step slowed. He glanced at the book cart on the pavement. "Why don't you return to the station, Honeycutt. I'll stop in here for a bit, and meet you later."

Honeycutt looked confused, but nodded. "Right you are, sir."

Slaughter stepped into the shop. He was half-thinking he'd look for a book on the old hospital, or maybe something on the criminal mind, but this was just an excuse. He loved books. He always had, even as a boy when his father would borrow some for him from the Mechanics' Institute library. He couldn't afford any as a young man. But two things had happened to change everything. He had become an Inspector, with a better salary, and the government had finally repealed the printing tax. Print was everywhere now. Pamphlets and books cost pennies. Not everyone could read, of course. Schools were for middle-class families like his own, and he was grateful that his father had been a respected manager at the gasworks for all those years. He often walked by people reading aloud to others. Newspapers, journals, and magazines with shocking stories.

He picked up a book by Aristotle, taking a look inside. Rhetoric. What makes a speaker persuasive: "Persuasion is achieved by the speaker's personal character when the speech is so spoken as to make us think him credible. We believe good men more fully and more readily than others..." Might be useful. Many murderers, he'd found, were likable and persuasive. He handed over sixpence and took the book with him.

∽

Tommy launched into his dinner plate, but his eyes never left Slaughter.

"He was nailed to the seat? How?"

Ellie glanced at her husband. Really, such a discussion at dinner. But Slaughter saw no reason not to inform the boy. He was interested in so many things.

"Not exactly nailed to the seat," said Slaughter, carefully slicing his pork. "A piece of wood was nailed down, and the length went up the back of his clothing."

"Why do you think he was sat up like that? What did he die of? Why at the old operating theatre?" Tommy shoveled more potatoes into his mouth between questions.

"Cubbie, perhaps we could continue this discussion after dinner?"

"Of course." He smiled at his wife, poured himself a glass of water from the pitcher on the table, then poured one each for Ellie and Tommy. "Tommy, what did you do today?"

Tommy looked over at Ellie. Well, all right. He supposed such a topic was not for women's ears anyway. He swallowed his mouthful and took a gulp of water.

"The usual things. I took more flyers for the Richard play up to Commercial Road, then I got a few pennies for helping the brick layers up near London Bridge move things for the railway. But then the foreman said how I couldn't work coz I wasn't offi-cial, so they had to let me go. But that was all right, since it was after they'd fed all us boys pies for lunch. Oh, and I helped with the floor they're laying in at the Rose and Crown. Got thrupence for that too." He dug in his pocket and laid the pennies on the table.

"Right you are," said Slaughter. He reached over and got the three tin boxes from the sideboard. "Now how many go in each?"

Tommy frowned and thought. "Well, I think I should do half for schooling." He put three pennies in one box with a clink. "And one for new boots." Clink. "And one for Sunday roast." Clink.

There were still two pennies on the table. Tommy scooped his last pork and potatoes into his mouth. Slaughter and Ellie exchanged a glance. "And these two are for me, to spend as I like." He pocketed them again.

"Well done, Tommy."

"Hmmm," said Ellie. "You left early this morning to fetch the flyers. Did you go to the hospital again?"

"Just for an hour." Tommy looked at this plate.

"Were they doing an interesting dissection?"

"Yes!" Tommy said before he remembered he wasn't supposed to go there.

"Well, I don't want to hear about it," scolded Ellie, "and see you don't spend your money on the penny gaffs. I don't want to hear you've been up at those places."

I won't let her hear about it, thought Tommy. That's for sure.

He loved the penny gaffs. For just a penny, he and his friends could get in and listen to the singing, and even join in the merriment. The girls in his gang liked it especially, since they got to behave as they liked, and didn't have to worry about acting like ladies. He'd met a sweet girl last month, a lady's maid from Lambeth, but he hadn't seen her since. Didn't want to mention that to Ellie, though. She might get ideas about him settling down.

As Ellie did the clearing up, he followed Slaughter into the parlor. The inspector usually had a pipe after dinner, just one as he read his book. Tonight, instead, he would need to supply information to a curious lad.

"So what do you do now, since you have a body?" Tommy flopped into the wing chair.

"It goes to the Southwark Coroner now." Slaughter got out his pouch from the drawer in the desk, took his pipe off the mantel, and began to pack it.

"The coroner is the one who looks at everything on the body, inside and out?" He glanced back toward the kitchen, but Ellie was washing the dishes, singing to herself.

"That's right."

"The coroner's a doctor, isn't he?" Tommy's leg swung back and forth off the arm of the chair.

"He can be. But his real job is to decide what caused the man's death."

"What do you think caused it?"

"I'm not sure."

"Was there blood?" Another glance at the kitchen.

"No, nothing like that. But it looked like he'd been there awhile."

"All of Sunday, do you think?"

"Could be."

"Do you know who the body is?" Tommy's foot bounced up and down.

"Yes, the watchman said it was Dr. Morton."

Tommy stopped moving.

"*The* Dr. Morton? Dr. Thaddeus Morton?" He looked shocked.

"I think so," said Slaughter. "Do you know him?" He looked curiously at Tommy.

"Yes. Or at least, I've seen him. I try to stay out of his way."

Slaughter lit his pipe, looking over the flame at Tommy.

"Sam, the dresser who's teaching me, he assists him sometimes. Dr. Morton is . . ."

Slaughter gave Tommy an encouraging smile. Whatever he said wouldn't be held against him.

". . . not very nice. Sam calls him"—he lowered his voice— "Dr. High and Mighty."

"Self-important, then?"

"Oh, yes. Thinks he knows everything, he does." Tommy looked at the ceiling and started bouncing his foot again. "Trouble is, he's really good. Everybody says he's why the other doctors send their serious cases to St. Thomas's. Even after the move."

Slaughter puffed thoughtfully for a moment. They could hear Ellie closing cupboards, then going down the hall to get her sewing.

"Would anyone want to kill him, do you think?" asked Slaughter.

"Pretty much everyone," Tommy said, as Ellie came in to join them.

∽

Sir Henry Featherstone's house was in Kensington, in Rutland Gate. The cab went across crowded Westminster Bridge and right into the traffic in Great George Street.

"Should we have taken a boat instead, sir?" asked Sergeant Honeycutt, bouncing along with his head occasionally bumping the ceiling of the cab.

"No," said Slaughter.

"I saw one of the new steam launches as we went over the bridge," said Honeycutt. "So wonderfully modern. Could get there in half the time, I'd bet."

"You weren't here four years ago," said Slaughter with a grimace of irony. "I assume you approve of that wonderful new invention, the flush toilet?"

"I do indeed, sir. Best invention ever. No more filth in the home. All of it flushed away."

"Except it isn't all flushed away. It's all flushed into the Thames. The stench has been appalling. That summer a few years ago, no one near the river could tolerate the smell. That was the last time I used the river to go anywhere."

Honeycutt frowned. "But Bazalgette will solve that problem, sir, with the new enclosed brick sewers."

"Yes, everyone's hopes are now on Bazalgette's new system to take care of the new problem caused by the new invention. This despite the accident that happened in June at the Fleet River project." Honeycutt opened his mouth to reply, then thought better of it.

It had been a frustrating morning. They had gone to Surrey Gardens first thing to speak with Sir Henry Featherstone about the murder, but were told he was at home for the day, planning to entertain hospital patrons that evening. While they could have interviewed other members of staff, propriety and procedure both demanded that they begin by interviewing the hospital administrator.

Along the way, they had stopped at Morton's home. Constable Jones had found the address from a society directory: Elizabeth Street, Belgravia. A parlor-maid at the townhouse let them in, but she explained she was only a day maid.

"I'm sorry to tell you," said Honeycutt, "but Dr. Morton has died."

The maid blinked slowly, then looked down at the carpet. She was young, with dark hair and a sallow look about her, as if she spent all her time indoors.

"Are there other staff here?" Slaughter inquired.

"No, except the charwoman who comes on Wednesdays. Dr. Morton is a widower, you see. He isn't home much. Prefers to tend to himself."

"Do you know of any family?"

"No, sir." She looked sadly at the floor.

"I'm so sorry to have had to tell you," said Slaughter. "Were you fond of Dr. Morton?"

The maid looked confused. "Not so much, sir," she said. "I was the third maid he had from the agency. He was a bit gruff and, well, handy, sir, if you know what I mean. But he won't be able to pay me now. I'll have to go back and ask at the agency what to do."

The house seemed well-appointed, but devoid of gadgetry or personal objects, with the exception of one photograph of a woman on the parlor mantel.

"Oh," the maid said, "yes, I know who that is. It's his wife, died a long time ago." She didn't know of any women since then, as she was only the day maid.

They had looked through Morton's study. A fresh box of cigars in the desk. A framed medical degree on the wall. Books on medical subjects, particularly surgery. A signed copy of *Gray's Anatomy*, with the inscription, "For Morton, who always looked over my shoulder. Henry." A few letters to and from solicitors, and lease papers for the house, dating back fifteen years. Files of cases, for both St. Thomas's and St. George's Hospital near Hyde Park.

"Perhaps he worked there before St. Thomas's?" Honeycutt said.

"Yes, I think so, looking at the dates. Seems like he was there until five years ago. I wonder why he left?"

They found little else of interest. There were two bedrooms upstairs, but only one in use. It was not very neat. The bed was unmade, and there were stains in the bathroom sink the charwoman had missed. Morton's shaving things were expensive, but not put back in their case. Clothes were draped over chairs, although evening dress was hanging in an armoire and the collars were stored in a drawer. An ashtray hadn't been emptied. Downstairs, the kitchen had little food—some bread and cheese in the larder, and some cold beef. A few tea things, and a half bottle of milk. Plate and silver and tea set only enough for two. A brandy snifter, a glass for water. The above-board cupboards had some crumbs, and the ones nearest the floor held a few mouse droppings. The charwoman wasn't very attentive, obviously, although the stove was practically spotless.

The parlor was neat, however, and the carpet expensive. Morton obviously entertained, when he entertained, in this room.

As they prepared to leave, they asked the maid what her duties were.

"I'm to keep this room and the study clean and dusted," she said, "bring in the post, water the plants, take deliveries, and close the drapes in the evening when I leave. But I'm only here Mondays, Wednesdays, and Thursdays. Should I lock up and go to the agency with the house keys, do you think?"

"Yes, an excellent idea," said Slaughter. "Might want to pour out the milk in the kitchen before you go, and take home the beef if you like. And please give Sergeant Honeycutt the name of the agency in case we need to come again."

They had left knowing little about the murdered man. Perhaps Featherstone could tell them more.

5

Sir Henry Featherstone was in the downstairs study, papers and ivory stationery laid out on his desk. He was in his element, writing notes and invitations in his swirling, florid hand.

My dear sir . . . so looking forward . . . this evening at eight . . . bring only your generous nature . . .

Hannah often helped with such tasks, but she was in the kitchen making sure that all would be ready for later. He wondered idly what she might wear. No matter. She would look lovely and would be a model hostess, a part she played well.

John entered the room so quietly that for a moment Sir Henry didn't know he was there.

"I'm sorry to interrupt you, sir," he said with a slight bow, "but there are two men here to see you."

Sir Henry noticed he didn't say "gentlemen." He looked up with a smile.

"Oh?"

"Yes, sir. From the police."

Sir Henry raised his eyebrows and put down his pen.

"Help me into my chair, please, John. I don't want to be stuck behind this desk when you invite them in."

John was already behind the desk. Having been with him for over thirty years, he knew Sir Henry's wants instinctively. Once all the adjustments were made, he returned to the front parlor.

"I'm sorry to have detained you," said John. "Sir Henry will see you now in his study." He turned to lead them across the foyer.

Slaughter and Honeycutt exchanged a look. John was a striking-looking man, tall and strong and dark-skinned. Gold Coast perhaps, thought Slaughter, as he listened to him speak. But here in London for many years, he thought.

"Have a seat, gentlemen," said a smiling Sir Henry, indicating the settee. "I like to talk with people at my own level."

The room was spacious and comfortable, with large windows. Not the usual dark study of a scholar, thought Slaughter. Rather the light-filled study of a public man, a sociable man.

"Shall I send for tea?"

"We won't keep you long, Sir Henry," said Slaughter. "I'm Detective Inspector Cuthbert Slaughter, and this is Detective Sergeant Mark Honeycutt."

"Pleased to meet you, sir," nodded Honeycutt.

"Ah, American!" said Sir Henry. "I had the pleasure of working alongside some Americans during my days in the West Africa Squadron, catching slavers. An innovative people. Knew some excellent doctors in your navy."

Honeycutt smiled a rather frozen smile.

"Well, what can I do for you?" Sir Henry asked, turning to Slaughter.

"I'm afraid we're here to report a death. One of your doctors, at the hospital." He took out his notebook. "Dr. Thaddeus Morton."

Sir Henry's eyebrows knitted together. He frowned. "Are you quite sure?"

"Yes, he was identified by the watchman, Alfred Morris, at Old St. Thomas's."

"Good heavens," said Sir Henry. "What was he doing over there?" He backed up his chair, as if separating himself from the tragedy. "How did he die? Was it an accident?"

"I'm sorry sir, but we're not sure yet how he died, until the coroner lets us know. We don't think it was an accident. His dead body had been arranged so as to be sitting upright in the operating theatre." Any man who'd been in the West Africa Squadron, and now ran a hospital, thought Slaughter, would have no trouble with harsh details.

"How bizarre." Sir Henry looked at the two men.

"We'd like the site left alone. Your watchman said we'd need to ask you to make sure the builders don't disturb it."

"Yes, of course," Sir Henry nodded absently.

"What can you tell us about Dr. Morton, sir?" said Honeycutt. "We're trying to get an idea of who he was, and what enemies he might have had. We went by his house on the way here, but there wasn't much there to go on."

"No, I expect there wouldn't be. Thaddeus didn't hold much with the personal, not since his wife died. Brilliant surgeon, though, just brilliant. A medical doctor, with a degree."

He glanced at the door. "I'm sure Hannah will be in soon," he said. "She might be able to help with the more personal side of things. Although Morton wasn't a man to mix socially."

"Would you say he was a bit of a lone wolf, sir?" asked Honeycutt.

Sir Henry looked a bit confused at the reference, then nodded. "Yes, I'd say so. Most surgeons are called 'Mister,' since they are not medical doctors. Many take pride in it. Morton was entitled to be called 'Doctor' and insisted upon it." He paused briefly. "You'll probably hear from others that he was a bit abrupt, even rude sometimes. But in my experience, that's often the price of genius. Those of us with lesser talents have more time for the niceties."

"Looking at his papers," said Slaughter, "we noticed he has only worked for St. Thomas's for a few years?"

"Yes, he came to us from St. George's." Sir Henry thought a moment. "I suppose you'll want to know why he left there, won't you? It's not public knowledge."

"Forgive me, sir, but we need to know everything you can share with us. It's often the things that aren't public knowledge that are most useful." Slaughter knew this was unnecessary to say. He liked to give people time to think through their own hesitations.

"Yes, of course. I understand. It was the young ladies, I'm afraid. At the time, St. George's had an excellent matron. A solid reformer, very moral. Like most hospitals that cater to the poorer class of people, St. George's relied on volunteers from the local ladies' associations." He paused. "Are you sure I can't offer you both some tea?"

Honeycutt would have loved a cup, but Slaughter shook his head. "No, thank you. Please do go on. Did something happen with a volunteer at the hospital?"

"I'm afraid so. She reported to the matron that Dr. Morton had taken liberties with her in the preparation room. This does happen sometimes, of course. I'm not defending it. Matron was quite firm about it, reporting it to the administrator. He asked the young lady in question whether she could volunteer elsewhere in the hospital, away from the operating theatre, so everything seemed solved. Then it happened again a few months later. And this time it was the daughter of one of their more prominent patrons."

"I see," said Slaughter. "So he was asked to leave?"

"It was very hard on the administrator. Morton was one of their best surgeons."

"How did he come to be at St. Thomas's?"

"He came to me. We had a serious talk. I used my best Royal Navy manner, of course." Sir Henry gave a confidential smile. "Told him no nonsense in my hospital. First sign of a problem and he'd be out, with no reference. Not that he'd need one. His medical reputation was stellar."

Sir Henry looked at his hands, which were now folded in his lap.

"I believe that everyone should be given a second chance. He did not thank me for it, but I didn't expect that. What I expected was good work, and that is what he delivered. We've made important advances in medicine at St. Thomas's, Inspector. I'm not sorry he was part of it, even if he was . . . dislikable. I am very sorry he's died."

Suddenly Sir Henry looked up and reversed his chair a bit. "Oh, dear, I must get word to the hospital. Call a staff meeting for first thing tomorrow. If you two are here, there must be a lot of gossip and talk going on there. You haven't been to the new hospital yet, have you?"

"At Surrey Gardens? Only to get your address, sir," said Honeycutt.

"But that means everyone will be speculating! The reputation of the hospital. Oh, my word. I'm sorry, gentlemen, but if there's nothing else?" Sir Henry was wheeling over to the desk, gathering paper and pen.

"We do want to ask," said Slaughter, "so that we don't disrupt things too much at the hospital: to whom should we speak first among the staff?"

"That would be Felix Tapper, the apothecary. You'll find his office just off the main entrance to the hospital."

"Thank you, Sir Henry." Slaughter and Honeycutt rose to leave, just as John appeared. Sir Henry didn't look up. "John, would you please show these men out? Then find Hannah and send her in to me?"

"Of course, sir. Gentlemen?" Honeycutt had to restrain himself from reacting to the mocking note in John's voice. They could hear Sir Henry's pen scratching frantically behind them.

∽

Jo Harris stopped by the matron's office as usual to show the permission signed by Dr. Woodsmith. Today her destination was the women's ward. A drawing of a new mother and her baby would both show the happier side of the new St. Thomas's at Surrey Gardens and remind poorer women that good care could be found at the hospital. The *Penny Illustrated Paper* was planning a feature on motherhood for the December issue.

The commission had not been easy to obtain. The editor of the *Penny Illustrated Paper*, Mr. Ebenezer Farrington, did not care for women illustrators. Jo had been obliged to contact his office several times before she was given an appointment. But in the end, he had been impressed by her pictures.

"You capture the facial expressions very well," he said, paging through her portfolio. "I did see some of your work a few months ago in *Sporting Life*, showing Palestro's win of the Cambridgeshire. But I want people, not horses. Sympathetic people. We need to bring the working classes literature and the arts, but also show those folks with money how to help them."

He had thanked her for bringing in her work, and offered £10 each for two engravings of new mothers with their babies. "With fathers or nurses there, too," he said. "We want an idea of service to the poor, not an idealized Madonna and child."

Jo worked all morning in the wards. As she was finishing a drawing of one of the mothers in bed, a group of medical students came through. The medical school had established ward-walking for all students in the mornings. It was partly an effort to instill a sense of responsibility to their patients, and partly a way to make sure they didn't drink too heavily in the evenings beforehand. It was hoped that the more isolated location of Surrey Gardens would encourage the students to concentrate on their studies.

The group stopped briefly at the bed, but by this time the mother was asleep, as was the baby beside her. As they moved on, she heard one of them say, "... dead! In the old operating theatre ..."

Who was dead? Her first thought was to wonder whether whoever it was might still be there, ready to be a subject for a picture. No, that wouldn't be possible. If the students knew about it, this must have already happened and been taken care of. But why would anyone be dead in the old hospital? It was closed, surely?

Jo went outside, looking to sketch a nurse who might be having her tea on the grounds. The nursing students, known as nurse probationers, were given a brief time for refreshment in the afternoon, and it was a glorious autumn day. Sure enough, she saw a young woman in the brown uniform sitting on a bench with her face in the sun.

"Excuse me," she said, "I'm Jo Harris, an illustrator for the *Penny Illustrated Paper*."

"Oh?" said the young woman. "That sounds interesting."

"It is," said Jo, sitting next to her. "I am working on a feature about mothers and babies. The editor wants a nurse or nursing student in the picture, but obviously everyone was busy on the wards. If you'd let me draw you here, I could put you in the picture as if you were tending the mother bedside."

The nurse sat up straighter and put her teacup aside. "I only have ten minutes," she said. "Will that be enough time?"

"I think so," said Jo. "I just need to capture your main features, and your dress. I can fill in the rest later."

"And you'll be able to tell it's me? In the paper, I mean?" She looked pleased.

"Yes, indeed," said Jo, moving to lean on a stone marker in front of the bench. She balanced the sketchbook in the crook of her arm. "I'll draw you how you really look. Now if you'll be as still as you can . . ."

"Certainly. My name is Susan, by the way."

"Thank you, Susan." Jo began to work, dividing her concentration so she could converse. Talking while drawing was a skill she was developing, but she often didn't remember later what was said.

"Have you worked here long?" Jo asked.

"Not really. I started at the school last July, so I'm about in the middle of my studies."

"I wonder if you know about something," Jo said, filling in the line of her cheek. She was a wholesome-looking girl, probably from the country or a small town. Her skin was somewhat mottled, with a few pock marks. She looked real, not like people's ideal of a nurse. Stable and competent. "I heard some of the medical students talking in the ward. About someone dead in the old operating theatre?"

Susan nodded vigorously. "I heard that, too. It's all over the hospital. Dr. Morton was found dead this morning. They think he's been killed." Her eyes were bright with interest.

Dr. Morton. Dr. Morton. Where had she heard that name before? Oh, yes—Sam. He often assisted Dr. Morton in the surgery. Not a nice person, from what she remembered. Sam didn't approve of his unhygienic habits. But who would want to kill him?

"Why would someone do that?" Jo asked. She was almost finished drawing the curls peeking out from under the cap. Quick sketch, she reminded herself. Not much time here.

"Dunno," said Susan, "but no one liked him. Especially the nurses." She lowered her voice and leaned forward so as not to be overheard. "One of my friends, her name's Sybil, she says he pressed against her once in the hall. You know, a *man-like* press."

"Goodness," said Jo. Line of the neck, collar, shoulder in the crisp fabric. Almost done. "All the doctors aren't like that, surely?" she said.

"Oh, no. Dr. Woodsmith, do you know him?"

"Yes, I do. He gave me permission to draw here."

"He's so very nice. He'd never do anything like that. And his young wife is so pretty and kind."

"I'll be sure to tell him he's nurse probationer-approved," said Jo with a smile. "But let's hope they find out who's killed Dr. Morton, if that's what happened. I don't think even St. Thomas's can afford to be losing surgeons."

"I'm sorry, Miss, but I must go back," said Susan, grabbing her cup. "Good luck with your picture!"

"Thank you so much for posing, Susan. I hope we meet again sometime." Dr. Morton dead. She wondered whether she could somehow see the body.

∽

The curtain was down at the Surrey Theatre, and Cyril Price was relieved to hear the applause. A little raucous, but that wasn't unusual. When the curtain rose again for his bow, he was delighted to respond to the boos and hisses with a sneer, followed quickly by a grin. Richard was an evil villain, after all, and the applause meant he'd played him well. Geraldine Orson looked at him out of the corner of her eye as she curtseyed. Lady Anne wasn't much of a part, she thought, but I made it mine. Someone in the audience threw a small bouquet of violets at her feet. She picked it up, smelled its scent, and gave another deep, humble curtsey, which exposed the top of her ample bosom. The first several rows cheered in appreciation.

They'd been in performance only since Friday, but the column in the *Saturday Review* had brought in the Tuesday audience. "Cyril Price has indulged us with a *Richard III* for our time," it said. "Miss Geraldine Orson has abandoned herself to a role worthy of her talent," it said. "As theatre stagnates throughout town in the wake of the International Exhibition, the Surrey is staging a Shakespeare worth seeing," it said. Well, thought Cyril, the reviews had brought in the middle-class portion of the audience. Some of the less literate had come thanks to Jo Harris's picture in the *Pictorial*, showing Richard looking particularly evil, glaring out at the audience from the stage.

"Darling, you're a genius," said Geraldine, as they tripped backstage. "I don't know why I doubted you. Real Shakespeare, here in Southwark!"

"This is where he started, my dear!" he chided her.

"Well yes, but not this far south. We're a mile from anywhere."

"I know," said Cyril. "The obelisk outside says so." He swatted her behind, gently.

The obelisk had been a blessing to their advertising. It stood in the middle of St. George's Circle, and had done so since 1771, as it proudly stated on its base. Each of the other sides of the pedestal indicated the distance into the heart of London: "One Mile XXXX Feet from London Bridge" facing Borough Road, "One Mile CCCL Feet from Fleet Street" facing Blackfriars Road, and "One Mile from Palace Yard Westminster Hall" facing Westminster Bridge Road. The theatre featured the obelisk on the flyers, because everyone knew where it was. Even cab fares were calculated from its location.

Tommy came running into the dressing room. "I'm so sorry I missed the performance, Mr. Price. I couldn't get here today, what with everything going on at the hospital."

"Nothing to worry about, my lad, nothing to worry about. We managed, although Agnes could always use a spare hand. She might not be as sanguine. Was there a run on bandages?" Cyril began wiping off his makeup with a rag.

"Didn't you hear?" Tommy panted. "It's Dr. Morton. He's dead."

Cyril's hand froze in mid-wipe. "What do you mean, dead?" Then he collected himself. "And who exactly is Dr. Morton?"

"He's one of the best surgeons at the hospital. You wouldn't know him. But they found his body, at the operating theatre in Old St. Thomas's yesterday. Everyone's talking about it. Had you really not heard?"

"I really hadn't," said Cyril. So, he's dead, he thought. That's horrible. And just a little bit of a relief, to be honest. "What did he die of?" Cigar-scented self-satisfaction probably, thought Cyril.

"They don't know yet. The coroner will say tomorrow. But he was sitting up, in the operating theatre. Someone had made it so he was actually sitting in the seats, but dead." Tommy caught his breath, and watched Cyril remove his dark wig, placing it gently on the form.

"That sounds like murder."

"Everyone thinks so! Nobody liked him. They're saying the most awful things. Sir Henry is going to come round tomorrow to Surrey Gardens. Give a speech or something. It's just like a play, isn't it, Mr. Price?"

"It is indeed. Do you think this Dr. Morton was like Richard III?"

"You mean an evil man who killed people and made them do things they didn't want to do? Wouldn't that be thrilling?"

"It would certainly be interesting," said Cyril.

∾

There were murmurs among the staff as Sir Henry Featherstone wheeled up the ramp to the platform and took his place beside Felix Tapper. Hannah had accompanied him, and there were several women there from the auxiliary board. Matron sat in the front row facing them, with some of the nurses and nursing students in the seats nearby. Several dressers sat on the other side, with the porters. The few assistant surgeons stood at the back as Sir Henry began to speak.

"Good morning." The murmurs quieted immediately. "As I'm sure you know, we have had an unfortunate death among our staff. Dr. Thaddeus Morton was found dead yesterday in the operating theatre, up at the old hospital." He looked around the group with a kindly expression.

"I know there are rumors going around that Dr. Morton's death was not an accident. This is likely, but the coroner is conducting an inquest today, so I will have more answers for you soon. This meeting is being called to reassure you that there is no danger to any of the staff here, and that you may comfortably but solemnly continue in your duties. I want all of you to please relay this assurance to the nurses and medical students working right now in the wards."

A few of the nursing students looked hesitant, and several of the porters were looking back at the assistant surgeons. Understandable, Sir Henry thought. It's my job to keep calm and order. He looked over at Matron, and they exchanged a look of collaboration.

"I have the assurance of the police that we can continue our work without interruption, with one exception. Police detectives will no doubt come here to the hospital to interview some of us. We will be asked about Dr. Morton, and activities we've seen here at the hospital."

Here he looked sternly out at his staff. "I want everyone to cooperate fully with the police. If there's something you've seen, even if you didn't report it to your superiors, you will need to tell them. Today, Matron and I will be ready to hear from you first."

He changed to a more comforting tone.

"Perhaps you saw something, or heard something, that didn't seem important at the time. Maybe it is important now. If you come forward with any information, you will be thanked, not reprimanded for failing to report it sooner. We would like to be as informed as possible before police questioning takes place. Now, as for scheduling . . ." Felix Tapper frowned and handed him a sheet of paper. It was evident that he had planned to talk about the scheduling rather than Sir Henry.

Sir Henry took his blued wire spectacles from his coat pocket and put them on. "Dr. Morton had two surgeries scheduled this week. We've asked Dr. Woodsmith to take those, with the dressers of his choice. For now, all of Dr. Morton's dressers are assigned to Dr. Woodsmith. Matron will be reorganizing the ward walking for the medical students, who will need to be redistributed. No nursing assignments need be changed." He took off his spectacles and smiled.

"I think that's all we have right now. Are there any questions?"

Sir Henry always asked for questions during his briefings of the staff. There was a pause, but he waited patiently. One of the nurse probationers raised her hand.

"Excuse me, sir. Who will do our work if we're asked to talk to the police?"

"Good question. I'd like you to arrange today for substitutions, since we don't know how long questioning might take. Some of you may not have to answer any questions at all."

Another hand. "Sir, where will we be talking to these policemen?"

"Oh, yes. Another good question. Well, first, let me emphasize that we mustn't do anything that will upset the patients. Policemen will not be permitted in the wards. Matron will come and fetch you if needed. We will set up an area near the tea room, but if you are on one of the far wards, you may simply be asked to go outside on the grounds."

There did not appear to be any more questions, so Sir Henry said, "I bid you all a good working day, tending to our patients. Please pass on what I've said to the night shift of nurses. I promise to share more information as it comes in. Do be sure to ask Matron if you need anything."

The group dispersed as Sir Henry came down the ramp. He took Hannah aside.

"My dear, I'd like you to meet with the Ladies' Committee. This event could affect our donors and benefactors. We want to provide them with assurance that this death has nothing to do with the workings of the hospital in its new location."

"I understand, Henry. I'll ask them to come to tea at the house, and we can all decide how best to manage this."

"Excellent." She hurried to catch up with the women who were preparing to leave.

Felix Tapper came alongside Sir Henry. "Thank you for doing the speaking, Sir Henry. I'll make sure that the assignments run smoothly. I'm sure I'll be the first to talk with the police."

"Yes, that would be best. Are you all settled into your new office? I heard you weren't as pleased with the location as we'd hoped."

"An excellent space, Sir Henry, but yes, it is a little far from the dressers' room."

"I understand. Certainly, this location is not everything we would have wished."

"Indeed, Sir Henry. We've already had complaints from the nurses about how few sinks are available."

"So I heard. I think we'll all muddle through, however."

"We will," said Felix, blinking behind his round spectacles. "I must be off, and I'm sure you're busy as well. Do give my best to Mrs. Featherstone. I see she's busy with the ladies."

Sir Henry wheeled about to see Dr. Woodsmith approaching him.

"Dr. Woodsmith." Sir Henry held out his hand.

"Nice to see you, Sir Henry," said Woodsmith. He was well dressed as always, and his whiskers trimmed and neat. He shook his head. "A harrowing event. Poor Thaddeus."

"Yes, poor Thaddeus indeed. I'm sorry this will mean more work for you." He motioned to a chair in the front row, and Woodsmith sat down.

"Oh, I don't mind that. Elizabeth will understand, and we have a number of dressers so competent they are as good as assistant surgeons."

Ah, yes, Elizabeth, thought Sir Henry. Woodsmith's lovely young wife. They'd only been married two months, but she was already popular among the staff.

"We may want to consider preparing one or two of the dressers for the examinations," said Sir Henry. "When you have time, perhaps after a week or two, you could send me your recommendations?"

"An excellent idea. I'd be happy to. In the meantime, do you plan to send some of the surgery schedule to Guy's? Or shall we simply make do with what we have?"

"I'm not sure yet," said Sir Henry. "Let me think on what's best. For now, we'll make do, I think. The schedule for the rest of this week and next is not too heavy for you to handle."

"Thank you, Sir Henry," said Woodsmith, rising. He really was a most able young surgeon, thought Sir Henry. Medical degree.

Physically strong, with a powerful left arm that could hold off bleeding during limb amputations, and a quick and nimble hand. And certainly the most affable surgeon Sir Henry had ever known. Not all surgeons kept their equanimity in this profession. Indeed, few had a polite manner in the first place. Something about the hands of God, Sir Henry had always thought. That kind of influence over life and death didn't often go along with an easy personality.

Sir Henry shook hands with the few remaining staff on the way out. John was waiting just outside the door to assist him.

～

The inquest room in the coroner's office could hold up to thirty people, but only six were in attendance: Coroner George Smith, Detective Inspector Slaughter, the coroner's secretary, a reporter for *The Times*, Jo Harris, and Dr. Benjamin Fife. Dr. Fife had conducted the post-mortem examination of Morton's body. Smith presided at the only desk in the room, with Dr. Fife seated on a chair in front of him. Fife was clearly the younger of the two men, but he looked more tired. His moustache drooped a little. Perhaps there had been a large number of autopsies lately. The preliminaries and introductions took only a few minutes before Slaughter took out his notebook.

"What were your findings, Dr. Fife?" asked the coroner.

Fife consulted his notes as Jo, seated at the side of the room, sketched in her book.

"I performed a post-mortem examination of the deceased, who appeared to be a medium-sized man, slightly overweight, about fifty-five years old. There was little remarkable about the body aside from one ingrown toenail and a strawberry-shaped birthmark on the left hip. Tobacco use was evident on the right-hand finger and thumb, and in stains on the teeth, of which only one molar was missing. The liver was somewhat distended, and the stomach contained only some bread and butter. The heart was in good shape for a man his age, with just a little lipid build-up in the vessels. Other organs and the bones appeared normal, and there were no abnormalities in the brain. The lungs, however, were darkly congested, with patches of deep purple, and the mouth had a faint sweet odor. There was darkening of the pelvis and thigh area, but we determined that to be post-mortem. There was no other bruising."

"Were you able to determine a cause of death?"

"We have not seen many cases with lungs like that, but the dark regions are consistent with an inhaled toxin of some kind. We looked through the records for similar findings. The sweet smell in conjunction with the combined darkening and congestion of the lungs suggests death by inhaled chloroform."

"An overdose of chloroform?" asked Smith.

"Yes, we are fairly certain. It is consistent with our previous findings, and we found nothing to suggest otherwise."

The reporter exhaled sharply and scribbled some notes. Jo continued sketching Fife's mustache.

"Have you seen many cases of chloroform poisoning?"

"Not many, but we do see them, usually from violent crimes where the criminals want their subject subdued, and they use too much of the liquid."

"I see. In your opinion, could the dose have been self-inflicted?"

"It seems unlikely. While it is possible to pour out too much liquid onto a cloth or absorbent sponge, one would likely lose consciousness before one could position the cloth in such a way as to block all incoming air. Then after an hour or so, one would regain consciousness."

"Did you find a bottle of liquid, or a cloth or sponge with the body?" he turned to ask Slaughter, who shook his head.

"No, we did not."

"Then I have a question for you, Detective Inspector Slaughter. Were you personally in attendance at the initial examination of the body?"

"Yes, I was. I believe that what we found supports Dr. Fife's opinion that death was not self-inflicted. The body had been tampered with after death. It had been positioned upright, with a stick of wood nailed to the wooden seat of the operating theatre. It's possible that the person who positioned the body was the one who caused the death."

The coroner turned again to Dr. Fife.

"At what time do you estimate death occurred?"

"The lividity in the pelvis and thigh would indicate that he was killed, then positioned upright within two hours of death. At that point rigor mortis would have set in, but when the body was discovered, there was no rigor."

"At what day and time did you conduct your preliminary examination?" Smith asked Slaughter.

"About 10:30 am on Monday morning."

"So, by that time he would have been dead . . . ?" he turned to Fife.

"For rigor to have set in and then passed would be up to 48 hours. My best guess would be that he died sometime Saturday morning. That would be the 18th."

"Thank you, Dr. Fife. And Inspector Slaughter. My finding is that this is a case of felonious homicide by a person or persons unknown, and that Dr. Thaddeus Morton died of chloroform overdose sometime Saturday morning. I hereby bring these proceedings to a close."

The secretary finished taking a note, stood, and ushered the others out of the room. As they crossed the threshold, the reporter approached Slaughter.

"Excuse me, Inspector Slaughter," said the young man, "may I ask just a question or two?"

"I don't have much information at the moment," said Slaughter.

"I know, sir, but Dr. Morton was such a respected surgeon. I thought you might be able to tell me your plan for the investigation? Will you be interviewing the hospital staff?"

"Yes, I will be interviewing anyone who might be able to help us determine who killed him," said Slaughter. He did not enjoy being the voice of authority, or being quoted in the press, but he knew it was important to sound confident.

"There has been some criticism lately of the Met's lack of speed on murder investigations," said the reporter. "Have you any plans for ensuring a quick solution to the case?"

Slaughter hesitated. The criticism had been mostly in *The Times* itself. "Please assure your readers that we are eager that the case be solved as soon as possible. Now I must be going to do exactly that." He turned, not too sharply he hoped, and walked away swiftly down Borough Road.

❦

Ellie finished putting the last dish on the table.

"And where is Tommy tonight?" asked Slaughter. He was tired and distracted, but the evening meal with Ellie was always a pleasure.

"At the theatre, just starting the three-week run of the new play." Ellie handed him a glass of water. On the table already was a small glass of whiskey. He'd been too late getting home to drink it beforehand.

"What's the play this time, then?"

"*Richard III*, by William Shakespeare," said Ellie.

"And Cyril Price is playing . . ."

"Richard III," they both said together. Slaughter chuckled. "I'd like to meet Mr. Price someday. Tommy makes him sound very colorful."

"I don't suppose you'd want to attend the play?" asked Ellie doubtfully. Slaughter usually preferred quiet evenings at home, but occasionally enjoyed a good play, concert, or lecture. He'd accompanied Ellie to lectures at the Women's Reform Club, and in May they had both attended the opening of the Exhibition and heard several new musical pieces, including one set to the words of Tennyson.

"Was the theatre review good?" Slaughter enjoyed a spoonful of cabbage soup.

"Tommy said it was. Claimed to be the play of the century or something."

"Perhaps we should go, if you'd like to. Richard III is a wonderful role. Last time I read it, I remember thinking that it was odd to put the villain of the piece as the central character. Seemed to elevate wickedness somehow. I'd like to see whether the performance changes my impression at all."

"And it would be nice to put faces to all these people Tommy talks about," agreed Ellie.

"Tommy is certainly growing up, isn't he?"

"He's always so busy, trying to contribute." Ellie served her husband more soup, then handed across the plate with the cold beef and bread.

"Are you at all concerned that he still insists on sleeping in the kitchen?"

"Not so much now. I think he feels secure there, near the stove and near the door. But now I also think he doesn't want to disturb us with his comings and goings."

"We do have a perfectly good bedroom for him upstairs," grumbled Slaughter. It was a discussion they'd had many times before. Ellie changed the subject.

"So, tell me about your new Detective Sergeant. You haven't told me much about him."

"He's very tall."

"Yes, that much you've told me. And American."

"And American. I have not pressed him about why he left Baltimore, and he hasn't volunteered anything. But he seems able enough, and Jones has taken to him, which makes things go more smoothly at the station."

"Is he attached to anyone, here or back home?" Ellie asked.

"You mean like a woman? He hasn't mentioned anyone. I assumed he was a bachelor."

"Clara at the Reform Club has that lovely daughter—what's her name? Oh yes, Edith. She works in a hat shop, but seems quite intelligent."

"Ellie, I hardly know him well enough to be match-making!"

"Just a thought," said Ellie. She looked over at her husband. He always appeared so confident and stable. And all those books. My goodness. She ought to talk to him about that. Over the last year or so, his collection had grown well beyond the shelves on either side of the study fireplace. There were now odd stacks on various surfaces in the house: on the night-stands, the dresser, even the kitchen cabinet. Little slips of paper stuck out of many of them. He seemed to be reading several of them simultaneously. But she didn't want to bother him with her housekeeping problems. She was aware the new case was very much on his mind, although she hadn't asked for details. But one thing bothered her.

"This new case you have," she said, "the murder of Dr. Morton. Tommy has been spending every spare moment at the hospital. Are you going to need to question him, as if he were a suspect?"

"I hope not," said Slaughter with a note of sincerity. "If the inquest is right about the time of the murder, we know he was here at home. Saturday morning he was with you doing the marketing, and he didn't go to the gasworks until after lunch."

Ellie looked relieved. "That's good," she said. "Now, when would you like to go see the play?"

～

Felix Tapper's office, from which he managed the dispensary at St. Thomas's, was much grander than Slaughter expected. He'd thought apothecaries were simply chemists, dispensers of medicines in dark shops off the high street. Certainly, the ones he'd seen had been exactly that, although their knowledge was often excellent. He recalled in particular once when he'd had a horrible cough and the local apothecary had recommended inhalation of creosote, which worked wonders even if it smelled terrible.

Tapper stood behind his desk, a large expanse of oak covered with papers and bottles of various sizes and colors. Behind him, shelves groaned under the weight of books in Latin, German, and English. A balance perched precariously on one of the shelves. Three phrenology heads shared the top of the bookcases with a line of empty ridged bottles marked with Latin labels.

Tapper's gray, fuzzy tonsure and spectacles were at odds with the formal surroundings. His collar was crisp, but he was in shirt sleeves, each sleeve held back from his wrist by a dark green band. He was holding a piece of parchment flat on the desk with one hand, while his other scratched notes into a book, a large volume containing records of some kind.

Slaughter cleared his throat.

"I'm sorry to disturb you, Mr. Tapper."

Tapper glanced up, surprised. He looks a bit like an owl, thought Slaughter.

"I'm Detective Inspector Slaughter, Metropolitan Police. I'm making inquiries about the murder of Dr. Morton."

"Murder, is it?" said Tapper, removing his spectacles. "I wondered what the inquest would reveal." He looked about for a chair, his eyes alighting on a comfortable seat filled with a stack of papers. He rose and began moving them in smaller stacks onto the desk, then resumed his seat.

"Have a chair, Inspector. I assume you have questions for me?"

"Some, I'm afraid, sir. May I confess I'm surprised by the size and comfort of your office? I take it you are more than just a chemist."

Tapper smiled a large, warm smile. His head rose a bit above the collar, and he seemed to puff his feathers.

"Oh yes," he said, "an apothecary at a large hospital is significantly more than just a chemist. I am the chief medical officer. A large portion of the staff here reports to me."

"Oh! I thought that Sir Henry was the hospital administrator." He was genuinely confused, and Tapper took no offense.

"Sir Henry is the main governor, the chair of the board. The board is concerned with charitable contributions, political connections, and higher management. My office supervises the day-to-day operations of the hospital." He made a point of moving the large record book toward the center of the desk.

"I see," said Slaughter. "And now I see why it was suggested I talk to you first, before any of the staff." He took out his notebook. "Thank you for making the time to answer some questions." He settled into the chair.

Tapper suppressed a sigh. There was so much to do. But he was curious.

"What was the cause of death, according to the coroner?" he asked.

"Death by chloroform inhalation, an overdose." Slaughter seemed to be looking at his notebook, but he was aware of Tapper's response. He seemed merely inquisitive.

"Interesting. We heard his body was found in the old operating theatre?"

"It was. Arranged to be sitting straight upright in the seats."

Tapper's eyes widened. "How strange."

Slaughter reached into his pocket for the blue slip of paper. "We also found this in his pocket. Do you recognize it at all?"

Tapper peered at it, then shook his head. "No. I have no idea what that would be. Nothing to do with the hospital, I don't think."

"Thank you. If I may, I'd like to get some preliminary background. How long have you worked at St. Thomas's? Were you head of staff at the old location?"

"Yes, I was," said Tapper, leaning forward. "I've been here over thirty years. Inherited the position, as it were, from my father."

So he'd know the history of the place, thought Slaughter. That may prove helpful.

"Are you in charge of all the medicines?" He glanced at the bottles on the desk and shelves.

"I am," said Tapper. He followed Slaughter's gaze. "Oh, they aren't dispensed from here," he explained. "All medicines are measured out in the dispensary down the hall, near the wards. These are for my own research, and reminders of the history of the profession. My reference library, as it were."

"I recognize the phrenology heads," said Slaughter. "I attended lectures on phrenology as a young constable."

"Oh, yes, such an interesting history. Rather faulty in its implementation, though, to my mind."

"But what are the green bottles up there? They all have ridges."

"They're for poisons. You must have noticed them in an ordinary apothecary shop? That some of the bottles have ridges on the sides? That's so one cannot mistake them, even in the dark."

"That makes good sense. May I ask, are you also in charge of dispensing chloroform?"

"Yes, of course. And ether. For the surgeries, and occasionally to the physicians for treatment."

"The physicians?"

A calm, thoughtful look came over Tapper's face. He rather liked teaching people. If he'd managed to stay at the Royal College of Surgeons and actually obtained his medical license, he would have liked being in charge of medical students on the wards. As it was, he did get to teach them a great deal, the physicians and surgeons having less patience.

"The physicians are the doctors who treat the patients with ailments and conditions that require care and medicine. The surgeons are the only ones who operate."

"And Dr. Morton was a surgeon? Was he the only one here?"

"He is—was—one of our two surgeons. The other is Dr. Woodsmith. Both have medical degrees, thus the title."

"And the surgeons, are they on staff? Here all the time?"

"Well, yes and no. This is a voluntary hospital, run on philanthropic funding. The surgeons are not paid by the hospital. They would normally have private practices, same as the physicians. Dr. Woodsmith has a private practice, in Harley Street. Dr. Morton, I believe, has been called in for several private practices. He prefers—preferred—surgery to anything else, and doesn't like the bother of having his own consulting rooms."

"Is that unusual?"

"Yes, but not necessarily for a surgeon of his experience. He'd already made his reputation."

"I see. Now, about the chloroform. Would you know if some was missing?"

"Now I would, since we've organized ourselves here at Surrey Gardens. I did all the packing up at the old location, but when we arrived here we found that a number of the crates had been waylaid. Some of them had been packed by assistants. They were tasked with counting the bottles of everything carefully, but not the amounts *in* the bottles, unfortunately." He looked down at his desk and slowly replaced his spectacles on his nose.

"So it's possible someone could have taken some of the liquid, so long as the bottle itself wasn't taken?"

"That's possible, I'm sorry to say." He blinked his eyes slowly behind his glasses.

"Would the chloroform have been in one of those ridged green bottles?" asked Slaughter.

"No," said Tapper, taking down two plain, clear bottles from the side of a shelf. Each had a white label. One said *Spir. Chlorof.* and the other said *Sp. Ether*.

"They aren't poisons, Inspector. They'd be in bottles like this."

"I see. And may I ask where you were last Saturday morning?"

Tapper smiled. "Right here, Inspector. I usually take inventory on Saturday mornings. You can ask Matron, who was here also."

"I see. One last question, and then I believe I'll need to talk to Dr. Woodsmith, if he's here. Did you know Dr. Morton well?"

"Not very. I'm not sure anyone did. He was a very gruff person. Most of us stood a little in awe of him. Even Matron, who rules the wards, tended to stay out of his way. But he may have been one of the most brilliant surgeons of our generation." Tapper looked carefully at the Inspector, reluctant to pass judgement. "The price we pay, I think."

〜

Sam Wetherby, the surgery dresser, was in the sunny tea room, listening to the chatter of the young nurse probationers as he doodled on his surgery orders. He liked sitting in here, although he didn't socialize with anyone. Very conscious, as were they, of the fact that they didn't have their own tea room, he was careful to give them their privacy.

But it reminded him of Nan to be in their presence, even if he didn't converse. It had been a year since she died, and she had been so like these young women. Eager to learn, eager to serve and help the sick. Like many of them, Nan had experienced tragedy at an early age. She had been a country girl, from Yorkshire. A sheep-raising family. When she was four, her mother had died of a fever after giving birth to a stillborn baby. Then seven years later, her father had been injured in an accident when a decrepit stone wall had tumbled down onto his leg. It hadn't seemed a dangerous injury, but the leg had become red and inflamed. The local doctor had come and tried to help, draining the swelling, but it had just gotten worse. Necrosis had set in. He'd never gotten to a hospital.

When her older cousin Sylvia had taken Nan into her home in Bishop Auckland, she had assumed she'd go into service. Later, when she got older, Nan automatically curtseyed in response to requests. Sam had found it adorable. But her cousin had listened with interest to Nan's dreams of becoming a nurse instead of a domestic servant. It had been a popular ambition. Many girls had dreams of nursing after reading about Miss Nightingale in the Crimea. Nan wanted to go to nursing school, and not just any school, but the one being founded by Miss Nightingale at St. Thomas's. Sylvia had made that happen, giving Nan enough money to go.

Sam's own story was quite similar, except he'd been working on his own in Leeds as an apothecary's apprentice after the death of his parents, saving money for medical studies, then he'd come to St. Thomas's. He, too, had no family left by the time they met.

When he met Nan, she had recently arrived at the nursing school. She was just starting her year of training. He'd first heard her voice in a tea shop near Old St. Thomas's, talking with the other students. Her accent had reminded him of home. One day he saw her coming out of the classroom building and had asked if he could walk her to the omnibus stop. She had smiled that fresh, sunny smile, and he thought the heavens had opened for him. Along the way they had talked.

"I want to be a surgeon," he told her. "But I didn't have the money to complete my studies. Being a dresser is the next best thing, though." He explained how he was one of the only permanent dressers, the others coming and going from among the medical students.

He'd realized at the time he was trying to impress her, already telling her about his prospects. He offered to ride the omnibus with her, and she had agreed. When they arrived at her boarding house, he'd met her housemate, Jo, coming out as they were going in. She'd seemed a plain woman, but she was friendly and held out her hand to greet him.

"You must be Sam," she said. "Nan's told me about you."

Sam had been surprised. He'd only just talked to Nan for the first time that day. But here she had already been talking about him to her friend! He had grinned and shaken her hand enthusiastically.

And now he and Jo were friends, but Nan was gone. He looked down at his notes and realized he was sketching a foot, a female foot. The bones under the skin. The nails. Her toenail had gotten ingrown and infected and had required surgery. She'd had the option to have chloroform, to act as an experimental patient for the hospital records. He remembered how excited she had been to be contributing in that way. And then she had died. A problem, they'd said. Lung congestion of some kind, a bad reaction to the chloroform.

Morton had put a hand on his shoulder afterward, saying he was glad Sam hadn't been assisting that day. It was the only time the surgeon had spoken sympathetically to anyone, as far as Sam knew.

❦

Chloroform, Sergeant Mark Honeycutt thought. What do I know about chloroform? Or ether?

He was at Slaughter's desk at Christchurch station, with his superior's notes in front of him. The coroner's decision had been quite clear: death by chloroform overdose. The victim was a surgeon. This was clearly a medical crime of some sort. But instead of being assigned to uncover the background of anyone involved, Slaughter had given him the task of understanding the technology of anesthesia.

During a smallpox epidemic in Baltimore a few years ago, Honeycutt had received some training in contagious diseases. He'd been impressed by the success of vaccination, which he considered an extraordinary innovation. He'd heard about the use of ether at Massachusetts General Hospital back in 1846 and knew that it was possible for inhaled substances to make patients unconscious. But he didn't know how it was done.

He could go to Surrey Gardens, interview some staff, and find out. But he knew the value of doing research before asking questions. He'd discovered that the hard way. The previous year in Baltimore, Honeycutt had been assigned to discover the whereabouts of the Winans Steam Gun. The weapon was to be confiscated from its inventor, Charles Dickinson, by the City Police. Eager to do his duty in the face of a possible Union invasion, Honeycutt had rushed the investigation, learning little about the gun before leading the search. He had assumed it was an ordinary weapon, like a rifle, despite eye-witness reports of its extraordinary size. If he had researched the patent, he would have known that it was a monstrosity, powered by steam and reportedly firing 200 projectiles per minute. He also would have known it was almost as large as a railway engine and would have ordered the search to proceed accordingly.

It was later a joke at the station. Every time someone went off to find something substantial, like a missing horse cart, his fellow policemen would make a show of looking under desks and in the spittoons. Although the embarrassment had not harmed his career, he had learned his lesson. Get the background first. The task here was to learn as much as he could about anesthesia, then interview those involved with its use at the hospital.

"Jones?" he called. Constable Jones appeared almost immediately at the open door and came close to giving a bow. "Yes, sir?"

Honeycutt smiled. "Have you ever considered a career on the stage, Constable Jones?"

"Have done," said Jones in a low, sonorous voice, "but the hours wouldn't suit me."

"Ah, understood. Look, I need to get some information about administering chloroform. Is there a library near the station? Or somewhere with medical information?"

"You mean other than St. Thomas's, sir?"

"Exactly."

"There'd be the Hunterian, sir, up in Lincoln's Inn Fields." Jones smoothed his mustache.

"The Hunterian?"

"Yes, it's like a museum, sir, a collection, in the Royal College of Surgeons. They have some grisly things there, but they know a lot about surgeries and such."

"Grisly?"

"Yes, sir, turn your stomach, some of it. They've got these wooden planks called the Evelyn Tables. Body parts, you know, mounted on boards. All varnished like. I have a cousin who works there."

"Excellent. What's your cousin's name?"

"Ben Whitlow, sir. He does their books, or records, or something. Just ask when you arrive."

The journey to Lincoln's Inn Fields was difficult. Honeycutt's tall form didn't fit easily inside a two-wheeled hansom. The rain had soaked his shoes and the hem of his trouser legs by the time he arrived.

A porter saw the hansom approach in the courtyard and watched Honeycutt walk up the steps through the large Doric columns. He opened the door, glancing down only briefly at the cuffs of Honeycutt's trousers. Obviously not a surgeon.

"Good afternoon, sir. How may I be of service?"

"I'm Detective Sergeant Mark Honeycutt, of the Metropolitan Police. My constable told me to ask for Ben Whitlow?"

"Yes, sir. Down that hall, second door on the right."

Ben Whitlow was a young man with a shock of dark hair, his head bent over a book on his desk. "Excuse me," said Honeycutt, "I'm Detective Sergeant Mark Honeycutt. I work with your cousin, Constable Derwyn Jones?"

Whitlow looked up. "Oh! How nice. How can I help you, Sergeant?"

"I'm investigating a case that involves the use of chloroform. I want to get some information on the use of chloroform in surgery. We have a murder investigation."

"Indeed! We have heard about Thaddeus Morton. What a horrible thing to have happened." He rose from the desk and moved ahead of Honeycutt out into the hall.

"Let me take you to our head librarian, Mr. Septimus Carver. Through here, please."

They entered a very large hall, and Honeycutt stopped in his tracks. To his right and left were skeletons of animals and even a human, mounted on low rectangular plinths. More skeletons stood on the ledge separating rows of glass cases with specimens of all sorts arranged down the center of the room. Around the sides of the space, reaching up at least two stories, were rows of bookcases on platforms accessed by ladders. A large rectangular skylight illuminated the room. The rain could be heard tapping on the glass.

"This is incredible," said Honeycutt. "It's like a temple to natural science." He reached into his pocket for his notebook and realized he'd forgotten to bring it.

"The curator would be pleased to hear you say that," said Whitlow. "Here we are." He knocked on a door marked "Librarian" in gold letters, opening it at once to usher Honeycutt in.

Mr. Carver was a tall, serious-looking man wearing a long black coat. As Honeycutt entered, he was just closing the glass over a shelf of books. There were books everywhere, on every wall of the room, up to the ceiling. A smaller version of the skylight lit the room from above. It was like being down a well, a deep well made of books. A cigar was still burning in the ash-pan on the desk, and the room smelled strongly of smoke.

"Excuse me, Mr. Carver," said Whitlow, "this is Detective Sergeant Honeycutt from the police, here about Dr. Morton."

"Thank you, Whitlow. Come in, Sergeant." He did not sit down, but Honeycutt was pleased to look him in the eye. "How can I help you?"

Mr. Carver seemed busy and distracted, but pleasant enough.

"Thank you for your time, sir. I am gathering information about chloroform and its administration during surgery. Background, you know, as we investigate the case of Dr. Morton."

"Of course," said Carver. "Happy to help in any way I can. Has the coroner issued the report?"

"He will soon, sir. Death by chloroform overdose."

Carver looked distressed. "That is very bad news, Sergeant. Very bad indeed. The use of anesthesia is new enough that any problems with it are magnified." He shook his head.

"I'm not sure I know what you mean, sir."

"Not all surgeons trust its use, and not all are experienced in using it. Are you familiar with the use of anesthetics to create unconsciousness?"

"I'm afraid not," admitted Honeycutt.

"The brief history would start with ether, first used by a dentist in your part of the world: America."

"Yes, I have heard of that. In 1846."

"Precisely. Over fifteen years ago. Ether works very well, but it has its drawbacks. Extreme flammability, unpleasant smell, nausea in the patient. It also takes a long time to work. But it's easy to dose. Very forgiving. Follow me as we go to the museum exhibits?"

Honeycutt followed as they went back into the large room with the cases and toward the glass exhibit nearest the door. It contained what looked like boxes, some with tubing, all with flared ends.

"Here are some of the devices used to administer both ether and chloroform. They're called inhalers, although of course an inhaler can also be used for other substances." He indicated a few ordinary inhalers in another case, simple fluted vessels with a tube at the top. "Ether or chloroform inhalers have improved over the years, and there are several designs currently in use. The Murphy inhaler is one of the most popular." He pointed toward a device that looked like a small horn. "Another very popular one is the Snow inhaler," he said, pointing toward a more complicated device with a box and a hose. "I assume you've heard of John Snow?"

"Isn't he the one who mapped the cholera outbreak about ten years ago?"

"Yes. He also helped the queen be delivered of Prince Leopold and Princess Beatrice, with chloroform. He invented this ether inhaler here, which uses warm water and a wide mouthpiece, plus a valve to help the patient not re-inhale his own breath. He used the same method for chloroform."

"What are those extra pieces?"

"They are three differently sized masks. You'll notice the space next to them. We do own a Samson inhaler, and we'll have another by John Clover once the Exhibition is over in November. They are currently being displayed there. "

"Please excuse my ignorance, but what's the difference between them?"

"Some are just better versions of the old way: a thick cloth, held over the patient's mouth and nose, and the liquid slowly dripped onto it. But Snow's, and the more recent designs, focus on water temperature to determine the concentration of the dose. That's important with chloroform especially."

"Why especially?" Honeycutt was regretting not bringing his notebook.

"Chloroform, you see, is harder than ether to dose properly. But it is much more pleasant for everyone. It smells better, works more quickly, doesn't cause as much nausea."

Carver went over to a nearby shelf and took down a book.

"I think this will help you, Sergeant. You are welcome to borrow it for a few days." Carver handed him a small booklet. It was titled, *Anesthetic and Other Properties of Chloroform*, by J. Y. Simpson, M.D., and dated 1847.

"Now, if you'll excuse me, Sergeant, I have to prepare the recent case of books we've acquired from Edinburgh."

"Just one more question, sir. Did you know Dr. Morton?" They began walking back toward the office.

"On sight only, Sergeant. And smell. He smoked cigars, of course, as do I. Helps keep the bugs out of the books. I didn't know him to talk to, but of course I knew his work."

"Did he publish about these anesthetics at all?"

"He did indeed. One of the more innovative surgeons in that regard. Realized the potential early on for performing surgeries deeper in the body than could ever be done before."

Honeycutt glanced at the booklet in his hand as he left. A little light reading for the evening, he thought. Perhaps it will put me to sleep.

~

Detective Inspector Slaughter was back at the station, waiting for Honeycutt to return, when Constable Jones peeked in.

"Excuse me, sir. There's a Lady Featherstone to see you."

Slaughter jumped. Why would she come here? He would have been happy to visit her at her home, where she'd be more comfortable. The station was no place for a lady. He came out to the waiting room immediately to lead her back.

"Lady Featherstone," he said, reaching out his hand. She wore a dress and velvet jacket of dark green, which showed off her pale skin and auburn hair to perfection. Her gloved hand slipped briefly across his. Her nonchalance seemed practiced, he thought. Certainly, every policeman in the station was either staring at her or trying not to. Powerful charisma, thought Slaughter.

"May I offer you a chair in my office?" he asked. "I can have Constable Jones fetch you a cup of tea."

"That would be very kind, Inspector," she said. He caught a glimpse of the heel of her white boot as she walked ahead of him. Odd color for this time of year, he thought. He must ask Ellie about that.

Jones arrived with tea on a tray, carried atop a side table. Where had he found such a thing? He placed the whole setting carefully at her side and took some time arranging the cup, sugar, milk, and spoon.

"That will be all, Jones, thank you," said Slaughter. He was rewarded with a withering glance.

"How may I help, Lady Featherstone?" He settled into his chair. With elites, he knew, one must always appear as if one has all the time in the world.

Hannah removed her gloves slowly, as any lady would. She was wearing scent, something floral, and it wafted within the room.

"Thank you, Inspector." She looked into his eyes, and Slaughter almost caught his breath. She was a lovely woman, and somehow familiar.

"I felt I should come here rather than talk to you at the house," her eyes lowered. "It's about Dr. Morton."

"Yes, of course," said Slaughter, curious. He waited.

"As you may or may not know," she continued, "in my previous life I was an actress. A stage actress. Before Sir Henry gave me such joy in making me Lady Featherstone."

Suddenly Slaughter realized why she looked familiar. He had not seen her on stage, but somewhere he had seen her picture, perhaps on a poster.

"May I be assured, Inspector, that what I have to tell you will be only between us?"

Her lashes fluttered so slightly that Slaughter thought he might have mistaken the gesture. "I would like to assure you, Lady Featherstone. But I'm afraid that if it has to do directly with the case, it may become necessary to reveal it at a later time."

Hannah took a sip of tea.

"Yes, I see. I shall hope for the best. Before I met Sir Henry, I was . . . involved with someone else. An actor." She looked up as if gauging his reaction, but he was not surprised, only interested.

"My kind and wonderful husband does not know about this relationship. It was long ago, and I would prefer that he not discover it. But Dr. Morton knew."

"How did he know, Lady Featherstone?"

"I'm not exactly sure how he found out," she said, her brows frowning inward. "But several months ago, he let me know that he was prepared to tell Sir Henry about it."

"How did he communicate this to you?" asked Slaughter.

"It was at the last event at Old St. Thomas's Hospital, a benefit to help with the move to Surrey Gardens. He approached me, told me he knew about it, and that he was considering telling my husband."

"How did he seem?" asked Slaughter. "Angry? Upset? Concerned?"

"Devious," Hannah answered, "like he wanted something. I asked what it was that he wanted. I've played enough blackmail scenes, Inspector, to know what was happening."

She took another sip of tea. "I assumed he wanted . . . more than I was willing to give."

"You mean money?"

There was a pause, and a smile spread slowly across Lady Featherstone's face. She almost laughed.

"Good heavens no, Inspector. I could have given him money, but he didn't need any as far as I could tell. I thought he wanted . . . favors. Given his reputation, you know."

"Yes, I have heard something about that."

"But that was not what he wanted at all. It was something about a meeting that had taken place in August, a full staff meeting. I was seated at the front next to Sir Henry. I had seen Dr. Morton enter late, at the back, and sit with some of the nurse probationers. He'd left shortly afterward. What he wanted was that I forget he had been there. That if anyone asked, he had missed the meeting."

"Did that strike you as a strange request?"

"It did. No one had noticed him anyway, as far as I could tell. It seemed a rather large threat for such a small thing. So I agreed. And that was the last I heard about it."

She took a last sip of tea.

"But you can see, Inspector, why I didn't want to mention this with my husband present. Given the context of Morton's request, you understand." She stood, gracefully lifting herself from the chair. Slaughter scrambled to his feet.

"I do indeed, Lady Featherstone. While you are here, may I ask if this looks at all familiar to you?" He held out the blue paper with the date on it.

"I'm sorry, but I'm afraid not. Looks like some sort of ticket, perhaps?"

"Thank you. And may I thank you also for coming forward in this way, and coming here to tell me about what happened? I'm most grateful." He rose to escort her out.

She left in a light breeze of scent, with several constables watching her exit. Slaughter heard a collective sigh as he turned back toward his office.

The planning meeting of the Women's Reform Club commenced with the usual inanities. Or at least, that's how Jo Harris saw it. There was always a bit of preening. Not by Ellie Slaughter, certainly, but by some of the higher status women. Hats and jewelry needed to be admired, husbandly activities compared.

Nan used to suppress giggles at such meetings. She'd lean over and tell Jo about the noise all the rustling dresses made. Miss Nightingale would never allow such things, she said. All that rustling disturbed the patient and made it likely that something near the hospital bed might be knocked over. Jo had never worn a crinoline herself, although she did wear petticoats when out with Cyril Price. Most of the time she just hemmed her skirts and didn't mind that they lay in folds around her limbs. She needed to move. All women needed to move.

These women seemed to be moving toward calling the meeting to order. Jo, as usual, pushed her chair outward so she could balance her sketchbook on her bent knee. Her ankle crossed over her opposite thigh, and new members often looked over disapprovingly, so she usually sat at the back. The topic at the moment was the next speaker for the Philanthropy series. Or rather it was supposed to be.

"I think we can all agree," said Ellie Slaughter, "that Dr. Guy's visit earlier this month was a resounding success. We've even had some funds collected toward his hygiene program at Millbank Penitentiary." Hats nodded around the room.

"The question is what to do next month. Should we return to our discussion of abolitionism? The war continues in America, and the petitions about ending trade with the Confederate States are no longer necessary given the Union blockade."

"It could be," said Rosalind Turner, in the front row, "that they'll have to settle the war first, before much can be decided." Several of the women nodded.

"Indeed, Mrs. Turner," said Ellie. "Perhaps we could discuss the female vote? We could invite someone from the Sheffield Female Political Association. Or would property rights would be a better choice? We know several people on the Married Women's Property Committee."

"Perhaps," said Mrs. Turner, "such controversial political topics could be held in reserve until spring? It seems like the need is still great for philanthropic action, particularly in the workhouses and hospitals."

Jo sighed. It seemed like there had always been this difference of opinion among the reformers. Did one focus on issues that would help women be more active in society? Or did one use the influence women already had to create change more immediately? There was indeed something to be said for the persuasive mode of influencing men in politics.

"If we were to focus on philanthropy," said Ellie, "should we turn our attention to education, or continue our work in the care of the poor?"

As usual, Jo thought, we'll continue with the poor. Everyone in this room is a woman, but not all women agree on what is important. None of them are poor, so it is much easier to separate oneself from the problem and help others who are less fortunate. With little but hats and feathers to portray, Jo began drawing the building at Surrey Gardens as she listened.

One of the new members tentatively raised her hand. "May I propose," she said, "that we consider the recent private paper written by Miss Nightingale?"

"I'm sorry," said Ellie, and other women looked confused also. "I don't know about this paper?"

"There is a movement afoot to create a law for ladies of the evening, which will violate their privacy and put them in hospital against their will. Miss Nightingale wrote a note about it to Lord de Grey, a 'Note on the Supposed Protection Afforded against Venereal Diseases.' It's been seen by very few people, but it is important."

"Please tell us about it?"

The woman stood so she could be more easily heard. "I'm sorry, since I'm a new member many of you don't know me. My name is Harriet Stubbing. I'm a senior nurse at St. Bart's." There were murmurs of introduction. "The issue seems to have begun with a report on the spread of venereal disease in the armed forces. The proposal is to prevent its further spread by passing a law that allows police to simply arrest those they deem to be prostitutes, and imprison them in the interest of public health." There was a stir of disapproval around the room.

"But isn't that blaming the women instead of the men who use their services?" asked one member.

"Yes, it is. And Miss Nightingale's paper has clearly shown that such measures do nothing to stop the spread of disease. But the implications go beyond that. Any woman walking alone, unescorted, could be deemed by police to be a prostitute and subjected to an intimate examination." There was an increasing buzz around the room.

"All right," said Ellie Slaughter. "It seems like it might be useful to have someone come speak about this proposed law. If I may appoint a committee for determining who is behind it, someone willing to come speak to us?"

A committee having been formed, the planning meeting dissolved for tea and conversation. Well, Jo thought, at least this one would be interesting. She rose and went to greet Ellie.

"That was a surprise," she said to Ellie, "but it sounds like a good topic."

"I'm just happy that no one raised the issue of the death of Dr. Morton," replied Ellie.

"Yes, I was at the inquest. I saw your husband there."

"Oh, he's been so busy with it. I just hope his new sergeant is being some help. There's such pressure from the Superintendent to get this solved quickly."

"I'm sure. Well, I must be off to find Bridget. She wasn't able to leave work to be here on time this evening, but she promised she'd have dinner saved for me."

Ellie watched Jo leave. It must be so interesting to be a woman with a career and a fascinating companion like that actor Cyril Price. She wondered what the two of them did together. It must be a very exciting life.

6

Friday dawned a bit brighter, and Slaughter decided to let Ellie sleep. He could warm up the stove in the kitchen and wake Tommy. He dressed quietly, tucked his notebook into his pocket, and went down to the study. The floor was cold, and he'd left his slippers upstairs. He'd lost his pencil the day before, so he took one from his desk and went into the kitchen. A shaft of sunlight was shining through the high window.

Tommy was still asleep next to the coal range, which remained warm all night. Slaughter had agreed to install it when they bought the house because Ellie had been so enthusiastic. A closed range, she explained. No smoke in the house. No storing wood, which attracted rats. Coal delivered. He'd been reluctant. Another supposedly marvelous innovation, destined to disappoint. Slaughter had liked the old wood-burning stove, inside the hearth, at their old house in Macklin Street. He liked how the meat tasted when cooked over wood.

In the end, Tommy's joy at a stove that stayed warm all night outweighed Slaughter's roasted meat. The lad had been only ten years old when he'd come to them after being suspected in the murder of Joe Carter, a stoker at the gasworks. The police had thought Tommy was involved, and it took a lot to prove he hadn't been. The boy's mother had died when he was four, and his father died a debtor at Queen's Bench Prison. He'd been in and out of orphanages and workhouses. When the case was over, Ellie put her foot down. "I want to take him in," she told Slaughter. "The lad has nowhere to go."

He'd had no choice, not really. Ellie had been so stalwart about them not being able to have children of their own. And she was quite right. The boy had no one. The court was more than happy to have them take responsibility.

The responsibility was murmuring in his sleep. Slaughter leaned over his small bed, and gently shook his shoulder. "Wake up, Tommy," he said. "Ellie's asleep. Let's get breakfast and be on our way."

Over tea and a slice of bread from the larder, toasted on the range, Tommy chatted sleepily.

"You gonna catch the murderer today, Inspector?" Tommy loved calling him that.

"It doesn't happen that quickly, you know."

"Oh, sure, I know. Do you suspect anyone yet? Who do you need to talk to?" He took a big pat of butter and placed it, without spreading, on the toast.

"I have no one to suspect yet. We've only talked to Sir Henry Featherstone, and the apothecary."

"Mister Tapper?"

"Do you know him?"

"Not to talk to, but I know him by sight. He's the one who looks like an owl."

"He does, a bit." Slaughter hid a smile. Tommy was observant, certainly.

"The physicians don't like him. He keeps opening windows they want closed. He says it improves ventilation."

"Interesting. So today we should go back to the hospital, to talk with people who knew Dr. Morton, and we need to find Dr. Woodsmith's surgery if he's not at the hospital. Are you going to Surrey Gardens today?"

Tommy shook his head, his mouth full of toast and butter.

"The gasworks?"

Tommy nodded and swallowed. "And then the theatre. Big night, Fridays."

Slaughter considered a moment. "You know, we might want to consider getting you a tutor. Maybe just one or two mornings a week. Would you like that?"

Tommy's eyes got wide. "Oh, yes, I would, very much. Would Mrs. Slaughter be all right with that?"

"Of course," said Slaughter. "Why wouldn't she be?"

"Well, a man in the house. A man who's not you . . ." He gave Slaughter a meaningful look.

"Oh, I see. You mean a man other than yourself?"

Tommy puffed up. "Well, that's true. But still."

"I shall see if I can find someone to come when Prudence is here, on her days." He raised a questioning eyebrow at Tommy.

"That would be suitable," nodded Tommy.

A childhood in the workhouse, the odd night at the penny gaff, and he's worried about Ellie and propriety. Good lad, thought Slaughter. He wouldn't regret the tutor's fees.

༄

Inspector Slaughter and his sergeant got out their notes and settled in at the big desk, Honeycutt stretching his long legs to the side. Jones popped his head in. "Tea for two hard-working detectives?"

"Thank you, Jones. Good idea." Jones vanished.

"So, I have a great deal of information about anesthetics," began Honeycutt, "from the librarian at the Hunterian Museum." He shared his notes, recreated the previous evening from memory. Slaughter listened carefully.

"So it seems like chloroform and ether would both be fairly common, but that one would need some knowledge to kill with it?"

"Not really, sir. It seems like the knowledge is needed for dosing in operations," said Honeycutt. "Either would be easy to kill with, so long as you could come up on the person unawares. A cloth over nose and mouth, a strong arm, and the victim would just keep breathing it in until he died."

Slaughter nodded. "All right. Let's work on who had access to it other than Tapper. I had an interesting visit from Lady Featherstone," said Slaughter. He explained about her affair and keeping it from her husband.

Honeycutt frowned. "Now, I don't know much about these aristocrats," he said, "but it seems an odd reason to come alone to the station."

"I thought so too. Which makes me wonder whether she was trying to tell us something else instead."

"Like casting suspicion on her husband?"

"That's one possibility. Or getting us to look into the theatre, or into Morton's penchant for blackmail. I think it would be a good idea to do both anyway."

"I agree," said Honeycutt.

"All right," said Slaughter. "Let's head to Surrey Gardens and interview people who knew Morton, and those who might know about access to anesthetics. We should talk to his surgical assistants. I think they call them dressers."

"Oh, for dressing wounds, I guess?"

"I assume so. We should also talk to the other surgeon, Dr. Woodsmith. If it isn't one of his days at the hospital, we can ask for the location of his surgery and call on him this afternoon."

As they stood up to leave, Jones came in with the tea. "Sorry, Jones, no time," said Honeycutt. Jones looked quite crestfallen as they left.

༄

"Good morning. What can I do for you?"

The woman at the desk was young, possibly in her early twenties, and was wearing the brown nursing school uniform. Her blonde hair was pinned tightly under her cap, and her blue eyes were alert.

"We're here in connection with the death of Dr. Morton," said Honeycutt. Slaughter had retreated behind him to the foyer and was looking at the paintings of the founders of St. Thomas's.

The student blanched a little. "Yes? You are police, then?"

"We are. I'm Mark Honeycutt, Detective Sergeant, and he's Detective Inspector Cuthbert Slaughter. We'd like to interview Dr. Woodsmith. Is he here today?"

"I'm sorry," she blinked. "He has private surgery today, in Harley Street. Number 64."

"That's fine," said Honeycutt. "Then we'd like to speak with the dressers who worked with Dr. Morton."

She looked down at her book, then glanced down the hall, then up at Honeycutt.

"I think you'd best talk to Matron," she said. "That would be Mrs. Wardroper, sir." Her tone was both worshipful and wary at the same time.

Honeycutt smiled and leaned across the desk to speak more quietly.

"Should we be worried about meeting her?"

"Well, sir, she's a very important person."

"In the hospital, you mean?"

"Everywhere, sir. She's a friend of Miss Nightingale, you know. Miss Nightingale said she wouldn't have set up the nursing school here if it hadn't been for Mrs. Wardroper."

Honeycutt prepared to ask another question, but she looked past his shoulder and whispered, "I'm sorry, sir, but that's the ward sister. If she sees me talking, I might get a bad mark on today's report."

"Thank you for your help," Honeycutt said more loudly as he leaned back from the desk.

"Woodsmith isn't here," he said to Slaughter, "and we've been told we should talk to the matron about anyone else. A Mrs. Wardroper."

Slaughter turned. "Shall we do that together?"

"The impression I get is that two of us may be a good idea, yes, sir."

The door to the matron's office was just off the foyer. Sarah Wardroper was a small woman, wiry and strong. She was seated at a plain desk with a tilted top, writing on a sheet of paper. The desk was situated so that she faced the door. Her black dress was serviceable, rich but bereft of flounces and frills. Her gray hair was tied back tightly in a bun under her cap. She reminded Honeycutt of some of the fiercer nuns he'd seen in Baltimore.

"Mrs. Wardroper?" asked Slaughter.

She looked up sharply, taking in both men in a single appraising glance.

"Yes, I'm Sarah Wardroper. And whom might you be?"

"I'm Detective Inspector Cuthbert Slaughter, Christchurch Police Station."

"And you?" she pointed her pen at Honeycutt. He stood up a little straighter.

"Detective Sergeant Mark Honeycutt, ma'am." He had almost said "sir."

"I assume this is about Dr. Morton's unfortunate demise?" She put down her pen and looked at them with an air of studied patience. "Sit down, please."

They sat, sharply. She gave them a small, approving smile.

"Now, let's begin. I have about ten minutes before I need to check on the reports of the ward sisters. What can I tell you?"

Slaughter cleared his throat. "First, ma'am, how long have you been with St. Thomas's?"

"Eight years as Matron of St. Thomas's, and two years as superintendent of the nursing school."

"And did you know Dr. Morton well?"

"Not well. I do not associate much with the surgeons. They come and go."

"What was your impression of him from what you did know of him?"

She pursed her lips. "I had heard of him before he came, and I knew there had been some issues with his behavior at St. George's. But Sir Henry was most insistent that we have him, because of his skill. The few times I saw him, he was polite enough. But given the rumors, I did recommend to all my nurses and nurse probationers that they give him a wide berth."

"Nurse probationers?"

"The students of the nursing school. All are considered on probation for one year as they learn, and they still must perform nursing duties in the hospital."

"Have you had any recent complaints about Dr. Morton's behavior?"

"I have not, but like Miss Nightingale I prefer prevention to cure."

"I understand you are friends with Miss Nightingale?" inserted Honeycutt.

"We served together in the Crimea. Perhaps you have heard of the Crimean War, even where you're from?"

Honeycutt was becoming accustomed to the assumption that Americans knew very little of the world. "Yes, ma'am."

Slaughter interjected, "Do you know of anyone who might have wanted Dr. Morton dead?"

There was a moment, and a serious expression crossed Mrs. Wardroper's face.

"He was not a pleasant man. I did not have to work with him, but I am in charge of those who do. He wasn't liked, but I can't think of anyone who had expressed anything about him that I would interpret as murderous intent."

"Just for clarification, you're in charge of all the nurses and nurse probationers?"

"Yes, I am."

"And also the dressers and assistants and porters?"

"Yes, that's what it means to be Matron," she said patiently, as if to a child.

"In that case," said Slaughter, "may I have your permission to speak to some of the staff?" Mrs. Wardroper's lips pinched. "Those who worked most closely with Dr. Morton?"

"He preferred Sam Wetherby to be his dresser, probably because he's so precise. He rarely used an assistant. If two surgeons were needed, he tended to work directly with Dr. Woodsmith. I never saw him speak to a porter."

"Did he work closely with any of the nurses?"

She frowned. "I'm not sure I'd consider the ward nurses people with whom he worked closely, but he knew the names of several of the nurse probationers. I didn't consider that appropriate. He didn't seem to know the names of his own medical students, although he took them on their ward walks."

"There were no medical students he talked to or took an interest in?"

"None at all." She shook her head. "It was disappointing to them, but most followed him to watch his technique in the theatre, and listen to his lectures."

Slaughter closed his notebook. "I know you're very busy," he said, starting to rise but waiting for her to do so first. She remained seated, so he stood. "May I have permission to access the staff who worked with Dr. Morton?"

Mrs. Wardroper glanced at the clock on her desk.

"The most convenient hours for the dressers would be between eleven and lunchtime," she began. Honeycutt got out his notebook and began writing. "For the nurse probationers, directly after lunch, or even better during lunch. For the ward nurses, before or after their shift. For the porters, in the evening. I won't have the routine of the hospital disturbed." She looked pointedly at Slaughter.

"I understand. Where would you like me to interview the nurses and nurse probationers?"

"You may use a corner of the tea room. It isn't centrally located, but it would be the most suitable for interviewing young women, since it is visible from three sides. But short interviews, please."

"Of course," agreed Slaughter. "Before we go, may I ask if you know what this is? It was found in Dr. Morton's pocket." He held out the blue paper.

She shook her head firmly. "No, Inspector, I have no idea. We don't use blue paper for anything here."

As he and Honeycutt left the room, they passed a woman in brown coming into the office with a stack of cards. "The reports, I assume?" said Honeycutt to the girl. She just stared up at him, then scurried into the matron's office.

"It's eleven now," said Slaughter. "I'm going to go to the tea room and see if I can set up a space for interviewing 'young women.' Why don't you go find that dresser? Perhaps talking to him will suggest others we might speak with. Let's meet at one and have lunch on the way to Harley Street."

Slaughter learned little that was new from the nursing probationers in the tea room. After introducing himself, he had asked a group of four sitting at a table together what they knew of Dr. Morton. They all glanced at each other.

"It's all right," said Slaughter, "Matron has told me you can answer my questions."

"He was . . ." began a dark-haired girl, then shrugged.

"Handy," cut in a young woman with ginger hair poking out of her cap at every conceivable angle, "but not with me." She grinned, showing a missing tooth.

"I've heard that before," said Slaughter. "What does that mean?"

"Handy," she repeated, "like with his hands on you when you didn't expect it. Always passing close in the corridor, touching." She gave a little shiver.

"But not you?" he asked.

"Naw, I wasn't his type. Not pretty enough. Besides, I'm twenty-seven."

"You should talk to Mary Simmons," said the first girl. The others nodded.

"Why Mary Simmons?"

"She was really bothered by Dr. Morton. He seemed to focus more on her."

"Where could I find Mary?"

"She's in with her tutor now," said the fuzzy-haired girl. "Come tomorrow, and we'll have her come here with us."

～

At the same time, Honeycutt had found Sam, the dresser. He'd been sitting out in the sun, eating a bun. A cup of tea sat under the bench.

"Sam Wetherby?"

"Yes," said Sam, looking up at Honeycutt.

"I'm Mark Honeycutt, Detective Sergeant with the Metropolitan Police."

"Oh, yes," Sam smiled. "Sit down, Detective Sergeant. Mind if I keep eating?"

"Not at all," said Honeycutt, "so long as you don't mind if I ask you some questions?"

Sam nodded as he chewed.

"I understand you worked with Dr. Morton."

"Yes, when he was here. For about three years now."

"Can you tell me your thoughts about him?"

Sam considered for a moment. "I value my place here, Detective Sergeant. I wouldn't want to speak ill, not only of the dead, but of a surgeon."

"I understand, Mr. Wetherby. But someone has killed Dr. Morton, and done it with anesthetics. We need information, so we can find out who would do such a thing to a fellow human being."

"Of course. Well, I can certainly answer questions about his surgical methods, and anesthetics."

"I've learned a bit about anesthetics. They seem to allow for vast improvements in surgery."

"They do indeed. Are you interested in such matters, Detective Sergeant, or is your interest confined to this case?"

"I have an interest in anything that improves human life using the mind, and science, and invention."

"A man after my own tastes!" said Wetherby. "Do you read much about such innovations?"

"When I can," said Honeycutt, "but my resources are somewhat limited."

Sam nodded. "My own interests are in medical improvements, obviously, but I have also been eagerly reading about Bazalgette's sewers, and the plans for communicating over wire. And the changes in the understanding of biology seem to be moving quite rapidly. The recent work by Mr. Darwin is quite extraordinary. You must be acquainted with some of the discoveries happening in America?"

"Not as much as I'd like to be," admitted Honeycutt. "But for now, let's see if what I know about anesthetics is correct."

Wetherby nodded and finished his bun as Honeycutt continued.

"The coroner reported that Dr. Morton died of chloroform overdose through the lungs. I understand that can happen accidentally because chloroform is harder to dose properly than ether."

"Yes, but it is so much more pleasant for the patient," noted Wetherby.

"I've heard that too. But we know it was deliberate, because other aspects of the murder have given us pause. Such as the position of the body."

"Yes, I heard that he was in a seated position?"

"In the seats of the old operating theatre," affirmed Honeycutt. "We have to assume the murderer was trying to say something about Dr. Morton. We think it must have been related to his work, so we need you to help us understand what it was like to work with him."

Sam sighed. "Cleverly articulated, Sergeant," he said. "I suppose when you're dealing with what must be a crime of extreme hatred, you cannot afford to tolerate niceties like mine."

Honeycutt nodded, but said nothing.

"He was, as I'm sure you know, a difficult man. I personally objected to the cloud of cigar smoke in which he traveled, and his general distaste for the new methods of hygiene. But on cases without anesthesia, he was brilliantly fast at his work. I've seen him amputate a smashed finger so quickly the patient only had to look away for less than a minute."

Honeycutt felt his finger twitch.

"He was an early experimenter with ether, and then with chloroform. But he had little interest in tests on animals, or in reading much about the discoveries of others. Much more interested in doing what he could immediately, as soon as an appropriate case presented itself."

"Dr. Morton had his pick, I assume, given his reputation?"

"Yes, he could override Dr. Woodsmith with a simple word to Sir Henry if he wanted a case himself."

"Would you consider him to have cared very much about his craft, as opposed to caring about the patient?"

"I couldn't have put it better, Sergeant. He cared not only for his craft, but for his own ability. He seemed to be always competing against himself, to do his work better. The hands of God, as they say."

Sam reached under his seat for his tea, finishing it in a single gulp.

"Some of his surgeries, of course, were unsuccessful. Because he was so experimental, families sometimes blamed him as if he were careless. His overall record, however, has been remarkable."

"What do you know of his personal life?"

"Nothing, I'm afraid. We did not talk on a personal level." Sam picked up his cup and bun wrapper and stood up, stretching in the sun.

"Since you worked closely with him, I do need to ask where you were Saturday morning?"

Sam gestured back toward the surgery rooms. "Right here, Sergeant. Tidying up."

"Can anyone verify that?"

Sam frowned. "No, I don't think so. It was a very quiet morning."

"I see." Honeycutt stood up too. He towered over Sam. "Can you suggest others who worked with Dr. Morton that I might talk to, Mr. Wetherby?"

"You can talk to any of the junior dressers and porters who work in the surgery, and of course his medical students, although he spent as little time with them as he could."

"Not much of a teacher, then?"

"No, Sergeant," said Sam. "He didn't have the patience for it."

Honeycutt met Slaughter in front of the hospital. Lunch was a pie from a vendor in Walworth Road before they caught a hackney to Harley Street. Along the way, Honeycutt reported what he had discovered.

"Sam Wetherby is an interesting man," he said. "It was clear to me he has all the experience to be a surgeon, just not the qualification. He's well-read and quick-witted. Very much in tune with the new methods, not just of medicine but of society at large. I can see why a surgeon of Morton's skill would prefer him."

Honeycutt would naturally be impressed by such a man, thought Slaughter. "Did he say anything that might indicate animosity toward Dr. Morton, or suggest it in anyone else?"

"Well, he didn't like him any more than anyone else we've talked to. He was clearly impressed by Morton's skill, if not his manner." The hackney went over a bump in the road and Honeycutt's head tapped the ceiling. "What did you learn from the nurse probationers, sir?"

"Not much, except they confirmed that he liked to touch young, pretty women. They did suggest we talk to one particular probationer, though. Mary Simmons. One of us will need to go back tomorrow and do that. I suspect she'll be uncommonly pretty."

"I'd be happy to undertake that, sir," said Honeycutt.

"I had a feeling you would," said Slaughter.

༄

Marylebone seemed so white and wide after Southwark. It was not difficult to find 64 Harley Street; every white pillar was labelled in sharp, black numbers. Wealthy patients did not like to search for houses. Most wanted to be delivered right in front and enter as discreetly as possible. A small brass plaque near the door said *Dr. Charles Woodsmith* and below that *Surgeon*. Another plaque on the opposite side of the door said *Mr. Arthur Pennington* and *Physician*.

"They must share the surgery," said Honeycutt.

"It's likely that they share the house rather than the surgery or a consulting room," said Slaughter. As they entered, he was proven correct. The front door led onto a hall. A door on the left said *Dr. Woodsmith* and on the right *Mr. Pennington*. They entered on the left.

A lovely young woman sat at the desk. Her brow was furrowed as she looked at the papers in front of her. She jumped as the two men entered.

"Hello?" she said. "I'm sorry, but Dr. Woodsmith has no more appointments today."

"I'm sorry to disturb you," said Slaughter. "I'm Detective Inspector Slaughter, and this is Detective Sergeant Honeycutt. We'd like to see Dr. Woodsmith."

The woman's pink mouth made an "o" shape, and her hand gracefully covered her lips. She stepped out from behind the desk with a rustle of petticoats, nearly tipping over the wooden chair.

"My apologies. I'm Elizabeth Woodsmith, his wife. I'm not usually here in the office, but today the nurse left to tend to a relative. An aunt, I believe. I'll go in and see if Charles is available. Please have a seat?"

She glided to the inner door, and they could hear her whisper to her husband. He came out at once.

"Good afternoon." He held out his hand. "Thank you for coming to my surgery. It's much easier than talking at the hospital." He pulled up another chair and sat in front of them. Mrs. Woodsmith rustled back to the desk, where she could be part of the conversation or not, as was needed. "What questions can I answer for you?" he said, "I assume this is about poor Dr. Morton?"

"It is indeed," answered Slaughter. He instinctively looked for signs of guilt or embarrassment, but Dr. Woodsmith's face revealed only an intelligent interest. Attractive man, he thought. He looks kind. His medical students must like him.

"We need to know anything you can tell us about Dr. Morton, both professional and personal."

"I'm afraid I didn't know him well. Do you want facts or impressions?"

"Both, please," said Slaughter. Honeycutt got out his notebook.

Woodsmith folded his hands together, made a point with his forefingers, and leaned his chin lightly on the point. "I think you will be told he was a difficult man, with a gruff personality and some objectionable habits."

Honeycutt tried not to laugh. Remarkably consistent, this Dr. Morton.

"And I'm sure you'll also be told he was a brilliant surgeon. I assisted him a few times, but on occasion I would join the students in watching him work."

"In the operating theatre, you mean?"

"Yes. Particularly when there were accidents that came in, where one really had to be quick. Machine parts embedded in the abdomen, or a foot crushed by a horse." Slaughter and Honeycutt instinctively looked toward Mrs. Woodsmith.

Dr. Woodsmith laughed. "Oh, don't worry—Elizabeth is quite hardened to these things. She attended Nightingale's nursing school at the old hospital. That's how we met." They exchanged a look that would have been more suitable in private.

"Have you been married long?" asked Honeycutt.

"Just over two months," she replied. "I'm still not quite accustomed to being a surgeon's wife." She smiled, showing beautiful white teeth. Honeycutt felt a tug of loneliness.

"Sir," said Slaughter, returning his attention to Dr. Woodsmith, "you say that on occasion you would observe Dr. Morton's surgeries from the seats in the operating theatre?"

"Yes, indeed," Woodsmith nodded.

"Did any of them use anesthesia?" Honeycutt asked.

"Several," Woodsmith said. "Of course, those are much easier to watch. Hardest thing about being a surgeon is the pain. Very difficult to become inured to it. Anesthetized patients are so wonderfully . . . peaceful."

"And you have used anesthesia yourself?" Honeycutt asked.

"Oh, yes, it is quite the most wonderful innovation. And chloroform has made everything so much more pleasant. But I can't always use it. The dosing means I have to pay attention, as it were, to two things at once: the anesthetic and the surgery itself."

"And you have to teach at the same time?"

"Yes, so there's a further division of attention. But that's not as serious, because the anesthetic itself gives time to lecture as you go."

"Sounds like a problem that needs solving," remarked Honeycutt.

"I think so too!" said Woodsmith, leaning forward. "There is talk in the medical community that with anesthesia becoming more common, more complex operations will be possible, and perhaps it would be better to have a doctor whose sole task is to attend to the anesthesia. Once we have solved the problem of infection, of course."

Honeycutt was leaning forward to engage this topic, but Slaughter interrupted.

"And do you know of anyone who might have wanted Dr. Morton to die?"

Woodsmith frowned.

"Well, here's where we talk about impressions. Not everyone understood what Morton was trying to do, moving the medical field forward. I know there were resentments. We expect that among the families of those who lost loved ones during operations, of course. It's possible that in their grief someone might want to kill the surgeon. But there were also professional jealousies, and he could be quite distasteful as a person. That's difficult to say, of course, but I'm afraid it's true."

Out of the corner of his eye, Slaughter could see Mrs. Woodsmith nod, as if to herself.

"I'm sorry, but I need to ask you both where you were Saturday morning?"

Dr. and Mrs. Woodsmith looked at each other.

"At home, Inspector," said Mrs. Woodsmith.

"All morning?"

She blushed a little and tried not to look at her husband. "All morning."

"One last thing, Dr. Woodsmith," Slaughter said, holding out the blue paper with the date on it. "Does this mean anything to you?"

Woodsmith peered at it. "I'm sorry, Detective Inspector. It means nothing to me. Elizabeth?"

She shook her head gracefully.

In the old days, Cyril Price had spent his post-performance free time in the back bars in Soho, seeking like-minded company. But that had been long ago. Now there were patrons and benefactors to seduce instead, seduce into investing in the Surrey Theatre. He did not run the place single-handedly, of course. A board made all the financial decisions. The board members were from the wealthier segments of society, often professionals who appreciated the contributions of art and culture to public life. With its emphasis on melodrama, the Surrey Theatre had not been the first choice among investors. But Cyril had changed all this with his increasingly more sophisticated fare. The board adored him.

Public appearances were Cyril's forte as an actor, but he didn't really enjoy the events designed to encourage contributions and investments. It seemed that they involved him playing a part he didn't like, the theatrical manager of a place of entertainment, the amusing man-about-town. Particularly aggravating was that he, like all the board members, was expected to bring a woman to these events. He had brought actresses of his acquaintance to such occasions, but they always looked like . . . well, like actresses.

As he waited for Jo to appear at the theatre, he was again grateful that they had become friends. They had met in a coffee bar in Lambeth. Cyril had been sitting at a table, writing edits in his script for *A Tale of Mystery*. Jo was at another table with her sketchbook. It had taken half an hour for Cyril to realize she was sketching him. He had pushed his blond hair out of his eyes, stood with an air of discovery, and with a charming smile approached her table.

"Cyril Price." He held out his hand. Jo looked amused. His hand looked soft and featured two large rings. His cuffs had lace, but she was observant enough to notice it was fancy rather than formal. Not of the finest quality.

"Jo Harris," she replied, taking his hand. He was pleased to note that her hand felt large and capable. She was plainly attired, in a gray dress with a modest petticoat. He raised an eyebrow, and she motioned to the empty seat at her table.

"I couldn't help noticing that you are drawing," he ventured.

"Yes, I am," she said.

"And that you appear to be drawing me." He swept his lock of hair back again.

She laughed. "An actor, am I right?"

"Not only an actor." He put his hand to his chest. "I am an actor and manager, bringing the world of theatre to the deserving public of Southwark, Lambeth, and Walworth."

"Pleased to meet you," said Jo. "I am an illustrator." She put her hand to her chest. "Bringing the world of everything to the deserving readers of penny magazines."

"And I caught your eye?" He turned his head so the light featured his profile.

"Yes, you are quite marvelous," smiled Jo. "I can see you as Hamlet, Macbeth, Lear . . ."

"Lear?" He looked shocked. "I am certainly not old enough to play Lear!"

Jo grinned. "I'm quite sure you could play anything you set your mind to."

"True," he agreed. "Quite true. So, am I to be featured in a piece? Have you been commissioned to draw the best that the theatrical world has to offer?"

"Actually, I was just drawing you to practice my skill with expressive faces."

Cyril smiled again and offered her more coffee. As they talked, he realized that she was different from the many women who fawned on him. She didn't take him seriously, but she was perfectly friendly. He began to suspect she might be like him. He felt no flirting, no sexual interest of any kind. They were just enjoying each other's company. He invited her to come draw at the theatre, and she had come by to do so the day of the board's benefit dinner.

"I wonder," he said to her as she sketched the rigging and painted backdrops, ready for the revival of *London by Night*, "would you be interested in being my companion for a benefit dinner tonight? It's an awful bore, I know, but I am expected to have a woman on my arm at these things. With you, I might actually enjoy the evening."

Jo had continued sketching, with a slight frown.

"I would be happy to. But I'm not sure I have anything suitable to wear," she said.

"Oh, don't worry about that! Come, come, come!" And he had spirited her off to the costume room.

Since then, she had accompanied him twice more to such tedious and yet necessary events. Her intelligence and interest had been delightful to the board members. Two had even let her sketch their portraits. One had introduced her to the editor of *Once a Week*, Mr. Samuel Lucas. Tonight there was a post-performance supper, and another of the board members had invited a wealthy young couple to attend. They were new to London, and Cyril knew he was expected to impress them. With Jo at his side, he was sure he would.

7

It was getting toward morning, but Cuthbert Slaughter had been unable to sleep. He came downstairs quietly and sat in his cold study, wondering why he felt that the investigation was going the wrong way. Aware that the small brandy he'd poured for himself would not help with sleep, he took out a piece of paper and tried to write a list. He entitled it "Lines of Inquiry." Then he crossed that out and wrote instead "Characters."

Murders were often like plays, he thought. You had a cast of characters, each with their own story and their own motivation. He wrote a list of everyone they'd interviewed so far, and how they were connected to each other. Sir Henry and Lady Featherstone, and her strange story about Morton and blackmail. Sam Wetherby, who'd worked most closely with the victim. Charles Woodsmith, the other surgeon, and his lovely wife, Elizabeth. Felix Tapper and Sarah Wardroper, managers with a lot of control over how things worked at the hospital. Nurse probationers who had received unwanted attentions from Dr. Morton (here he made a note to talk to Mary Simmons). He took another sip of brandy as he added Tommy to the list.

Everyone on his list was too nice, too clean. They'd all been so pleasant and helpful. It was as if Morton had been the only serpent in the garden. That wasn't possible. Another serpent had killed him, a serpent who had felt strongly enough to not only kill him but display him in that horrible way. What did the display mean?

Underneath all these nice stories and pleasant people, there had to be some darkness, some pain. So far all he had were some annoyed young nurse probationers and some possible professional jealousies. He'd seen no intensity of emotion from anyone.

His own technique, being unfailingly polite and amiable to everyone, was not getting to the heart of the case. Perhaps he should be more devious. Sergeant Honeycutt was good at getting people to gossip, and gossip often revealed the nasty underside of superficially civil interactions. Rumor, innuendo—these could often be more important than facts. Shakespeare knew this. Othello's jealousy was more important than Desdemona's actual guilt. Lear's distrust of his own daughters, Hamlet's guilt at not avenging his father, Richard III's unyielding hatred and ambition—it was emotion that caused people to do horrific things.

He heard Ellie's slippered feet on the stairs. She came up behind him and put her hands on his shoulders, looking at the paper. "Yes," she said, "I thought you'd be here doing this. Time for a change of strategy then?"

"I think I've again fallen into the trap of detection," he sighed. "Too many facts, not enough information on the feelings that lead to murder."

"Have you evidence of anything at all?"

"Just the blue piece of paper in Morton's pocket. No one's identified it so far."

"Tommy will be up soon. Show it to him. He knows a lot about what goes on in town."

She saw the brandy glass peeking behind a stack of books. "Can I get you a cup of tea?" she asked. "It's getting too close to morning for brandy."

"Thank you, yes, please," said Slaughter, but first he took her hand. "I meant to tell you. I'd like to get a tutor for Tommy. He's asked that it be on the days Prudence is here, so you're not alone with just him and the tutor."

She smiled at him. "Yes, and yes," she said. "Now let me get you some tea and wake the lad. He'll be late to the gasworks for Saturday shift."

Half an hour later, Slaughter and Tommy were both half-asleep at the breakfast table.

"Tommy," said Slaughter, "I want to show you a piece of evidence from this case, to see if you can tell me what it is." He fetched the blue paper out of his notebook.

"Uh huh," said Tommy, yawning. "That's one of the blue tickets they use for events at the theatre."

"The theatre?" asked Slaughter, confused. They sold tickets to operations?

"The Surrey Theatre," explained Tommy. "When they have events to get people to give money to the board. I call 'em Cyril Parties, because they always want him to be there, playing Cyril the Famous Actor."

~

Semi-rehearsals were often scheduled for Saturday afternoons at the Surrey Theatre during the run of a play, but there had seemed no need for any. Geraldine had been performing beautifully. The audience sympathized with her Lady Anne so much that young men called out warnings to her from the audience, then appeared at the stage door afterward to make sure she was alive and well. Everyone knew their parts perfectly, and there had been no flaws with scenery or lighting. But Cyril was worried about his opening speech, so he was on stage, with Agnes watching out front and providing helpful advice.

Cyril hunched a bit and glared out into the seats. "Now is the winter of our discontent, made glorious summer by this sun of York," he intoned. Then, "I don't like the stress on 'now,'" he said. "Is it better on 'winter?'"

"Try it, love," Agnes called up from the third row. "I can't tell if you just talk about it."

"Now is the *winter* of our discontent, made . . . wait, if it's *his* winter only, that's fine. But I think maybe his brother is only pretending all is well, now the war's over. How about this?"

He moved downstage and looked out into the house.

"Now is the winter of *our* discontent, made glorious summer by this son of York," he sneered.

"I do like that better," said Agnes, "but I'm not sure why?"

"Because it makes it just Richard's discontent, just mine, while everyone else is having a good time. I think it's more revealing of his isolation."

"Yes, dearie, I agree. Can we have lunch now?"

Slaughter and Honeycutt had come in the door from the lobby quietly and were seated at the back of the stalls, watching.

"He does fill the stage, doesn't he, sir?" whispered Honeycutt.

"Yes, even in a rehearsal," agreed Slaughter. "But we'd better have a word." There were steps on either side of the stage, and as they approached, Cyril went over to meet them.

"Gentlemen," he said, with a bow. "Welcome to my theatre. Whom do I have the honor of addressing?"

"Detective Inspector Cuthbert Slaughter, Mr. Price. And this is Detective Sergeant Mark Honeycutt. We're with the Metropolitan Police."

Cyril took a step back and put his hand on his heart.

"Surely no crime has been committed here?" he asked, as if horrified.

"Not that we know of, Mr. Price," said Slaughter. "May we have a word with you? We would like your help with a case."

Cyril nodded. "My dressing room is over there. If you gentlemen will follow me?"

The room was larger than Slaughter expected, with a chaise longue against one wall. In the corner there was a small desk.

"Please come in and sit down. You are police, you say? What can I help you with?"

"Yes, Mr. Price," said Slaughter, as they sat gingerly on the chaise longue. "We are investigating the death of a Dr. Thaddeus Morton."

"Ah," said Cyril. His face was impossible to read. "I had heard about that."

"Oh?" asked Honeycutt. "From the papers, perhaps?"

"Yes, but first from our dogsbody, Tommy. He also works at the hospital. Where Morton works. I mean *worked*, of course."

Slaughter decided to leave Tommy out of this for the time being. "We discovered this in Morton's pocket. Perhaps you know something about it?"

Cyril took the blue paper. "Why, yes, this looks like one of our benefit tickets. Let me think, the 28th of August . . ." He walked over to the desk and flipped through a diary. "Oh yes, the gala."

"Gala?"

"We had a gathering that evening, instead of a performance. It was during the run of *Twelfth Night*. I played Orsino, you know." He looked meaningfully at Honeycutt. "If music be the food of love, play on."

"Oh," said Honeycutt, at a loss.

Slaughter said, "Orsino is the Duke, in love with Olivia but unaware that his own page boy is actually a woman who's in love with him?"

Cyril shifted his gaze to Slaughter and smiled broadly. "Why, yes, Inspector. You know Shakespeare?"

"I have read some of the plays and sonnets."

"Oh, but Inspector, Shakespeare isn't meant to be *read*. It's meant to be performed! You must come see our current production, *Richard III*. I am playing Richard." Cyril turned to the right and raised his shoulder a bit, showing his most excellent profile.

"Thank you. I would like that very much," said Slaughter, taking out his notebook. "So you say there was a gala to raise money for the theatre, on the 28th of August?"

"Oh no, it wasn't to raise money for the theatre. It was a benefit for St. Thomas's Hospital. The move, you know, was quite expensive."

"I see. Do you host many benefits for causes like that?"

"Yes, some. The board of the theatre likes to be engaged in the socially beneficial activities of this area. The hospital, the School for the Indigent Blind in St. George's Circus. The charity work at the local church." He raised an expressively bored eyebrow.

"Was Dr. Morton present that evening?"

"Morton . . . Morton. Yes, I believe he was. There were so many people here from the hospital." He looked up at the ceiling. "I remember now. Gruff gentleman, smoking a cigar."

"Did you speak with him at all?"

"I believe I met him briefly in the lobby. Shook his hand, that sort of thing. The board likes me to meet everyone. I am flouted like a carnival attraction." He did not look put out about that. In fact, thought Slaughter, he looks quite pleased.

"Did you notice anyone he might have been talking to that evening?"

"I don't think so." Cyril tapped his chin with his forefinger. "Oh, perhaps Lady Featherstone. I think I saw them exchange a few words. And Sir Henry, of course. I didn't see the man much, Inspector. Just met him, really."

He looks a little nervous, thought Slaughter. I wonder whether he knows something, or whether it's just acting.

"We noticed a woman just now in the audience seats—"

"The 'house,' Inspector, please."

"In the house," said Slaughter.

"That's Agnes. Been with us for years. Best costume designer and set decorator in the theatre world."

"Would you consider her a friend?"

Cyril raised his eyebrows, "A friend? Of mine? Why, yes, Inspector, I believe I would."

"Does she attend these galas?"

"Occasionally. Doesn't take a liking to crowds, Agnes."

"May I ask you, Mr. Price, where you were last Saturday morning?"

"In and out of here, as I recall." He was now peering closely at the Inspector, wrinkling his brow.

"Is there a problem?" asked Slaughter.

"Not at all," said Cyril. "It's just very interesting." He leaned forward, his blond lock flopping onto his forehead. "Your brow furrows *after* you have the answer to a question, never before. And the corner of your mouth raises ever so slightly."

"I beg your pardon?"

"I study people, Inspector. I played a police inspector once, and I did it very poorly. The reviews said I was marvelous, of course. But it's so hard to show that one is thinking deeply. You do it quite well."

Slaughter tried not to look taken aback. Actors, he thought.

~◦~

Sir Henry took out the letter for the third time, looking up to make sure he was alone. John would be within earshot if he needed anything, of course.

I have information concerning your wife, the note said. I will be in contact again.

It had arrived six weeks ago, but he had received no additional note, no further contact. Was it a blackmail letter? What information could there possibly be about Hannah that he didn't know? Did he want to know?

Perhaps someone has discovered her affair with Cyril Price, he thought. It was long ago, but would make excellent fodder for one of those tawdry penny papers. Perhaps the note was from a journalist? No, he sighed. He was fairly sure about the handwriting. He opened the desk drawer and took out the hospital contract with Thaddeus Morton, looking again at the signature. Very likely, he thought. And now the man is dead. He pondered, not for the first time, what Morton knew and what he might have been planning.

His conscience told him he should share this with the police, but he was hesitant. He had not told Hannah about the note in the first place. Instead, he had shown it to John and asked him to be alert to anything that might threaten Lady Featherstone. Just in case. He knew that if anything came to physical violence, he would need John's help to defend her. But all had been quiet.

Quiet and lovely. He looked out the picture window at the trees. The bright Saturday sun was shining in, making parts of the glass glow bright yellow. Even in October, the garden was green and beautiful. Hannah loved tending it, as she loved tending him. The pillows on his sofa, embroidered not well but lovingly. The maids ordered to keep the fires stoked so his feet were always warm.

She would not betray him. They had talked together, late at night when darkness encouraged confidences, her warm body beside his. She claimed not to miss the excitement of the theatre, to be quite happy in polite society. Had he given her enough, he wondered.

Money and position, yes, but enough to make her content? And could a woman younger than himself prefer him as a lover?

Not for the first time did he damn that tumor. It had been the result of an old wound he'd sustained in the West Africa Squadron. He'd been in his prime then, a strong, handsome man who earned respect. As captain, he'd commanded ships that fought against the slave trade, capturing clippers off the coast of Africa. Even his injury, caused by a shard of decking embedded in his back during battle, hadn't slowed him down. It was over a decade later that the mass began to form near his spine. The Harley Street surgeons had done what they could. He'd been in his forties by then, a good surgical risk. The only anesthetic available had been nitrous oxide, so it had been painful. The healing went well, but it had left him wheelchair-bound. It wasn't anyone's fault. It had been too close to the spinal cord. And he'd become interested in hospitals, leading to his current position.

He was a lucky man, he reminded himself. Lucky to have been born into the upper class, to parents who cared about him and his brother. Lucky to have attended the best schools, and to have served off the coast of West Africa and survived to return to England, accompanied by John. Lucky to have served king, then queen, and country, in ending the slave trade. Lucky also that after the surgery, his new situation had encouraged him to change interests, from sports to the theatre. Otherwise, he'd never have met Hannah.

When she returned from tea with her friends, he vowed, he'd plan a special evening with her. Perhaps she'd like to go to the theatre, or out to dinner. Maybe to Verrey's in Regent Street, where she could both see and be seen. She could wear her finest. He'd order expensive champagne, being careful not to eat too much of that rich food himself. Then when they returned home, he'd show her yet again that experience and love surpass youth in the bedroom.

Agnes was in the costume room, sewing what looked like a lump of cloth into the shoulder of a jacket. The doorway was narrow, and the room very small. A skylight let daylight in from above. She was grumbling to herself. "You'd think they'd be able to get the stuffing to me, wouldn't you? But no. 'Not on Saturday,' they said. Not on Saturday! When would I need it but on a Saturday, I ask you . . ."

"Excuse me," said Inspector Slaughter. Agnes peered up at him. "Yes?" Her lashes were so thick he could barely see her eyes.

"You're Agnes Cook? Mr. Price said we might speak with you."

"Yes, I'm Agnes. Are you from the flower seller? I've been asking and asking. Violets, I said, I need violets. I've sent three notes this morning."

"We're from the police, investigating the murder of Thaddeus Morton."

"The murder of who?"

"Would it be possible to speak with you somewhere where there's a little more space?"

Agnes thumped the jacket onto the small table, then leaned on it to stand up. She was not a large woman, but the table squeaked in protest. "More space, he says. If I could get more space don't you think I'd have it?" She began to move past them. "Come with me. We can talk in the scene loft."

The scene loft was certainly larger, with huge panels and rolls of fabric leaning against the walls. An assortment of carving tools, carpenter's planes, and other equipment were laid out on a long bench. Cans of varnish and tubes of paint were overflowing out of a cabinet in the corner. The wooden floor was covered with streaks of various colors. Agnes clomped over to a corner that had a drawing table and four tall stools. She climbed up on one, as did Slaughter. Honeycutt's were the only feet touching the floor.

"All right. Who's dead then?"

Honeycutt took out his notebook, and Slaughter spoke first.

"Dr. Thaddeus Morton, of St. Thomas's Hospital. Did you know him?"

"Not likely. I stay away from doctors as a rule. No idea what they're doing, most of them. I always say, if you want to be ill, go to a doctor. He'll make sure you are, right enough."

"This doctor was a surgeon. He did operations. But we think he might have been here for the St. Thomas's benefit. The gala, Mr. Price called it."

"Oh law, the gala. Right bunch of rich folks, mixing with the hospital big-wigs. Everyone swanning around the lobby. One of them knocked over the flowers I put out there!"

"That sounds very rude," said Slaughter. "Did you see a man there, a gruff man, with a cigar?"

"Oh yes, I remember him. Is that your Dr. Morton, then?" Slaughter nodded. "Then yes, I saw him. Blowing cigar smoke all over my curtains. Did you see them? The nice velvet ones over the doors into the house? Cost a bundle, then everyone's out there, bumping into the fringe, making 'em smell like smoke. Is that right, I ask you?"

"Not at all." Slaughter shook his head in sympathy.

"He didn't stay long, though. Only spoke to a couple of people."

"Do you remember to whom he spoke?"

"Let me think a moment. I had my eye on him, what with the curtains. Didn't want the whole place going up in flames." She adjusted herself on the stool. "He talked for a minute with Lady Featherstone. She didn't look as if she liked him very much. Waved the smoke away from her face, she did. Then I saw Sir Henry introduce him to Cyril. Not Cyril's type, I would have thought."

Honeycutt looked over at Slaughter, then back down at his notebook.

"How not?" asked Slaughter.

"Well, you see," Agnes said, lowering her voice even though no one else was in the loft, "Cyril's a lovely man, and a dear friend. And we have a joke between us, you know, about him and the ladies. And I do like Jo Harris, who comes with him to all the events. She's great fun to talk to. Knows about everything, she does, and creates such realistic pictures. Andrew, our scene man, he wants to have her do some of the artwork for the next play. Maybe even designing a whole set piece."

Slaughter waited, nodding.

"But aside from Jo, he doesn't really take to ladies, if you know what I mean." She winked.

She means he likes prostitutes, Honeycutt thought, rather than ladies. Slaughter knew better.

"Did he seem to . . . like Dr. Morton?"

"Oh, no, I wouldn't say that. He looked kind of shocked, really. As if Dr. Morton had said something surprising. He flushed, like. Then in half a second, he turned into Cyril the Great Actor, as he usually does."

"I'm sorry?"

"Cyril's act, you know. He flips his hair out from his eyes, and poses, and flirts. Like he does with everyone."

"Men and women?"

"Oh yes, men and women. I overheard this man say something to Cyril about touring the hospital grounds. So what happened to him?"

"He was killed. In the old St. Thomas's operating theatre."

"Served him right, I'll bet."

❧

"Was she saying that Cyril Price is a sodomite?" asked Honeycutt as they rode back to the station.

"Possibly," said Slaughter. "People discuss such things more now that it's no longer a capital crime. But it was certainly not discreet of her to have implied it. It's still against the law."

"Also in Baltimore. But it's rarely enforced if both parties are adult and no one is forced."

The horse hooves seemed abnormally loud on the road. Slaughter looked out at the people walking along the pavement. Rather quiet for a Saturday afternoon, especially when the sun had come out. Borough Market was probably crowded, though.

"But if Morton was buggering Cyril Price—" Slaughter looked up sharply. "Sorry, sir. If Morton was interested in Cyril Price, how does that correspond with what we've been told about him annoying young women?"

"Man's nature," said Slaughter, "is not always divided into the categories we assume."

And it's not always about sex, Slaughter thought to himself. Sometimes it's thinking you're not loved enough. Sometimes it's about power. Like Cleopatra and Antony.

"What did you think of Mr. Price, sir?"

"I think he is an actor. Agnes suggested that too. Always acting, never shows his true self. But a few things concern me about the gala."

"Morton talking to Lady Featherstone?"

"We do have her report about him talking to her at an earlier event, at the old St. Thomas's. It could have been more of the same."

"The only way to find out about the blackmail," said Honeycutt, "would be to ask her for proof or talk to her husband. We found nothing at Morton's house."

"That's true. And if Morton was a blackmailer, would he have also been blackmailing Cyril Price? Or might Cyril Price have been blackmailing him?"

"Possibly, sir, but who would be harmed by these blackmailing schemes? For Lady Featherstone, it would be Sir Henry. But would he be disgraced or lose his position? I doubt it."

"Yes, I agree. Lady Featherstone's past, even if it were known, might affect her social standing. But his standing could well survive such a revelation. That was why I didn't understand why she came to the station."

"I suppose," said Honeycutt, "that Cyril Price's reputation could be ruined if his intimate activities were known, but in the theatre world? I would think that sort of thing wouldn't be uncommon."

Slaughter gave a wry smile. "You may be right. But the other way around, could Cyril Price have ruined Dr. Morton's career?"

They were back at Christchurch station. The mid-day sun was peeking out from behind the clouds. As they pulled up, Jones came out to open the door.

"Wait here," said Slaughter. He got out and called up to the driver. "I'm sorry, but could you take us back, past where we were, to Surrey Gardens, the new St. Thomas's Hospital, please?"

"Right, gov," Honeycutt heard the driver reply. They left the constable standing at the curb, throwing his hands up into the air.

"Why back to the hospital?"

"We almost forgot. Matron said nurse probationers should be interviewed at lunch. We need to talk to Mary Simmons, the girl Morton pestered. Then, I agree, we should speak to Sir Henry again."

"You don't want lunch, sir?"

Slaughter ignored this. "Let's start at the hospital. If Sir Henry isn't there today, I'll leave you and go across Vauxhall Bridge to Kensington to see him at home. You stay and talk to Mary Simmons."

⤳

Sir Henry was not at the hospital, so Slaughter proceeded to Kensington. Honeycutt went directly to the tea room. He'd been told to look for four or five nurse probationers at a table, one with ginger hair peeking out from under her cap. They weren't hard to find. All were eating meat pies except one, who was having a bowl of soup.

"Excuse me," said Honeycutt. "I'm Detective Sergeant Mark Honeycutt of the Metropolitan Police. I was told to ask for Mary Simmons."

"Mary, this is what I was telling you," said the red-haired woman to the girl on her left, nudging her with her elbow. "He wants to talk to you about Dr. Morton."

The girl eating the soup was dark and pretty, her face like a pale moon, with large expressive eyes. Dark brown. A man could get lost in those, thought Honeycutt. At the moment, though, they looked frightened. She had frozen in mid-spoonful.

"Please don't worry," said Honeycutt. "I know it's hard to talk about other people. Especially important people. But you look so like my sister back home in America. She knew she could trust a policeman, because I was one." He didn't have a sister in Baltimore, or anywhere else, as far as he knew.

"I'm . . . not sure I should," said Mary. She touched her hand gently to her chest. Honeycutt noticed two little pin holes in her uniform. Matron wouldn't like that, he thought.

"How about if I go get a cup of tea and come back? Can I get you one?"

Mary didn't answer. The red-haired woman said, "I'll take one, if you please."

Honeycutt smiled at her. "And what's your name, Miss?" The other girls at looked at each other and tried not to giggle.

"I'm Clare Tucker," she said.

"Very well, Clare Tucker, I'll fetch some tea for you and me both."

When he returned with the cups and teapot, it was obvious the girls had been talking. Mary seemed a little calmer.

"I only have a few minutes," she said, "but I'll try to answer your questions."

"Mary works over in the surgery ward," explained Clare. "It's a bit of a walk from here."

"That's fine," said Honeycutt. He reached in his pocket to take out his notebook and noticed Mary watching him with wide eyes. He decided to leave the notebook alone for now.

"Clare here says you knew Dr. Morton?"

"Yes. He . . . um . . . took notice of me."

"I see. How old are you, Mary, and where are you from?"

"I'm twenty, sir. I'm from Cardiff, in Wales."

"Do you miss Wales very much?"

Mary looked up at him, and her eyes softened. "Yes, I do. But I so want to be a nurse. And Miss Nightingale's school here, well, everyone knows it's the best."

"I have heard that," said Honeycutt. "Would you say that Dr. Morton paid more attention to you than the other probationers?"

Mary lowered her eyes, and nodded. She looked like she might cry.

"He was right handy," said Clare, "wasn't he, Mary? Touched you and all, didn't he?"

Mary nodded again.

"Did anyone know about this, other than your friends here?"

Mary looked up, suddenly. "No. I never told anyone else. Honest I didn't."

"You didn't want Matron to know?"

She shook her head. "I didn't want her to think it was my fault. She's always saying to stay away from the surgeons and medical students. I work in the far ward, near the operating theatre. Nobody would see anything there."

"I don't want to ask anything that would make you uncomfortable," said Honeycutt quietly. "But did he only touch you on your uniform? Or did he take other liberties?"

Mary's eyes filled with tears. "Only on my uniform, but he said as how he would be doing more. If I allowed him to, he said. He'd give me gifts, he said."

Clare leaned forward. "And he did, too, didn't he? Gave you that pin. Made you wear it and all."

Mary nodded with big eyes, her hand reaching up to touch the tiny holes on her uniform. "But then I didn't have to worry about it anymore. Because they told me he was dead. In the old operating theatre."

"That's right, Mary," said Honeycutt. "No need to worry anymore. When did you last see him?"

Mary sniffed. "Um . . . I think a fortnight ago. Wait, maybe Friday. Not yesterday, but the Friday before that. Surgery day."

"Did he say anything to you?"

"Only hello. He said it in this low voice, while he . . . patted me. In the corridor." She took a deep breath. "That was the last time." She looked up. "I'm sorry, but I really have to go now."

"Of course. I just have one more question. Were you here at the hospital Saturday morning, or somewhere else?"

"Here," she said, looking round at her companions. "We have class Saturday mornings."

The others nodded, and Mary rose from her chair.

"Thank you so much for talking with me, Miss Simmons. And for reminding me of my sister, who I miss very much." He stood as she left, then sat down to finish his tea.

"Dr. Morton was horrible, make no mistake," said Clare. "I can say so because he never went after me. And that pin, giving it to her like he owned her or something."

"The pin was where the holes are in her uniform?"

Clare nodded. "It was like a ring or something, like a circle. Matron lets the nurses wear a pin, a cross of St. George or something. But this looked different. Anyway, nobody noticed it."

"Well, thank you, ladies. And thank you, Clare," said Honeycutt, rising. "It was nice to meet you all. You've been very helpful."

"I'm glad to help," said Clare, "but I'm also glad he's dead. It's hard enough to be a nurse probationer, without being handled when you can't do nothing about it." Honeycutt couldn't help but agree.

❧

John came out into the hall to let Inspector Slaughter in.

"Sir Henry is writing letters now, Inspector," John explained. "It should only be a few minutes. I'll let him know you're here."

"Before you do, I'd like to talk to you a moment, if I may."

John looked surprised, but his expression was quickly replaced by caution. A noble-looking man, thought Slaughter.

"If you like. What can I do for you?"

Slaughter looked up at him. There was no invitation to sit down.

"How long have you worked for Sir Henry, John? If I may call you John?"

John looked across the foyer at the wall. He held his hands together behind his back, as if being questioned by a superior officer.

"You may. My name is John Addo. I have been companion to Sir Henry for almost thirty years."

"How did you meet?"

"I was rescued from a Spanish slaver, the *Almirante*. I was one of over 400 souls on board. Sir Henry was captain of the *Black Joke*."

"The *Black Joke*?" asked Slaughter.

"A naval ship captured from the Brazilian slavers. It was renamed after a song the sailors liked to sing. It followed the *Almirante*, and there was a battle. When it was over, I did not wish to be re-landed, and I hid in the captain's cabin. Sir Henry was badly wounded, and he was treated in the surgeon's room. When he returned to his cabin, I begged him to take me to England, where I would be emancipated. Sir Henry agreed."

"Extraordinary," said Slaughter. "How old were you?"

"I was ten. He saved my life. I stayed with him as his servant on the *Black Joke* until he retired, then came here with him."

"When did he begin to need your physical help?"

John thought for a moment, and Slaughter saw he was considering whether to answer.

"In '44, after the operation. The wound he got fighting the *Almirante* became a tumor. The operation was a success, but he lost the use of his legs." Slaughter considered. "If that is all, Inspector, I shall see if Sir Henry is ready to receive you."

Slaughter stood in the hall alone, taking in the rich furnishings. These people live very well, he thought. And they have a most remarkable servant. Dedicated to Sir Henry's well-being, certainly. What might he do if he thought his family was threatened?

"Sir Henry will see you now." John had approached without Slaughter hearing him.

Slaughter entered the study and noticed that Sir Henry was seated comfortably in an armchair.

"Come in, Inspector. Have a seat. Can I get you some tea?"

"No, thank you, Sir Henry."

"What can I do for you?" He motioned to John that he wasn't needed. "Have you had good access to everyone at the hospital?"

"Yes, thank you. Mr. Tapper and Matron were very helpful, and we've been able to do our work easily. But we have been following a line of inquiry I'd like to share with you."

"Of course! How can I help?"

"We have this blue piece of paper, sir. It was discovered in Dr. Morton's pocket when he died." Slaughter removed it from between the pages of his notebook. "Do you know anything about it?" He leaned forward to hand it to Sir Henry.

"No, I don't think so."

"We discovered it was a ticket for a gala to benefit the hospital, on the 28th of August."

"Oh! Yes, I recall now. At the Surrey Theatre. Yes, indeed."

"Do you recall who was present that evening?"

Sir Henry looked up and thought a moment. "Well, we were, of course, Lady Featherstone and myself. Cyril Price, naturally, and the actress Geraldine Orson. A few other people from the theatre, I believe. All but one member of the hospital board, and their guests, and I'd say about a half dozen benefactors with their wives."

"Any physicians or surgeons?"

"Yes, indeed. We like as many as possible to attend these things, mix with the money, you know." He smiled.

"Was Dr. Morton there?"

"Yes, he was. I introduced Mr. Price and Miss Orson to him, Dr. Woodsmith, and two or three of our physicians."

"Did you notice anything peculiar about Dr. Morton's behavior that night, sir?"

"No, not really. Oh, I did see him talk to Lady Featherstone. I asked her what he wanted, and she said he'd made a comment about the insipid nature of some of the new patrons. Sounded like him. And he was nice to Cyril Price, which I didn't expect. Invited him to see the hospital. Other than that, Inspector, he was his usual cigar-smoking, abrupt self."

"Sir Henry, I have to ask you a sensitive question about Lady Featherstone."

Sir Henry looked down at his hands, then up at Slaughter.

"Inspector, you have no doubt discovered that Lady Featherstone was an actress in her younger days."

"Yes, we do know that."

"I take it you have you uncovered something unsavory about her past?"

"Yes, I'm afraid we have."

Sir Henry took a sip of water from the glass on the table next to him, and said quietly, "Let me stop you there, Inspector. I am already aware that my wife had a relationship with Mr. Price. It was many years ago. We have never spoken of it, but I have always known."

Inspector Slaughter paused. He had assumed Sir Henry had known, but he wasn't sure why.

"Were you aware that Dr. Morton was trying to blackmail her about it?"

Sir Henry looked confused. "Are you sure? Why would he do that?"

"Since you already know about Lady Featherstone and Cyril Price, I think it's suitable to tell you that she visited my office last week. She reported that Dr. Morton had made an arrangement with her."

"What sort of arrangement?" Sir Henry knitted his brows. Slaughter looked in his notebook.

"Lady Featherstone had apparently seen him come in late and leave early at a full staff meeting in August, at the old hospital. For some reason he didn't want anyone to know he had been there. He sat briefly among the nurse probationers, apparently."

"Now that is very odd, Inspector. He would not have been expected to attend a full staff meeting. The surgeons do as they please, although he would have been welcome."

"Are you saying you have no idea why he was there, or why he wouldn't want it known that he was there?"

"No idea at all."

"I do have one more question, I'm afraid. Can you tell me where you were last Saturday morning?"

Sir Henry smiled, then his smile blossomed into laughter.

"You think I killed him? I suppose I might have, but how would I have gotten him up into the seats in that horrible position?" He gestured toward his legs. "I'm sorry, Inspector, but these legs haven't done what I tell them for eighteen years."

"So, you were . . . ?"

Sir Henry smiled again. "Here at home writing letters, with my lovely wife helping organize them."

Slaughter rose, closing his notebook. "I'm sorry to have bothered you at home, Sir Henry. And I appreciate your help."

"Of course." He rang a small bell next to his water glass, and John came into the room.

"John, see the Inspector out, would you please?"

⤳

By the time Slaughter returned to Christchurch station, the sun was going down. He had been forced to take a circuitous route back from Kensington. Traffic over Vauxhall Bridge had been so much better since the pleasure gardens had closed, but the traffic to and from the Exhibition had replaced it. It was easier to go through St. James's and across Westminster Bridge, so he decided to go home, even though it meant passing by Waterloo Station. Perhaps on Saturday evening it wouldn't be as bad.

Something really needed to be done about the London traffic, thought Slaughter. Every new innovation had just brought more people and cartage into the city. The railways had been an engineering marvel, enabling the speedier movement of goods, and then people, into and out of town. Once these goods and people arrived, they had to be carried around London. Cabs, like this one, competed with foot traffic pushed off the narrow pavements, and carts. So many carts, carrying all manner of things: furniture, crates of wine for restaurants, casks for the many pubs, live chickens and pigs, drapery and more drapery. London was increasingly being built upward, but architectural innovations made things even worse on the streets. He was very glad he'd never had to serve as one of the Met constables controlling the congestion.

He wondered whether the Women's Reform Club had ever discussed this problem. Oh dear, now he remembered. Ellie was having Jo and Bridget over to the house this evening, to plan something. What was it? Something about Miss Nightingale and domestic hygiene, he thought. He hoped he and Tommy would get some dinner. Then it occurred to him Tommy would be working at the theatre anyway.

He arrived and saw Tommy heading out the door, cap on his head and shrugging into his coat as the cab pulled up.

"Hold on there, Tommy," said Slaughter as he got out and paid the driver.

"Don't worry," said Tommy, "they've got your dinner, nice and hot!" He grinned at Slaughter.

"Oh good," said Slaughter, relieved. "Do you have a minute to run a note for me?"

"Always," nodded Tommy. "To the station, then?"

"Yes, I need to let Sergeant Honeycutt know I've gone home."

"Is that all? I'll just tell Reggie on the way to the theatre. He'll take the message up to the station for you."

"Excellent. Thank you." Tommy prepared to run toward Blackfriars Road.

"Oh, and Tommy?"

"Inspector?"

"What nights this week is the play?"

"Tuesday until Saturday. Why?"

"I'm thinking of taking Mrs. Slaughter to see it."

Tommy grimaced. "I don't know if she'll like it, but I think you will." He waved his cap and ran off.

The house was warm and smelled like roast duck. Ellie must have bought some fresh at the market this morning. Onion and sage, too. It suddenly occurred to him he hadn't eaten any lunch. He hoped Honeycutt had eaten at the hospital.

Slaughter sat down and took off his shoes in the parlor, aware for the first time how tired he was. He had thought to find the women in the kitchen, but on the way down the corridor he noticed they had taken over his study.

"Hullo," he said, waving to all three.

"Cubby!" Ellie rose and went to greet him. "Now, don't worry, we have your dinner," she said, leading him into the kitchen.

"I know—it smells wonderful."

"Let me pour you a glass of water—no, you look like you could use beer. I'll get you a plate. Then we must get back to it."

Slaughter sat at the kitchen table, enjoying his duck, the warmth of the kitchen, and the sound of voices in his study. The kitchen had been scrubbed clean. He did wish he could afford more help for Ellie. The house wasn't large, but there were three downstairs rooms, and bedrooms and bath upstairs. Prudence came in two or three days a week to clean and tidy, but the charwoman came only once a month. The coal had added an extra element, quite literally, he thought.

And Ellie's philanthropic work, unpaid though it was, remained important to the education and moral foundation of the community. It also kept her from being lonely, he thought, as laughter drifted in from the study. He took his plates up to the board, then carried his beer with him into the study.

Books that had been on the chairs had been moved to his desk. Slaughter's own desk chair was free, so he took a seat and fussed with the book stacks as he listened.

"I understand why Miss Stubbing brought up the issue, but I don't think Miss Nightingale's note was intended to circulate. I'm reluctant to use it as a topic, even aside from who might come to speak," said Ellie.

"I know I'm not on this committee," said Bridget, "but I have to agree. Would it be better if we developed a more appropriate idea? Perhaps related to this but not exactly?"

Out of the corner of his eye, he could see Jo drawing on her sketch pad. "I think it will be hard for listeners not to blame the women making their living in this dangerous way," she said. "Perhaps it would be better to focus on those who are taken advantage of?"

"We already talked about 'fallen women,' and the way they are blamed instead of the men who procure them," said Bridget, "just a few months ago."

"What about the women who aren't in the public eye?" said Jo. "They have stories too, especially the ones taken advantage of by men."

"You mean ordinary women who must tolerate men's advances?" asked Ellie.

"Who could speak about that?" Bridget said. "It happens every day. To any woman who works in public, or goes to school, or even walks down the street."

The three women looked down at their work. There was a depressed silence.

"Right," said Ellie, "let's start again by looking at the issues being considered in Parliament. What have been the latest petitions?"

"There is one from the Worshipful Society of the Apothecaries, asking for more money to treat the poor," said Bridget.

"And one about copyrighting artworks internationally," said Jo. She was peering at Bridget as she drew.

"And there have been several against the Revised Code," noted Ellie. "I'm not sure people like the idea of schools being paid based on the examination results of pupils."

"Let's bring them all back," said Jo, "as ideas. We'll explain why we don't want to violate Miss Nightingale's privacy, and that we need another topic. Personally, I think we should continue with our work on abolishing the slave trade. All right, how's it look?" She showed Ellie and Bridget the sketch. Bridget was portrayed frowning at her papers with a look of concentration. It was very well done.

As if they were of a single mind, they turned to Slaughter.

"How is the murder investigation coming?" asked Ellie.

Slaughter tapped the tobacco down in his pipe. "Slowly," he said. "We know how Dr. Morton died, and likely where, but not why."

"It's love or money," said Jo.

"Or sex," said Bridget.

Slaughter considered. "Or professional jealousy," he said. "The question is how to get someone to admit to such feelings."

"You have a reassuring manner," said Jo. "Might just be a matter of seeing, rather than listening."

"You would say that," teased Bridget. "Not everyone can see with your artist's eyes, you know."

As Jo and Bridget prepared to leave, a thought occurred to him.

"If you are continuing with the abolition topic, I did meet someone who might be of assistance to your group." Jo looked at him with interest as she put on her coat. "Sir Henry Featherstone's man, John Addo. He was rescued from a slave ship by the West Africa Squadron. I don't know whether he'd be willing to speak to the Women's Reform Club, but if he were he'd be excellent."

As Ellie saw her friends out, Slaughter finished his pipe. He really shouldn't worry, he thought, about Ellie reading the penny magazines. It was quite obvious that she and the Women's Reform

Club were more than aware of the vagaries of human interactions. But he was also thinking about their frustration, and women being forced to tolerate the liberties men took with them. Thaddeus Morton had clearly been one of those men.

8

Mark Honeycutt was unsure what to wear to Sunday dinner at the Slaughters', but he simply hadn't brought many clothes with him from America. He'd noticed that the style of his clothes was different, but he hadn't had the opportunity or the funds to do much shopping. It seemed to be more a matter of fabric than style anyway. He decided to wear what he wore to work rather than to church. He'd walked a mile in his church clothes that morning to attend the newly opened Our Lady of La Salatte and Saint Joseph Church, near the old hospital. Like the hospital, it had been moved to accommodate the railway. He had not felt ready to take communion.

The Slaughters attended Christchurch, but only irregularly. Originally, they had done so as a touchstone for Tommy. When he was younger, they'd attended with him to encourage Christian morality, but that had been unnecessary. The lad seemed to possess a natural morality, although goodness knows how he obtained that on the streets, Ellie often thought. Instead, Tommy had been taken with the theatricality of the services. He was usually the one who suggested they attend, unless he was working. This Sunday, he'd been needed in Borough High Street to run errands for a Jewish furniture merchant who supplied set pieces for the theatre.

"Do you think that the publication of Darwin's theory has affected church attendance?" Slaughter asked Honeycutt over dinner. Tommy had arrived home just in time to join them, and Ellie was happy to have an even four at the table. If he was surprised by the question, Honeycutt gave no indication.

"I'm not sure, but I know the census said attendance is lower. It's unfortunate that they removed the question about religion. Ironically, the survey wasn't very scientific."

Slaughter nodded. Dinner was typical for Sunday: roast mutton, potatoes, and greens with onions. Honeycutt had said how happy he was to have a home-cooked meal. Tommy, eating carefully with his knife and fork, looked up at Honeycutt.

"So, you're from America?" he asked.

"I am. Baltimore, Maryland."

"That's named after our Bloody Mary, isn't it?" asked Tommy. Ellie gave him a look.

"Yes, I'm afraid so. But it was a haven for Catholics for many decades."

"I know all about Catholics, from a boy at the workhouse. Are you Catholic?"

"I am," said Honeycutt, glancing around the table. Slaughter and Ellie nodded and continued eating.

"So, who do you think killed Dr. Morton?" asked Tommy. Ellie sighed.

"I'm not sure Detective Sergeant Honeycutt wants to be cross-questioned over dinner," she said.

"I'm sorry," said Tommy. "Would it be all right to ask about America?"

Ellie looked over at Honeycutt, who smiled. "Is it all right?" he asked her.

"Tommy is a curious lad, and he likes to learn things. I just hope you don't find his questions offensive."

"Not at all. Ask anything you like. About America," he amended. Ellie got up to bring the pudding.

"Are the slaves fighting in the war?"

This was not the question Honeycutt expected. Although he found it uncomfortable, he didn't want to avoid answering. After all, he had said Tommy could ask anything.

"Yes, they are fighting in the war." He paused, wondering how to phrase what he was thinking. "On both sides. For the Union they believe they are fighting for freedom and for their country. For the

Confederacy, they believe they are fighting for their homes and their country."

"But aren't the slaves forced to fight for the Confederacy?" asked Tommy.

"Yes, some are. But both sides are forcing people to fight, free people as well as slaves."

Tommy thought about this. "Which side is right?"

Ellie put the baked pears on the table. Mark answered Tommy with a shrug, and turned to Ellie, "My, that looks delicious!" he said.

Then he took a deep breath and replied to Tommy. "My family has held slaves for decades," he explained, "but I believe that enslaving people is wrong. That's why the slave trade has been outlawed in so many places. Slavery has caused a lot of problems, and it has made a lot of people rich. My family was never rich, and one of our slaves was raised in my family. Bobby was my best friend in the whole world." Ellie gave him a sympathetic smile.

"It sounds," said Slaughter, "like the whole issue is more complicated than it appears."

Tommy nodded sagely. "Most things are," he said. "It's like when people think I'm a certain way because I lived in a workhouse."

Once they had finished their dinner, Honeycutt rose to help Ellie clear the table. "Thank you, kind sir," she laughed, "but the big question is"—she looked pointedly at her husband—"are you two willing to discuss the case?" Tommy nodded his head hopefully.

"I was hoping to retreat with you to the study," Slaughter said to Honeycutt, "but it looks like we'll be four for this discussion, if you don't mind?"

Back in America, Mark had often talked over cases with his colleagues, and on more than one occasion with the wife of his superior. But not a twelve-year-old boy. His eyes flicked toward Tommy.

"Yes, I know it's unusual," said Slaughter, "but Tommy is like a son to us. He also happens to know some of the people involved. Tell Sergeant Honeycutt what you do for people, Tommy."

"I work at the Surrey Theatre, and I help at the hospital. And I do errands, and sweeping, and brick carrying, for just about everyone between Surrey Gardens and the river," he said proudly.

"Maybe we should question him," said Honeycutt, with raised eyebrows.

"A good idea," said Slaughter. "Tommy," he said, with mock seriousness, "are you willing to take the stand to testify?"

"Yes, sir!" said Tommy. Ellie grabbed a chair and took several books from the sideboard, stacking them on the seat to boost him up. "Go on then, young man," she said. "Up you go."

Honeycutt pulled the table over to the side of the room, sat down with a serious expression, and took out his notebook. He was very glad he had worn his work clothes to dinner. Inspector Slaughter rose and, putting his hands behind his back, began pacing in front of Tommy.

"Mr. Jones," intoned Slaughter, "where were you on the morning of Saturday, the 18th of October?"

"I did the marketing with Mrs. Slaughter in the morning." Tommy looked up at the ceiling. "Oh, and then after lunch I went to the gasworks to run papers around." Honeycutt took a note.

"And did you know Dr. Morton?"

"Yes, sir. Like I told you, nobody liked him. Stayed out of his way, like."

"When was the last time you saw Dr. Morton?"

Tommy thought for a moment. "That would be the day before, sir, the Friday. Saw him talking to one of the student probationers."

Slaughter looked up. "You did?"

"Yes, sir. One of the pretty students, sir. In the corridor."

"What did you see?"

"He said something to her, and she looked kind of startled, then nervous. She turned to go and he"—Tommy glanced over at Ellie— "patted her as she left. On her . . . bottom."

"Had you seen him do that kind of thing before?"

"Yes, sir. He liked doing that to student nurses." Ellie sighed and turned to the sink, her shoulders stiff.

"And do you know Dr. Woodsmith?"

"A little bit, sir. He's always very nice to everyone. And he's strong."

"Strong?"

"Yes, sir. Has a strong arm. Makes him a quick surgeon for amputations. He can hold a man's leg completely still with his bent arm while he cuts."

"Goodness!" exclaimed Ellie.

Slaughter looked over to make sure Mark was done with the note. "Young man, we understand you also work at the theatre."

"Yes, sir, the Surrey Theatre. I help backstage."

"Do you know Cyril Price?"

"Oh yes, sir. He's a great actor and manager. Told me so himself." Tommy grinned and pushed back a lock of his hair in an excellent imitation.

"And do you know Agnes Cook, the designer?"

"Yes, everyone likes Agnes. But she does talk out of turn, sometimes."

"Oh? Can you explain?"

"She takes little drinks while she works, sir. Carries this little flask around, but she thinks nobody sees. Sometimes she says things about people that those people wouldn't want said."

"I see. Do you know anyone else who might be involved, who knew Dr. Morton?"

"Well, Sam Wetherby, sir. He assisted Dr. Morton. Knows as much as a surgeon does, too, I think."

"Might he be jealous of Dr. Morton, Mr. Jones?"

Tommy thought a moment, his feet swinging. "Maybe," he said, "but he was also disappointed in him. Because of the hygiene."

"The hygiene?"

"Dr. Morton didn't always wash, sir, even though Sam says it's important."

"I see. And what about Felix Tapper, the apothecary?"

"Like I told you, I know who he is, sir." Tommy hesitated.

"Is there something?" asked Slaughter.

"Well, sir, I think he's the one what gives Miss Orson her medicine."

"Miss Orson?"

"Geraldine Orson, the actress. I heard her writing a note to Mr. Tapper. She always reads aloud when she writes, and I was passing by the dressing room. I know who Mr. Tapper is, so I was curious. Went in when she wasn't there and saw the note. It was about getting some medicine after the show. And I've seen her take drops in water sometimes. But she doesn't seem to be ill."

Slaughter nodded. "Do you have any questions for Mr. Jones, Sergeant?"

"Just one." Honeycutt looked up from his notebook. "How did you get to be such an observant young man?"

"Lots of practice, sir," smiled Tommy. "Lots of practice!"

❦

"I presume you'd like me to go to the theatre to interview Miss Orson, sir?" asked Honeycutt the next morning. It was raining again, but he'd managed to avoid the worst of it. Another good reason to live close to the station.

"I was thinking I could do it, so I could buy tickets for the play," replied Slaughter. "But then I remembered the actors won't be at the theatre. There's no performance tonight." Jones went by the office door, preening his mustache. "What's the matter with Jones?"

"It's the artist, sir. Jo Harris. She wants to draw a few of the constables who worked on the Saunders case. Jones is most excited about it."

"Oh, yes, I know Miss Harris," said Slaughter. He vaguely recalled being asked about this, but he'd been thinking on other things. "Well, it's all right with me so long as it doesn't interfere with everyone's duties." The Saunders case had been on his watch. The brothers would have gotten away with a fortune in jewels, stolen from two of the nice brick houses on Stamford Street. But his constables had apprehended the culprits behind the Victoria Theatre, where they were trying to sell their stolen goods. Constable Stevens had also captured the criminal buying them.

"Should I visit Miss Orson at home, then?" asked Honeycutt. "I have her address here from the list they gave me at the theatre." He pulled the list from his pocket. "Nelson Square, Number 45."

"An excellent idea. If this is about drugs, just assure her that we are not interested in making a case about that. But we need to know whether Morton was in any way involved. Could be another situation for blackmail, so you'll need to tread gently."

"Understood, sir." As Honeycutt took his coat and left, Jo Harris was coming in. She was carrying a folding easel and a basket over her arm in addition to her usual satchel. Instead of a coat she wore a blue cape covering it all. The cape was shedding water. A constable jumped up to assist, hanging her cape on the rack.

"Thank you," she said to the constable. "I'm Jo Harris, from the *Temple Bar* magazine, here to draw the three constables who were on the Saunders case." She put her things down near the rack.

"Yes, Miss," said Constable Stevens. "I'm one, and the others are here, too. Where would you like us? In the public area here? Or in an interview room?"

Jo looked around. "I think an interview room might be best, if it has enough light. Is Detective Inspector Cuthbert Slaughter at his desk?"

"He is, Miss. Shall I take you through?"

Jo peeked around the edge of the door. "Inspector?"

Slaughter rose. "Hello, Miss Harris." He smiled. "I haven't seen you in two whole days."

"I know," she said, "but this is where they sent me. Miss Braddon is writing a story on the Saunders case, so Mr. Sala wants illustrations. Sensational stuff. I think they're setting up in one of the interview rooms? Thank you for being so accommodating."

"Happy to be of service," said Slaughter. "May I see the sketch when you're finished?"

Jo agreed, and for the next hour worked on sketching the three constables. All were most happy to oblige. But Jones kept changing his pose.

"Honestly, Constable Jones, you were fine where you were before."

"But this is more dramatic, isn't it? If I'm looking over their shoulders at the plan?"

Jo shook her head and kept sketching. "I think if I'm going to have this done today so you gentlemen can get back to work, it would be better if you'd stayed standing where you were."

By the time she returned to Slaughter's office, she had snapped the sketchbook closed and was frowning.

"I'm sorry," she said, "it's not as good as I would like. I brought the wrong notebook, you see. These are draft sketches going back years. Didn't have a good clean sheet. I'm afraid I'll have to go home and redraw this evening to make it right."

"That's all right," he said. "I won't judge it harshly. I'd still love to see, if you don't mind?"

Jo put the book in front of him and flipped through the pages to get to the one she'd just drawn. He stopped her. "May I see this one?" he asked.

"Certainly," she said, "it's just a piece of jewelry." She shrugged. "It belonged to a friend."

"It's very unusual. Is it a snake?"

"Yes, it's a snake eating its own tail. A cheap copy of the one Prince Albert gave to the queen some time ago."

Slaughter frowned, trying to remember. "And you say your friend had it?" He gestured to the chair, and Jo sat down, confused.

"Yes. Do you think it has something to do with your case?"

"I'm not sure. May I ask you about your friend?" Slaughter could tell he was in a sensitive area. Jo was Ellie's friend, but she would have other friends too. She'd come here to draw the constables, not to help him with his case.

"Oh, it's not Ellie's," said Jo. "It was my friend who's passed. Her name was Nan Deighton." The expression on Jo's face changed. Slaughter could see the friend had been special. He spoke gently.

"Did you give her the . . . it's a pin, is it?"

"It is a pin, but I didn't give it to her. Her fellow did. She knew him from St. Thomas's, from being a nurse probationer."

Slaughter nodded. "I can't see where it pins on?"

"The hinge is right there, where it gets darker."

"And how big was it?"

Jo held up finger and thumb about an inch apart.

Slaughter nodded again and turned the page. "Oh my!" he said, smiling. "You've captured Jones exactly."

"I'm afraid he looks like something out of a pantomime," Jo said.

"Well." Slaughter glanced at the open office door and lowered his voice. "He rather is sometimes, isn't he?"

◦◦◦

Geraldine Orson's house, like Geraldine herself, held an aura of faded elegance. Built of brick at the end of the Napoleonic Wars, it had not aged particularly well but was still interesting to look at. Honeycutt rang the bell at Number 45 and stepped back into the rain. A young man of about Tommy's age answered the door.

"Good afternoon. I am Detective Sergeant Honeycutt of the Metropolitan Police. Is Miss Orson at home?"

"Yes, sir," said the boy, and stepped back.

"Thank you. Are you her son?" asked Honeycutt.

"No, sir. Would you wait in here, please?" He pointed to the parlor just off the hall.

Honeycutt looked around the room while he waited. One chair was covered in red velvet and looked expensive, but when he sat down it didn't feel stable. He stood instead and looked at the books on the shelves. Shakespeare, Sophocles, Milton. They were all bound in red leather. When he pulled one out, it clung to its neighbors. A set, then, rarely read, if at all. Out of curiosity, he lifted the edge of the cloth on the side table. A single-seamed hem. He began to wonder whether anything in the room was real.

"Detective Sergeant Honeycutt," Geraldine said smoothly as she approached. Her hair was up in fashionable disarray, and her bright blue dress was of a fabric that rustled without being too full. A simple thick cream shawl crossed her chest, and he realized it was quite chilly in the house. There was no fireplace in the room. "What can I do for you?"

Her face was bright and confident, her cheeks a little flushed.

"Yes, Miss Orson. I'm sorry to disturb you at home. We're investigating the death of Dr. Morton."

"Ah," she sighed, sinking rather carefully onto the sofa and directing Honeycutt to the red chair. "I had heard about that. Cyril Price mentioned it to me." She looked at Honeycutt with an air of having all the time in the world to talk with him and nothing else she'd rather do.

Honeycutt knew little of the theatre world. He had never been to a play in Baltimore, although his grandmother had taken him to see an opera at the Holliday Theatre when he was sixteen. It had been an extravaganza called *Harnane* or *Ernani* or something. His grandmother had gone on about what a genius Verdi was. He hadn't understood anything that was happening on stage. He missed his grandmother, but he hadn't missed the theatre.

Geraldine Orson bore no resemblance to the woman he'd seen singing on stage in the opera. She was elegant, although he could see small lines around her eyes. Her vitality and charisma were her best assets, Honeycutt decided. She was classically beautiful, yes, but it was the unwavering gaze, the set of her mouth, the way she held her head. He found it hard to take his eyes off her.

She smiled as if she knew exactly what he was thinking. "Did you have questions for me, Detective Sergeant?" She said the word "detective" as if it were something sweet.

Honeycutt cleared his throat and took out his notebook. "I do, Miss Orson. First, I'm afraid I have to ask you where you were on the morning of Saturday the 18th?"

Geraldine smiled brightly. "That would be the Saturday before last?"

Honeycutt nodded. She had a beautiful smile.

"Sleeping." She said it like a hush. "I always sleep until noon on Saturdays."

"I see," he said, trying not to imagine her in bed. "May I ask if you were . . . alone in the house?"

"Oh yes," she said, looking into his eyes. "Alone in the house. Alone in my bed."

"Ah," Honeycutt said, seeking moorings in his notebook. "We need some information about your relationship to Felix Tapper, the apothecary at the hospital."

Geraldine blinked, slowly. Her head tilted as she looked toward the front window. "My goodness," she said, her hand moving gracefully to the knot on her shawl. "Relationship? I have no idea what you mean."

"I'm sorry to say this, but we have reason to believe you might have procured drugs from him? Drugs for a non-medical use?"

"I see," she said, lowering her eyes. She nibbled her lower lip gently with shiny white teeth. When her eyes rose to meet his, they were glistening a little.

"It's true," she said, taking a handkerchief from a small pocket on her dress. It opened, and he could see little roses embroidered on the edges. She touched it to the corner of her mouth. "I'm afraid I am of a . . . nervous disposition."

She stood and passed in front of him, her rose scent drifting past his face. "It's this world, you see. The theatre world. It is very hard on a woman alone." She paused. "I don't expect you to know what it's like. I'm a widow, as you may have heard. My husband died in India. Since he died, it's all been such a strain. The late nights, the unforgiving roles, the demands of men who think that I am as they see me on stage." Here she turned her head and looked directly into his eyes, and the pools of deepest blue made him feel twinges of both pity and desire.

Honeycutt forced himself to look at his notes. "Drops, the witness said. What might those drops be, Miss Orson?"

She wheeled to face him, her expression changing. Her eyes narrowed, and she flapped the handkerchief down by her side. "Who are you to ask me such questions? The drops were perfectly legal. Anyone can go into any shop anywhere and buy opium." Startled, Honeycutt wrote down "opium."

"Yes, Miss Orson, they can. So why did you obtain them from Mr. Tapper?"

"He's the best apothecary in London!" she cried. "And he treats me like a lady, not a"—she turned away and spat the word out—"*suspect.*"

Honeycutt realized he was staring. He managed to remember to say, "I assure you we are not interested in prosecuting you or Mr. Tapper for the drugs. We are interested in whether Dr. Morton may have been directly or indirectly involved." She gave a single nod of her head, but her eyes still glared at him.

He realized he'd been sitting while she had been standing. He stood up, notebook in hand. "Did he prepare a different kind of formula for you? Something stronger than you'd get in an ordinary apothecary shop? Is that why you went to him?"

Geraldine walked gracefully back to the sofa and sat down, looking up at him. She sniffed into her handkerchief. "Please sit down, Detective Sergeant. I'm sorry I got angry."

He sat.

"It's true that Felix Tapper prepares me a stronger dose than is usual," she said, "but that is because my nerves are particularly faulty. The strain gets to be too much for me sometimes. And now . . . now . . . the stronger dose is absolutely essential." She dropped the handkerchief into her lap as if in despair, and a tear slid down one rosy cheek. "I'm sorry, Detective Sergeant. I'm afraid I am more fragile than I appear."

"I understand, Miss Orson. I do." He wanted to take her hand. Instead he said, "Did Dr. Morton have knowledge of these transactions?"

She paused and wrinkled her brow, which had the odd effect of making her even more lovely. "I believe he did. I received a note. It wasn't signed, but I showed it to Felix—Mr. Tapper—and he said it was Morton's writing."

"When was this?"

"About a month ago."

"Do you still have the note?"

"I do not," she said. "I destroyed it."

"What did it say?"

"It threatened to expose my ... dependence on the drops. Isn't that the most ungentlemanly thing you've ever heard?" She looked up at him with those pools of blue. Honeycutt nodded.

"What did you do?"

"Nothing. The note said I would be hearing from its writer again soon. But I never did." She sighed. "You won't need to tell anyone about this, will you, Detective Sergeant?" She reached across and touched his hand with the tips of her fingers. "My career, in the theatre ... ?"

"I'll mention it to as few people as I can," Honeycutt agreed. "If it has nothing to do with Dr. Morton's death, it will not need to be a public concern."

"Thank you so much, Detective Sergeant," she said. Her voice was so rich and smooth. "I knew that a gentleman like you would keep a lady's secrets."

∽

"What about the Thames Tunnel?" asked Honeycutt. He and Slaughter were having what by now had become a typical discussion over lunch. They had both returned to the station to exchange notes and were ensconced in Slaughter's office.

"What about it?" asked Slaughter, as he handed Honeycutt a slice of Ellie's excellent bread with a chunk of cheese.

"It's a wonder! It's 1300 feet long and runs over 70 feet below the river."

"Have you been there?"

"Not yet, sir, but I'm very much looking forward to it."

"You likely know that it was built to connect the docks on either side, and to have carts for goods travel through. But it cost far more than expected. They couldn't complete the entrances for the carts, couldn't make them big enough. Now it's only for foot traffic, defeating the original purpose."

"It's a wonder of the world."

"Apart from the lives lost building it ..." He handed Honeycutt some pickle.

"Thank you, sir. Lives are sometimes lost with something new and innovative."

"Apart from that, the Thames Tunnel has become an underground haven for vagrants and miscreants of all kinds, male and female. Just ask our friend Sergeant Cummings at Bermondsey station. The police are called out almost every night."

"It has proven to everyone that a tunnel under a river is possible. Brunel's shield made it so far fewer lives were lost, and will be lost, building more."

"But to what purpose if it doesn't even help trade?"

"It's an innovation, a harbinger of the future. They've already begun building an underground railway from Farringdon to Kings Cross. People will be able to travel quickly, away from the jostle of the streets."

"That project has already led to a boiler explosion and damage to many homes. And you heard about the Fleet sewer flooding the cutting at Farringdon?"

"It's the start of a new era, and tunnels may be key. Who knows, sir—maybe someday they'll build a tunnel all the way to France."

Slaughter laughed. He enjoyed these arguments with Honeycutt. While not a typical brash American, Honeycutt had great faith in progress and the practical arts. Slaughter, although not a typical traditional Englishman, saw far more cost to new technologies than he saw benefits.

"Well, let's see what modern thinking can do about our murder," said Slaughter, wiping his fingers on the table napkin Ellie had thoughtfully provided.

"It feels like we're missing something," Honeycutt said. "We have a pretty good picture of Morton now. He was a woman-dangler, certainly."

"A what? Oh, a philanderer. He does seem to have preferred them young and pretty, and annoyed them terribly."

"He also seems to have engaged in blackmail. But to secure what? He didn't need money," Honeycutt pointed out.

"No. But from what we're hearing, he did like power. Of a kind."

"So, anyone over whom he held such power, who didn't like it, could be our man."

"Or woman," said Slaughter.

"Or woman. I wish I knew more about English society," said Honeycutt. "How much would the public care if they knew Geraldine Orson was addicted to opium?"

"The theatre-going public might care, and in this part of town, they can be unruly. They might even cause a commotion during a performance, insulting her."

"That would be humiliating. And possibly dangerous."

"Yes, it would," said Slaughter, "and if the press began saying things, theatre managers and boards would see her as a liability."

"So, it could ruin her," said Honeycutt. "What about Cyril Price's . . . proclivities?"

"Yes, that could cause the same sort of problem."

"Either of them would have reason to kill Morton, then. Or could they have done it together? They are friends, sir."

"A good point. The two of them could certainly manage it. Do you think a knowledge of anesthetics would be necessary for this murder, though?"

They sat and thought for a moment.

"I did see something odd today," mused Slaughter. "Jo Harris was here, and she had a drawing in her sketchbook. It was a pin, like a woman would wear. About an inch across. Belonged to her friend, she said, a woman who had died. Strange design, like a snake eating its tail. Didn't you mention something about a pin like that when you interviewed the nurse probationer, Mary Simmons?"

Honeycutt pulled out his notebook and flipped through. "Yes, her friend Clare mentioned it to me. Said Morton gave it to Mary."

"Jo Harris said the design was from a ring Prince Albert gave to the queen, but a cheap copy. I'd like to know more about it," said Slaughter. "Is it a common kind of pin?"

"I have no idea. Jones might know someone we could ask, like a jeweler?"

"Yes, you pursue that. Was it widely reproduced? Then get back to the hospital. Talk to Mary Simmons. No, better yet, talk to her friend Clare. Can she recall when she saw the pin on Mary? And where might it be now? If you don't get helpful answers, then ask to talk to Mary again. With your most soothing manner, of course. All of this may be completely unimportant."

"Absolutely, sir. May I also suggest something based on your notes?"

"Of course."

"What about Sir Henry's man, John Addo? You said you spoke to him and that he's very loyal to Sir Henry. Did Sir Henry or his lady have a reason to want Morton dead?"

"It seemed a very weak reason, about her earlier life in the theatre."

"That's just it, sir. What if the person she had the affair with were someone else, instead of Cyril Price?"

"Sir Henry knew it was Price."

"Perhaps she told him that. Maybe Morton was still trying to press her about someone else, someone important perhaps."

"Like a government minister or something?"

"Exactly. She didn't mention Mr. Price to you, sir, did she?"

"No," said Slaughter, "she didn't." He smiled. "You do think deviously, Honeycutt. That's good. I'll go back to the theatre. Agnes may be our best source on something like this."

The theatre was closed, so Slaughter went around the back to the stage door. It wasn't locked. There was no one near the door. He stopped by the dressing rooms, but they were all empty. So was the tiny costume room. A burly man in boots was coming toward the door with his coat on his arm.

"Excuse me," said Slaughter, "I'm looking for Agnes Cook?"

The man jabbed his thumb toward the scene loft. "She's in there, doing something foolish with my paint," he grumbled. "Something about the blood not looking right. I do blood just fine, thank you, but she says it don't look right on the fabric." He shook his head and stomped out the door.

Slaughter glimpsed Agnes taking a sip from her flask as he entered, so he backed up a step and entered again, making more noise this time. He cleared his throat. "Miss Cook?" he asked. She jumped with a small shriek, and turned. Her thick eyelashes fluttered.

"Oh, it's you then," she said. "You gave me a turn. I thought everyone was gone."

"Yes, I think I just met one of your colleagues on his way out."

"One of my what?" She had a small jar of red paint in her hand. "Oh, yeah, that's Rex. King of the scene shop, he calls himself. Some king. Look at this." She held out the jar. "Blood, it's supposed to be. But put it on the soldiers' costumes and it looks like mud. Will that work for a battle scene? I ask you, will it?"

"Not if you need blood," agreed Slaughter.

"Exactly! And we need blood! What good is all that 'my kingdom for a horse' nonsense if he isn't dripping blood?"

"No good at all," said Slaughter. "I wonder, though, if you might be able to answer just one or two questions for me? About the old days?"

Agnes sighed and put the blood down on the sawhorse behind her.

"Yeah, all right," she said, "but how old? I don't remember things like I used to." She sat on a stool and waved Slaughter to another.

"It would be about fifteen years ago."

"Oh, lawd, I was working over at Drury Lane then." She made it sound like Drury Lane was in another country.

"Did you happen to know an actress named Hannah Fairchild?"

Agnes screwed up her eyes in thought, "Hannah Fairchild . . . Hannah Fairchild. Oh! Yeah, I know who you mean. Always played the ingenue, the innocent girl?"

"That sounds right," said Slaughter.

"She was funny, really. Always played these wide-eyed country types, but she wasn't like that at all. No she wasn't. Knew her way around, I'd say."

"Do you happen to remember with whom she knew her way around?"

Agnes smiled, then laughed, then laughed so hard she almost fell off the tall stool.

"Well, I can tell you who her favorite was. Cyril Price himself!"

"Mr. Price?"

"You can bet your life on it. I didn't know him that well then, but the way she looked at him. And they were such a handsome couple when they went out together."

"Was she aware of his inclinations?" Slaughter asked.

"Well, now there you have me, love," said Agnes. "I've no idea. Like I said, I didn't know him that well then. We became friends afterward, just before he took over this place." She waved her hand around the scene loft.

"Thank you for your time, Miss Cook," he said as he rose to leave. "You've been most helpful." He paused, "Oh, I wonder, since it's Monday, whether I can get tickets for Friday night's performance? Or should I just return on Friday?"

Agnes grinned. "Oh, well, police are special, aren't you? I'm sure Cyril wouldn't mind if I gave you tickets. You bringing the missus, then?"

Slaughter nodded. "Well, yes, I'd like to."

"Don't worry, love. I'll have them held for you at the front. Just come tell them I left them for you."

Slaughter thought a moment. Agnes wasn't a suspect at this point, but she was involved in the case. "Look, let me pay you for them, while I'm here? We aren't supposed to take favors. How much for two?"

"I understand, dear. That would be three and six each, so . . ."

He searched in his pocket, then handed her a crown and a two-bob bit. She nodded and put the coins in her pocket. "Thank you again," he said.

"Wait a minute," she said. "Why were you asking about Hannah Fairchild? Did something happen to her?"

"Oh, no, I'm sorry. She's perfectly all right."

"Never knew where she got off to. She just disappeared from the stage," said Agnes, shaking her head and picking up the blood jar.

"I think," said Slaughter, "that she married well."

Honeycutt had more success at the hospital. The rain had gone, and the afternoon became sunny and warm. Almost like Baltimore in October, a little damp but warm. He felt like he should miss America, but he didn't. Even with something as horrendous as murder, this was far better than riots during a war. The brutality with which people of different skin color now looked at each other had caused him more pain than he realized at first. He knew he was running away. And he knew that Britain, with her great empire, was not morally superior in any way to the hatred he saw in Maryland. But here, he felt, he could be of use, perhaps even bring some new ideas.

He could certainly use his charm, he thought, to help people talk about themselves. Clare, of course, didn't need charming. She was most forthcoming about Mary Simmons and the pin.

"Oh, the pin! I hated that thing. Cheap piece of goods he gave her, saying as how it was what Prince Albert had given the queen. More like what a tinker in Soho would give his doxie! A famous doctor could afford better." They were outside the hospital on the grounds, the path nearest to the women's ward. Honeycutt had promised to only keep her a moment.

"What size was the pin?"

"About this big," she said, holding thumb and forefinger about an inch apart.

On his way to the hospital, Honeycutt had stopped by the jeweler that Jones had named, a Mr. Postlethwaite. His shop was in Ludgate Hill, near the Old Bailey. It wasn't really a jeweler's, but a pawn shop. Mr. Postlethwaite, said Jones, knew everything about gewgaws, old and new. And he had. Yes, a cheap piece as Honeycutt described had been made, but not very many. They hadn't sold well once people realized they had only sentimental value and were made of pot metal. He'd only seen one because someone had tried to pawn it, saying it was valuable precisely because so few had been made. By the time the prince died in December, quality replicas had cropped up and were sold to wealthier people as mementos. But these cheap ones weren't common.

"Can you tell me when you last saw Mary wear it?" Honeycutt asked Clare.

She thought for a moment. "I think it was that Friday, before Dr. Morton was killed."

"Do you know where it is now?"

"No, I'm afraid I don't," she said. She looked back toward the building. "I have to go back in now, but Mary should be in the surgery ward. It's Monday, so there aren't any surgeries. You might want to ask her." She gave Honeycutt a smile, tucked her frazzled hair under her cap as best she could, and hurried back to the ward.

Honeycutt knew his way by now. As he approached the surgery ward, he saw Dr. Woodsmith coming out.

"Detective Sergeant Honeycutt," he said politely, holding out his hand. "How nice to see you again. Any luck so far?"

"We have some leads," said Honeycutt. This man is very smooth, he thought. So pleasant. "I'm looking for Mary Simmons?"

Woodsmith looked confused for a moment. "Oh, the nurse probationer? She's in the preparation room," he said, gesturing behind him.

"Thank you. I didn't expect to see you here today, Doctor. I thought there were no surgeries on Monday."

"Oh, there aren't, Sergeant," said Woodsmith. "I came by to check on one of our patients from last Friday's operation. Bad reaction to the chloroform, I'm afraid, but she seems to be all right now. I'm a bit worried about the incision site, though . . ." he trailed off.

"I'm sorry to have disturbed your rounds," said Honeycutt. "I'll be off to find Miss Simmons." Woodsmith nodded and walked off down the hall.

Mary Simmons was rolling bandages, standing at a table in the preparation room. Honeycutt saw her before she saw him and noticed how pretty her face was in repose, when she wasn't worried. He regretted that he had to change that.

"Miss Simmons?" She started a bit, and her eyes widened.

"Yes?"

"I'm sorry to disturb you, but I have one or two questions for you." He smiled what he hoped was his most charming smile. He could see her trying to remain calm.

"Yes, all right." She put down the bandages and folded her hands together in front of her.

"I'd like to ask you about the pin Dr. Morton gave you."

Mary looked up at him, and he saw tears welling up in her eyes.

"I'm sorry. I don't know what happened," she said.

"Is something wrong?" he asked.

"It wasn't my fault, but I forgot and left it on." She sniffed and began to cry. Honeycutt took out his perfectly clean handkerchief and handed it to her across the table.

"I'm so sorry to have upset you," he said. "Left what on?"

"The pin. I had forgotten to take the pin off my uniform, and I put it in the cupboard with the pin still on it, and when I came back . . ."

"It was gone?"

"Yes. My uniform was there, but the pin on it was gone. And I thought he was going to be so angry."

"Who? Dr. Morton?"

"Yes, because I wasn't wearing it."

Honeycutt took out his notebook. "When was this?"

"That Friday before he was killed. Then when I found out he was dead, I was so relieved because I wouldn't have to face him." She dried her eyes with the handkerchief.

"I see."

"That's so very wrong of me. I should have been sad because he was dead."

"I'm quite sure you weren't wrong. Dr. Morton was taking advantage of his position with you. You were worried he was going to be angry with you. Was he angry with you often?"

"No, he didn't seem to be. I didn't know him, really. But I've seen him get angry, at porters and nurses, even Matron. He was frightening. I didn't want it directed at me."

"What time on Friday did this theft happen?"

Mary thought, squeezing the handkerchief in her hand and looking down at the table. "I put my uniform in the cupboard just after seven, because I was done for the day. It didn't need washing, so I just hung it up like I usually do, with the other uniforms."

"The uniforms are hung up together with the other women's?"

"Yes, but they all have our name sewn in. I usually take the pin off, in case someone might steal it . . ." The tears started to well up again.

"Please, don't cry," said Honeycutt soothingly. "It's all over now, really. He can't be angry with you now. Can you tell me who might have been around the probationers' room on a Friday evening?"

Another sniff. "Yes, there'd be the other nurse probationers on my shift, and sometimes the nurses or matrons will come in to check things. But then after that, there'd be no reason for anyone to be in there until morning shift."

"So you noticed it was missing Saturday morning." She nodded.

"Is the door to the probationers' room locked?" She shook her head.

"So anyone could have come in during the night," he said. "It wasn't your fault."

She looked up at him with a small smile.

"And you can keep the handkerchief."

Inspector Slaughter wanted to walk up Blackfriars Road from the theatre, but the traffic was heavy. Carts of all sizes went in both directions in the street, and the noise of the wheels, horses, creaking loads, and noisy human altercations made it hard to think. Instead, he began to wander southward, through smaller streets. Coming upon the gardens of Bethlehem Hospital, he noticed that the sunlight made everything look calm and peaceful. The hospital itself, an asylum for the insane, was large and imposing. The palace that had originally been there had been torn down, and a much more serviceable-looking building built in its place. But the gardens were still lovely, and one could walk through quietly.

Turning northward again, he was about to cross Waterloo Road when he spotted a bookshop. It was a small place, and he had almost missed it. "C. Willis, Second-hand Books" the sign said. Second-hand was always better, he'd found, and much cheaper. Although he'd had little time to find a tutor for Tommy, he could certainly bring him something for learning, perhaps a Cassell's or a primer on science.

"May I help you?" asked the proprietor, whom Slaughter assumed was Mr. Willis. He was a gentle-looking man, with a bit of a squint. His clothing, while neat, was distinctly out of date.

"Yes, please," said Slaughter. Impulsively he decided that Tommy might prefer something more exciting. After all, the tutor would determine his school books. "I'm looking for good story, suitable for a young man of twelve."

Mr. Willis nodded. "Does the lad know his letters, or read at all?"

"Yes, he reads quite a bit."

"Has he read *Robinson Crusoe*?" inquired Willis, walking down a narrow aisle. The place was filled with books. They were piled on the floor and pushed onto shelves. But he went directly to one shelf and pulled out a book. "This one has engravings by George Cruikshank."

Slaughter looked through the volume. It reminded him of the copy he had read when he was a child. "Excellent. And what is the price?"

Willis headed back to the front of the shop. "It was three shillings sixpence new. So now it would be a shilling." He held out his hand.

Back on the street, Slaughter crossed Waterloo Road to return to the station by way of the back streets south of New Cut, which was sure to be full of people at the market.

Honeycutt was already there, writing in his notebook. Slaughter went to the supply room to get himself a cup of tea but was stopped by Jones.

"Oh no, sir," said Jones, with a flourish. "I'll get that for you, sir!"

Honeycutt reported Mary's story of the missing pin at the hospital, and Slaughter shared Agnes's information that Cyril had certainly been Hannah Featherstone's lover. After they had exchanged notes, Honeycutt said, "May I be frank about this investigation, sir?"

"Of course," said Slaughter. "What are your thoughts?"

"I've been thinking we need to be more scientific about things, if it isn't too forward to say."

"It isn't. We may be thinking along the same lines. We've been focusing a great deal on why someone would want to kill Morton. But he was an unpleasant man, possibly a blackmailer and a molester of young women."

"Exactly, sir. So anyone might want to kill him. But at the same time, what about his body?"

"His body?" Slaughter frowned. Did Honeycutt want to go back to the beginning of the investigation?

Back in Baltimore, Honeycutt had developed something of a reputation at his station. After his initial mistakes, the others in the force had begun treating him with respect because of his scientific interests. In suspicious deaths, he had come to be the one called in when a case was flagging. He was not a coroner, nor did he want to be one, but the body often held secrets.

"We know how he was killed, because the coroner told us. Overdose of chloroform. We know the murderer set him up in the theatre. But what if he wasn't killed there?"

Slaughter could see what he meant. "You're right, Sergeant—we should be focusing less on the why, and more on the how. If he was killed at Old St. Thomas's, how was he convinced to go there, walking into a trap? If he was killed elsewhere, how was his body transported to the old hospital and carried up the stairs?"

"Wherever he was killed," said Honeycutt. "the murderer would need some time where he wasn't seen. To overdose someone, it's not enough to just hold a cloth over the victim's mouth. You need time to continue administering the drops until his breathing stops completely."

Slaughter noticed that Honeycutt was rather proud of his new knowledge of anesthetics.

Honeycutt continued, "And you can't carry a body very far, even in darkness, without a barrow or cart of some kind."

"It could even have happened in another room instead of the operating theatre. We didn't search the rest of the unused hospital," said Slaughter. "I suggest we go back there and take another look. If we can find Alfred Morris to assist us, so much the better."

9

Slaughter and Honeycutt arrived at Old St. Thomas's Hospital in a cab, as they had before. The morning was sharp and cold, and there was the feeling of a coming storm in the air. The wind pushed down the streets between buildings. Honeycutt felt a sensation of the river itself sending its chill into Southwark. His heavy coat felt thin, and he was glad of his woolen scarf.

Marie had knitted him that scarf before he had left. "You'll be so cold in London," she'd said, trying not to show the tears in her eyes. He'd been her responsibility, she felt, living at her boarding house in one of the worst neighborhoods in the city. It was silly, she knew. He was a policeman, even if he was young. It was his job to protect her, not the other way around. "Now you listen to me, Mark," she said. "I know cold. I'm from Winnipeg, remember?" He remembered. She often talked about Canada, her life in her tribe, her French husband who brought her to Baltimore years ago.

Progress to the old hospital was slow. Carts piled high with goods were traveling in both directions. As they approached Union Street from Blackfriars Road, the cab swerved to avoid a cart coming the other way directly in front of them. The cab driver cursed, and the carter yelled back. The piles of cloth on the cart, held only by ropes, leaned dangerously toward them as they passed.

Old St. Thomas's was quiet, but just up the road from the church was a flurry of activity. The railway company was constructing in earnest now. Everything past Guy's Hospital was blocked off, and teams of men were carrying lumber and pushing barrows of bricks back and forth.

"If Morton was killed back there," said Honeycutt, "we'll never find the evidence. There's barrows and carts everywhere."

Slaughter agreed. "Let's hope there was simply no reason for a bricklayer to harbor a deep hatred of him."

Ascending the spiral staircase from the church door, they almost collided with Alfred Morris coming down.

"Oh!" he said. "You're back again. Good thing I'm here. I was just about to lock up."

"You're on your way out?" asked Slaughter as Alfred turned to lead them up the stairs.

"I've been told there's no need for me until the builders can come and finish closing."

They arrived in the herb garret. Alfred turned to face Slaughter.

"May I ask when that might be, sir? The builders being allowed back? I'll be losing wages for as long as I'm not needed here."

"I'm sorry," Slaughter said. "I confess I hadn't considered that. Detective Sergeant Honeycutt and I want to look around at all areas that would have been accessible on the morning of Dr. Morton's death. Once we do that, I see no reason why we can't allow the builders to return."

"I'll help you in any way I can, sir," said Alfred.

"Can you show us all the areas that would have been open then?"

Alfred toured them through the operating theatre, out through the doors at the patient entrance, and down the corridor into the women's ward.

"This is all that was left open," he said.

"Would you know if anything was changed or moved on the 18th?"

"Not on the 18th, sir. I don't work Saturdays since the move to Surrey Gardens. You asked me not to clean, so I didn't, but I did look in on the ward on that Monday after your men left, and there was nothing amiss."

"And the courtyard?"

"I looked there, too, but you're welcome to check," Alfred said, leading them across the ward to the side door. They looked into the courtyard, which gave onto an alley at the back through what looked like a gateway.

"Was that open to the alley on that Saturday, do you know?" Slaughter asked.

Alfred nodded. "I come in that way when I don't want to take the stairs. There was a locked gate, but they dismantled it three weeks ago. Someone buying it for a park, they said." He shook his head at the folly of human commerce.

Slaughter and Honeycutt spent half an hour searching the theatre, the corridor, the ward, and the courtyard. Then they walked out the gateway into the alley, ending up back on St. Thomas's Street.

"There's nothing here, sir," said Honeycutt. "But now we know there's another way in."

Slaughter nodded, and they returned to seek out Alfred. "Anyone could come in this way," he noted, as they easily unlatched the door back into the ward.

"I suppose he locks up the church tower door because that's the way most people would enter," said Honeycutt.

They found Alfred in the garret, looking out the window across the rooftops.

"They're going to change this whole area," he said sadly. "They've got lumber and bricks stacked all the way down to my house on Maze Pond. And when they're done, there will be no way to get from the street to the river without walking through a dark tunnel under the tracks. Still, that's progress, I suppose."

"Not always what one wants, is it?" said Slaughter. Honeycutt said nothing.

"Let me ask you, Mr. Morris, about the alley?"

"Oh, yes. Not used much anymore."

"But the door to the courtyard, it only latches. Could someone come into the ward from the alley?"

"They could, but not many people know it's there. It was used mostly for deliveries. Patients and visitors came in through the main entrance courtyard off Blackfriars Road. The railway will be blocking the alley off anyway now."

"When does the railway work happen? Any night work?"

Alfred shook his head. "No night work, thank goodness. That would be a lot of noise on Maze Pond if they allowed it. No, Guy's Hospital made them promise."

"So it's very quiet around here at night?"

"Except for deliveries. There's still carts going across to the leather market late at night."

"Where's the leather market?"

"Just right down Weston Street. You can't miss it because of the smell."

Honeycutt pointed out the window. "So it's just down that road there, to the right?"

"Yes, sir. I'll walk part of the way with you if you like. My house is on the way."

The three men climbed down the spiral stair, and Alfred locked the door carefully as they left. As they approached Weston Street, St. Thomas's Street got louder and noisier. But it was quieter by the time they got to Maze Pond. They said goodbye and thanked him, Slaughter assuring him that the builders would be allowed in the next day.

The leather market area smelled horrible, even in the cold. The hide tanning companies had been forced to move from the City, where they used to trade at Leadenhall Market. The odor and waste had offended the professionals at the banks and businesses in the area. Bermondsey was away from the City's control across the river, and the leather trade had been flourishing. The Leather Market building itself was tall and imposing. On a Tuesday morning, it bustled with skin merchants selling to the tanning trade, which operated in the narrow streets surrounding the Market. The odor of lime, urine, and dog feces was almost unbearable. Honeycutt brushed against a woman carrying a bucket of dog waste and cringed.

"They're called pure-finders," Slaughter said. "They collect dog waste from the pavements and parks, if they can get there before the street cleaners."

Honeycutt took a handkerchief from his pocket and put it over his nose. "What's it for?"

"It's rubbed into the leather to break it down and soften it. Come on, let's get away from here." They walked faster to reach Long Lane, where they waved down a cab.

❧

Ellie and Jo arrived at the Featherstone house in Kensington early in the afternoon. Lady Featherstone's reply to their request had said two o'clock, and they were afraid they might be late. They knew the house was very close to the Exhibition, so traffic might be a problem. They'd taken the omnibus early, then alighted some distance away. Jo was wearing her heaviest coat, but even so the wind chilled through her. It kept pushing at her satchel, trying to carry it away off her shoulder.

"I don't know why I'm nervous," Ellie said, pulling her scarf more firmly round her neck. "I guess I've always been a little intimidated by the aristocracy." They started walking down Knightsbridge, across from the park.

"Not me," said Jo. "This weather is miserable, though. If we go down Brompton Road a bit, we might find a tea room."

"I don't think we have time. Perhaps it would be best just to ask whether we might wait inside for Lady Featherstone?"

Jo agreed, and they continued up Knightsbridge toward the house. The door was opened by John.

"You must be Mrs. Slaughter and Miss Harris?" he asked.

"Yes," said Ellie. "I'm sorry we're a bit early, but would it be all right if we wait for Lady Featherstone?"

"Do come in," said John, stepping back. "It's quite cold today."

Ellie smoothed her hair once they were in out of the wind, and Jo adjusted her satchel more firmly under her arm. John turned to lead them into the parlor.

"It's rather awkward," Ellie said. "You're John Addo, aren't you?" He turned with just the slightest look of surprise.

"I am," said John, "and you are Mrs. Slaughter. I met your husband when he was here to interview Sir Henry."

Ellie smiled. "We're here to talk to Lady Featherstone about inviting a guest speaker to the Women's Reform Club for next month. But my husband had suggested you would be an excellent choice, and so in a way we're really here to talk to you."

John paused and stood very still. "Why would he think that?" he asked.

Jo spoke. "Inspector Slaughter told us you have a very interesting history. We are raising money for the abolitionist cause, to eliminate African slavery in all its forms."

John nodded, with a serious expression on his face.

"Would this be an evening meeting?" His eyes were deep and intelligent, thought Jo. The shape of his head was noble, and such interesting ears . . .

"Yes, typically we meet for evening lectures," said Ellie.

"Then I would be happy to do so, if it would be helpful," said John.

Ellie smiled. "Well, that's excellent," she said. "I'm glad that's settled. Then I shall talk to Lady Featherstone about publicizing the event and whom to invite."

John glanced at the clock. It was almost two.

"Allow me to present you to Lady Featherstone. She's in the morning room," he said, as he led them to a beautifully carved door on the left side of the hall.

"Excuse me, Mr. Addo?" said Jo. "I'm sorry to intrude, but if you aren't otherwise occupied, would it be all right if I drew your picture while Mrs. Slaughter talks with Lady Featherstone? You have a dignified face, and your image on the flyers for the lecture might encourage people to attend."

John paused with his hand on the door knob. He looked at Jo, her mussed hair, unassuming coat, plain dress, and sketchbook. "Yes, I can make time for that," he said, with just a hint of a smile around his mouth. He opened the door.

"Mrs. Slaughter." Hannah rose to meet Ellie as she entered the bright, elegant room. She was wearing an ivory wrapper, trimmed with blue satin. "Do come in. And Miss Harris . . . ?" she looked curiously at Jo, who still stood in the hall.

"Delighted to meet you," said Ellie. "Miss Harris has just asked Mr. Addo if she could draw his likeness while we talk?" Was that a wrapper she was wearing? Or perhaps it was a new style. She certainly looked lovely in it, whatever it was.

"Mr. Addo?" Hannah looked curious. "Oh, John! Yes, of course, if it's all right with you, John?"

"Yes, Lady Featherstone. I've agreed to sit for her, unless you need anything?"

"Not at all," said Hannah. A thought occurred to her. "I wonder, Miss Harris, if I may have a copy when you've finished? It would make a good gift for my husband."

Jo nodded in agreement as John closed the door.

"Please sit down, Mrs. Slaughter. Shall I send for tea?"

"No, thank you," said Ellie, seating herself on the settee. It was white with pink and red roses in the pattern. It might have been silk, she thought, but surely one wouldn't use silk for upholstery?

"It's so nice to see you," said Hannah. "I have heard good things about the Women's Reform Club." She seated herself in her usual chair, just a bit above Ellie.

"Thank you, Lady Featherstone. It's about the club that I've come, as I mentioned in my note. I wonder whether you might be interested in assisting us in raising money for abolition causes. John has just agreed to give a lecture for us."

"He has?" Hannah looked surprised. "How very unusual. He normally says very little, except to my husband. I'm so pleased you asked him."

"It was very kind of him to agree. But we thought that you would be a good patroness for our cause. A woman of your standing would be able to encourage the sort of funding that's needed now that the slave trade is finally being crushed."

Hannah looked pleased. "I do have a number of commitments at the moment," she said. "The Ladies' Committee at the hospital, and various charities. But I think I can make time for such an important cause."

"We'd be so grateful," said Ellie. "The people you know in society would be able to make such a difference."

"Then it's settled," said Hannah. She walked over to a small desk and made a note in her appointment book. "I hope it's not indelicate to ask, but how is your husband's investigation proceeding? I've heard very little."

Ellie considered for a moment. Were Sir Henry and Lady Featherstone suspects? Should she be careful?

"I believe it is going well, if slowly."

"I know my husband is concerned that it be wrapped up as quickly as possible. I believe he's going to the station this very afternoon to talk to your husband."

"I see," said Ellie, uncertain what to say.

"It's a horrible thing, isn't it? Dr. Morton was a fine surgeon. I confess I found his manner unnerving, but his accomplishments were extraordinary."

"So I have heard," said Ellie.

"It is quite a loss to the hospital. And I'm afraid the papers haven't been very kind, even suggesting that the hospital itself might be dangerous. That a murderer is still on the loose."

Ellie realized that her assumptions about Lady Featherstone may have been incorrect. She assumed that she was a superficial woman. It was her own bias against aristocrats, she thought. Mustn't judge people. Hannah Featherstone seemed well aware of the world around her, its dangers and subterfuges.

"I'm quite sure my husband will discover Dr. Morton's killer," Ellie said.

"I'm sure of that also. I just hope he does so before the reputation of St. Thomas's is damaged."

Ellie and Jo departed shortly afterward, saying goodbye to John as they left. The afternoon had warmed slightly, and they crossed the street to catch the omnibus back to Southwark.

"Does one normally meet visitors in the morning room at two in the afternoon?" asked Ellie.

Jo laughed. "I can't imagine what makes you think I'd know!" she said.

∽

Sir Henry caused quite a stir arriving at Christchurch police station in his extravagant carriage, with John lifting him down into his chair. As it happened, one of the writers from the *Illustrated London News* was waiting in the station room. He'd been hoping to speak with Inspector Slaughter but was instead being entertained by Constable Jones. The journalist looked up in delight as Sir Henry entered, and approached him, cutting off his path to the desk.

"Sir Henry Featherstone," he said, somewhat breathlessly. "I'm Gerald Harker from the *Illustrated London News*. Can you help me tell our readers what's happening in the investigation of Dr. Morton's death?"

"Well, now, I'm just here to have a conversation with Detective Inspector Slaughter," Sir Henry said, looking up at the young man. "I am hoping I can be of service to him. Are you writing a story on the investigation?"

"Yes, I am," said Mr. Harker, somewhat in awe at being greeted so kindly. Many people, especially those with "Sir" before their name, did not appreciate being waylaid in public. But Sir Henry smiled with a welcoming look, and Harker felt suddenly proud of his job. "It's been over a week, and our readers are getting worried. Is there a madman loose at the hospital?"

Sir Henry shook his head. "I can assure you, personally, that the hospital is safe, that we are helping many people every day return to health. Have you a medical background, young man?"

Harker admitted that he did not.

"It's hard to understand, sometimes, the extraordinary responsibility of a hospital like St. Thomas's. We take in people from all walks of life, especially those who cannot afford a private doctor. And we provide them with the best possible care, from the best surgeons."

"Like Dr. Morton?" The young man was scribbling notes on his pad.

"Yes, like Dr. Morton. And when something this terrible happens, it is up to everyone to assist the police as much as possible to find out what happened. Are you here to help with this?"

Harker looked confused. "I'm here to tell the story," he said.

Sir Henry reached out and patted his arm. "Good for you," he said. "I will recommend to Inspector Slaughter that he contact you personally as soon as he can speak with you. Do you have a card?"

Harker fumbled in his pocket, then scribbled on a piece of paper, "Gerald Harker, Illustrated London News, 198 Strand" and handed it to Sir Henry.

"Thank you, young man," he said, "and I wish you much success in your career. You have a special quality about you that should serve you well."

Harker was two streets away from the station before he realized he had learned nothing at all.

"I'm sorry to come to you at the station, Detective Inspector," said Sir Henry, after he was settled in Slaughter's office. John had returned to the station room to wait, and Jones had gone to fetch tea with alacrity. Apparently this was the gentleman to whom that stunning woman was married, Jones thought. My goodness.

"I'm sure you can understand how difficult it is to field questions at the hospital about the investigation," said Sir Henry, glancing meaningfully at Honeycutt, who occupied the chair next to him. "I thought I would stop here on my way to Surrey Gardens and ask about your progress?"

Slaughter knew that despite Sir Henry's gentle manner, he was being pressured. Sir Henry saw his expression change and held up a hand in protest.

"I am not trying to rush you, Detective Inspector," he said. "In fact, I just persuaded a young man from the *Illustrated London News* to leave the premises." He handed Honeycutt the slip of paper. "The last thing any of us need is bad publicity."

"Thank you, Sir Henry. I will, of course, be honest with you," said Slaughter. "We have quite a few people who had a reason to do away with Dr. Morton, so we are now looking at how it might have happened. We are also trying to connect the reasons people disliked him with the location at Old St. Thomas's. It has only been a little over a week since Dr. Morton was found. The detecting branch of the force is, as you know, only a generation old. We have not yet attracted the staffing to go along with what the public expects of us.

But I have a very good team here, and we will have answers for you soon." Sir Henry nodded.

At that moment, Jones brought in the tea. He bowed as he left. Must be the presence of aristocracy, thought Slaughter. Honeycutt poured.

"While you're here, Sir Henry," Honeycutt said, "would it be presumptuous for me to ask you a few questions?"

"Not at all, Detective Sergeant," said Sir Henry. "Happy to oblige."

It was remarkable, thought Slaughter, how placid Sir Henry's exterior was. One felt immediately that one could trust him, tell him secrets. He might know quite a few secrets about the people they were investigating. Honeycutt was on the same track.

"You're a very kind and attentive man, Sir Henry. I wonder, do people who work at the hospital confide in you?"

"Yes, sometimes," he said. "A few treat me like a father rather than an administrator." He smiled. "But what you want to know is whether anyone has told me anything that might be of interest to the case. Let me think a moment."

He took a sip of tea.

"Oh, that's good," he said. "I'll be sure to tell your constable—Jones, is it?—that he makes a proper cup. Well now, I'd say the person who talks to me the most is Matron."

"Mrs. Wardroper?" asked Honeycutt. She hardly seemed like the type to confide in anyone.

Sir Henry smiled. "She looks fierce, and runs a tight ship, but she's a very kind person underneath. She talks to me sometimes about the nurse probationers—who's getting along, and who might be a concern. She knows I wouldn't interfere in her purview."

"And has she mentioned anyone in the past few weeks?" asked Honeycutt.

"Yes, she was concerned about one of the new girls, Flora I think her name was. But she arrived too recently to know Dr. Morton. But there was another. Mary Simmons. She wouldn't say anything, but Matron suspected she might have been frightened by Dr. Morton.

And she was very upset about something she'd lost." Honeycutt nodded and made a note.

Sir Henry looked sympathetic. "Some of the nurse probationers, they come from the countryside. They don't really know what to expect. She'd come from Wales, but I think Matron had expected her to have more gumption, considering her brother's panache."

"Her brother?" asked Slaughter.

"Yes, she's Cyril Price's sister," said Sir Henry.

Honeycutt looked confused. "But they have different names."

"Oh, actors," said Sir Henry with a smile. "Always changing their names. I had a deuce of a time getting Hannah to keep her first name when she married. She thought it was too plain." He shook his head. "Price is the name he took for the stage," he said.

"Has anyone else confided in you in the last few weeks?" asked Honeycutt.

"I did have an interesting conversation with Dr. Woodsmith, but I doubt it relates to this," said Sir Henry.

"What was it about?"

Sir Henry paused. "I'm not sure I should say this, because it was a private conversation," he said.

"We understand, Sir Henry," said Slaughter. "If it doesn't pertain to the case, it need not be known that you shared it with us. And if it does . . ."

"Yes, I see what you mean," said Sir Henry. "Dr. Woodsmith was concerned about Dr. Morton jumping the surgery schedule."

"How so?"

"Well, he didn't want to make an issue of it. That's Dr. Woodsmith for you. Competent, friendly, beloved by the patients. He wouldn't want to make trouble for anyone. But there had been several cases in the last year or so where he was scheduled to operate, but Dr. Morton had jumped in, insisting on taking the case."

"How many is several?" asked Honeycutt.

"I'd say maybe five or six times over the last year," said Sir Henry.

"Were they usually anesthesia cases?" asked Honeycutt.

"You know, I'm not sure. Is it important? We would certainly have records of it at the hospital. Matron could find out, I'm sure."

It was decided that Honeycutt should accompany Sir Henry to the hospital to check the records. As John collected Sir Henry and began wheeling him out to the carriage, Honeycutt glanced at the slip of paper he'd been handed. "*Illustrated London News*!" he said to Slaughter. "Did you know that they have a color press? Got it just a few years ago. They're the ones who first used the new high-speed press, the one first shown by Applegath at Crystal Palace. It's steam-driven. Extraordinary piece of technology. Of course now it's been supplanted by . . ."

Slaughter smiled and waved him out. "You can tell me about it later," he said. "For now, I'd like a list of all the surgery patients who died at the hospital in the last year. And let's find out how many of those were scheduled for Woodsmith but were taken by Morton."

Honeycutt nodded and ran out after the carriage.

～

Tommy had come home for bread and butter before going to the theatre for the evening. The stove was on, the kitchen was warm, and the tea was good and strong.

"Did you really go to Sir Henry's house?" he asked Jo and Ellie.

"Yes," said Jo, taking a sip of her tea.

"Was it very grand?"

"It's steps away from Hyde Park, in Kensington. Brompton, really. So yes, it's grand," said Ellie.

"It has wide front steps and a big door with a brass knocker," said Jo, "and a grand foyer with a red Persian carpet. I can show you a bit of the foyer because I drew John Addo there." She got out her sketchbook and flipped to the drawing, turning it around for Tommy to see.

"It looks like a grand hotel," said Tommy. "Do they have a conservatory?"

"We didn't see one, but I expect they do. It's an elegant house."

"Bet it looks like the Palm House at Kew," he said. Ellie laughed. She'd never been sorry she'd taken him to so many nice places. He absorbed everything.

"I've seen Mr. Addo before, with Sir Henry," said Tommy. "You've got him to rights, Miss Harris. He looks like a king or a prince or something."

Jo peered at her picture. "I noticed that too."

"I've heard some black people taken from Africa were already slaves there, but others were royal. Do you think that's true?"

"Yes, the slavers don't care much about the original status of the people they're buying."

Tommy shook his head. "Buying people," he said, "how could they?"

"So, what did you do today?" Ellie asked him, changing the subject.

"I was going to ask for work up Blackfriars Road with the bricklayers, but the wind was so cold I decided to offer some cleanup at the gas works. It was much warmer in there. I did some sweeping and some mopping. Got sixpence." He took it out of his pocket and put it on the table.

"Are they paying you properly at the theatre for all your help?" asked Jo.

"Oh, yes. Cyril always gives me a bob if I work the whole evening, and Agnes slips me something now and again. Rex even gives me some pennies when I help in the scene loft. They know I'm saving for my schooling." He bounced his knee up and down as he finished his bread and butter.

"I think I'm lucky," he said thoughtfully. "The men at the gasworks said that someone my age working in a factory gets about four shillings a week, and they're inside all the time with the noise and people beating them when they're sleepy. In a good week, I get at least that, and I'm outside when I like, inside when I like. And if I crawl under a barrow in the market street and take a nap, who's to care?"

Jo smiled at Tommy's view of life.

"Well, young man, you'd better be off if you're going to get to the theatre by seven," Ellie said. Tommy gulped down the rest of his tea, put his cap on, and bounced out the door.

"He's a good lad," Jo said.

"That he is. They questioned him the other night, you know, Cuthbert and Mark Honeycutt."

"Did they?" Jo frowned.

"They did it all in fun, but it was questioning. Apparently, Geraldine Orson, the actress, takes quite a bit of opium. She gets pills from the apothecary at St. Thomas's."

"Does she indeed?" said Jo. "Might that be related to Dr. Morton's murder?"

"I'm not sure. Her acting career would be ruined if it got out, you know."

"I expect it would. I won't say a word, but it is interesting. It would certainly make her vulnerable to blackmail. If Dr. Morton were the one blackmailing her . . . Do you think she could kill?"

Ellie shrugged. "I don't know her at all," she said. "But Cubby bought tickets to the play for Friday. Perhaps I'll meet her afterward."

"I'd love to know what she's like," said Jo, putting down her cup. "So, are we finished planning John Addo's lecture? We can bring it to the club as a *fait accompli*, then tell them we have almost two weeks to advertise. Can you send Tommy to Mr. Addo tomorrow to let him know the date?"

"I can," said Ellie, making a note. "He'll be thrilled to see the house for himself, even if it's just a peek inside."

Instead of hailing an expensive cab on Blackfriars Road, Jo walked up toward the river. It was quite dark, but she knew the way well. She walked along the omnibus route, just in case she felt unsafe. She always thought of Nan when she crossed Blackfriars Bridge. They once stood in the middle, waited for the train on the adjacent rail bridge, and screamed as loud as they could, just for fun.

As she turned on Fleet Street, she thought about the assignment she needed to complete the next day. It was another trial at the Old Bailey, first thing in the morning at the Old Court. A policeman, James Dray, had been stabbed in an altercation, and the Lord Mayor would be attending, and Lord Chief Baron Pollock was presiding. Attacking a policeman was a serious crime, but Jo had been hired to draw Frederick Pollock for a feature on the judiciary in *Chamber's*

Journal. As a member of the London Photographic Society, he had been photographed several times. But the *Journal* wanted an image that expressed not only his solidity but emphasized justice as a form of moral improvement.

Jo loved this kind of work because it allowed her some creative license. Pictures, she thought, were not just for showing reality. They always carried meaning. And the artist could select that meaning and subtly draw not only what showed, but what did not. Emphasizing eyebrows could show seriousness, and certain lines at the corner of the mouth could portray humor. A tense posture could be drawn as powerful, or as fearful. People might appear younger or older depending on circumstances. It occurred to her she should draw Tommy again before he grew much more.

～

Matron was not particularly pleased to see Detective Sergeant Honeycutt again. The presence of policemen in her hospital, even a handsome one in plain clothes, seemed to imply disorder. She greeted him standing in the doorway of her office.

"Good afternoon," she said.

"Good afternoon, ma'am," said Honeycutt. "I'm sorry to disturb your work, but Sir Henry suggested I talk to you."

Matron's mouth unpursed a little. "How can I be of assistance?" she asked.

Honeycutt took out his notebook. "We are seeking records of those surgeries within the last year or so where the patient died."

Matron looked taken aback. "That's a strange request," she said.

"I agree. But we are trying to determine who would want to kill Dr. Morton. Perhaps the family of a patient had a grudge, if their loved one died."

Matron nodded, a short snap of the head. "I see what you mean. We do have those records, but they would be in Mr. Tapper's office, not mine. I only have the records of the nursing staff." She took a file off her desk, then closed the office door behind her. "I'd rather not have you wandering the hospital on your own, and I need to take this packet to Mr. Tapper anyway. I'll accompany you."

Honeycutt was not sure whether he was supposed to walk beside her or follow, so he compromised, following about half a step behind.

Felix Tapper was sitting at his large desk, writing in an enormous book. He looked up as Matron entered, and rose with a pleased expression. His owlish eyes crinkled behind his spectacles.

"Mrs. Wardroper," he said, "how nice to see you. And Detective Sergeant Honeycutt."

Honeycutt could sense Matron plump her feathers a bit.

"Mr. Tapper," she replied, in a much gentler tone than he'd heard her use. One could almost call it friendly, even a little shy.

"This must be about the investigation," he said, removing his spectacles. "How can I help?"

Honeycutt was about to speak, but Matron began. "The Detective Sergeant would like to see the records of surgeries. He's looking for the ones where the patients died."

Felix's eyes widened. "Over what period?"

"I think the last year or so should do," said Honeycutt. "I also need to know the surgeon, the anesthesia if used, and which cases scheduled for Dr. Woodsmith were instead performed by Dr. Morton."

"Certainly. Those should all be here." He walked over to a large cabinet, taking out a volume bound in dark blue. Honeycutt saw out of the corner of his eye Matron tuck a stray lock of hair into her cap and arrange the lace streamers down her neck.

"Now let me see," Felix muttered as he opened the volume. "No surgical deaths since we moved here. All were at the old hospital." He looked up. "Conditions for the patients seem to be better here, for some reason." He returned to his perusal. "Yes . . . it's quite a few, I'm afraid," he said. "This will take me about half an hour to make you a list."

"If you have time right now, I'd be most grateful," said Honeycutt.

"I can do that." Without looking up from his book, he reached out for a piece of paper.

"Would you prefer I wait here, Mr. Tapper, or should I wait in the tea room?"

Tapper glanced up at Matron, raising an eyebrow. He felt rather than saw Matron shake her head.

"Have a seat, Detective Sergeant. You'll find a book on plants and their medicinal properties on the table. Good reading for a policeman. Or if you're not up to reading, there are illustrations at the back."

Honeycutt ignored the implication and took a seat.

"I'll come back for you shortly," said Matron to Honeycutt. She gave Tapper a fleeting ghost of a smile, then left, her shoes snapping down the hall.

Honeycutt flipped through the book, *The Complete Herbal* by Nicolas Culpeper, whose pleasant face adorned the frontispiece. It was well thumbed, with many handwritten notes in the margins. One dog-eared page had a section on the herb pennyroyal. A passage was marked:

mixed with honey purges the belly, helps bring down women's courses, and is of special use for those that are troubled with the falling down of the mother, and pains thereof, and causes an easy and speedy delivery of women in childbirth

Next to the passage a hand had written, "abortifacient" in large letters.

Tapper was busily flipping through the blue-covered tome and scribbling, writing down names and dates.

"All herbs have both useful and dangerous properties," he said as he copied. "Which one are you looking at?"

"Pennyroyal," said Honeycutt. "There's a note here saying it's an abortifacient, but it doesn't say that in the text itself."

"Over time," said Tapper, "the popular use of herbs makes its way into the official books. Culpeper's book has been around since 1653, but wise women have known the uses of these herbs for much longer. We laud the physicians and surgeons, but it's among ordinary folk that the knowledge originates. Only recently have professional men carried it forward."

After about twenty minutes, he handed the list to Honeycutt. There were over thirty names on it, each with the date of surgery, reason for the surgery, surgeon, anesthetic (if used), and cause of death. About twenty had Dr. Woodsmith's name next to them, while the rest had Morton's. Tapper had put a star next to two of Morton's patients.

"Those were cases where Dr. Woodsmith was scheduled, but Dr. Morton decided to do the surgery instead."

"And that was permitted?"

"Yes, he was more experienced than Dr. Woodsmith. There was no objection."

"Were there more detailed files kept on patients?" Honeycutt asked.

"Yes," said Felix, blinking. "For those who were discharged, the papers are here, although the file room hasn't been organized yet. The papers you want, for the ones who died, would be with the coroner."

Matron returned while Honeycutt studied the list. He gauged the atmosphere in the room. These two liked each other, and they were of an age.

"Thank you. You both have been at the hospital a very long time," he said. "You must have seen quite a few surgeons come and go. Is this sort of schedule jumping common?"

"No," they both said. Tapper started to speak, then deferred to Matron.

"It's not typical. Only when a surgeon of great worth also has a great ego."

Honeycutt thanked Tapper for the list, then Matron accompanied him back to the entrance to the hospital. She was walking briskly but seemed more relaxed than when he had arrived.

"Do you remember any of Dr. Morton's patients on this list?" he asked, handing it to her.

"Let me see," she said, as they passed her office. "Yes, I remember Mr. Oscar Morgenstern. Very difficult case. He was a large man, and the bowel obstruction was difficult to reach. One of the nurse probationers was with him when he died after the operation. She was very upset. He had been such a nice man." Honeycutt tried to take notes as they walked.

"And I remember Nan Deighton, of course, because she was one of ours. Nurse probationer, with an infected toe. Sweet girl. And this last one, Leonard Browning. Accident at the gasworks. Metal rod through his thigh. His screams could be heard throughout the ward." She handed the list back to him.

"Was there any connection among Morton's patients? Any related to each other, or to him?"

"Not that I know of."

"It appears that almost all of Morton's were anesthetized," said Honeycutt.

"Yes, Dr. Morton liked the time it gave him, although he could be fast without it," she said. "And he preferred chloroform to ether, as you can see on the list, even though it was harder to dose properly."

"Did he always dose it himself, do you know?"

"You'd have to ask one of the dressers," she said, "or his students. I would assume so, since he liked to be in control of everything."

She'd certainly know about wanting to control everything, Honeycutt thought as she stopped just short of opening the door for him to make sure he was leaving.

10

Jo half-listened to the case itself the next morning, as she focused on capturing Lord Chief Baron Pollock's personality on the page. He was a fierce-looking man, with a hawk-like brow and piercing eyes. Although he was almost eighty years of age, the bags under his eyes lent an air of gravitas rather than weariness.

Constable Dray and another policeman had been called to the Brown Bear pub in St. Giles on October 6th. There's the first problem, Jo thought, trying to keep order in a place like St. Giles. Three men in the pub, upon seeing the officers, taunted them that they were "Garibaldi's men." Jo wondered whether this meant they thought the officers were supporters of Italian unification, but it was unlikely the men were that sophisticated. Upon receiving the answer, "I don't know about that," two of the men attacked Dray. When Dray tried to arrest them, all three fought him, and at one point, the prisoner, Michael Hennessy, stabbed him above the eye.

First Dray told his story, then his sergeant testified. A knife had not been found at the scene. As Jo finished her sketch, a doctor testified to the wound being like an incision, but then he agreed it could have been caused by a piece of metal from the edge of the pub counter. As Jo closed her sketchbook and put it in her bag, Pollock declared Hennessy guilty of wounding but not intending to kill the officer and sentenced him to nine months in prison. The Lord Mayor nodded sagely from his seat. The wheels of justice sometimes turn very quickly, Jo thought as she left.

It was cool but not raining. Her plan was to stop by the offices of Bradbury and Evans to see whether there was any work for their *Once a Week* magazine. She was walking down Fleet Street when she almost bumped into John Addo walking into Peele's Coffee House.

"I'm so sorry," she said. "Nice to see you, Mr. Addo."

John touched his hat. "And you, Miss Harris. Busy as always, I see."

"Yes, I'm afraid so. Off seeking work as usual."

"I wish you luck. Have a good morning, Miss Harris." He touched his hat again and entered the coffee house. As Jo walked past the window, she couldn't resist peeking out of the corner of her eye. John was meeting a lady at a table. Jo felt bad for being so curious.

The offices of Bradbury and Evans in Bouverie Street were uncharacteristically quiet, and she didn't see the secretary, Reginald, at his usual desk. The door to the inner office was open, and she heard laughter. *Once a Week* had been publishing for two years, but she didn't know anyone except Reggie. After waiting a few moments in the outer office, she approached the inner door and tapped on the frame.

The man who looked up smiling from his desk could be none other than Frederick Evans himself, with his round face and white hair.

"I'm sorry to interrupt," said Jo, "but Reginald isn't at his desk. I'm Jo Harris, the artist."

"I've heard of you!" said Frederick, rising. The woman seated in front of his desk turned to look at Jo. "Catherine, meet Jo Harris. She's done some drawings for *Once a Week*. Perhaps she could do some for your next cookery book!"

Catherine gave Jo a cheerful nod, then turned back to Evans. "Now, Frederick," she said, "you know perfectly well that book presented bills of fare, not cookery. And it was written by Lady Maria Clutterbuck!" They both dissolved into laughter again, and Evans collapsed into his seat. Jo stood perplexed, unsure what to do.

Evans mopped his eyes with a handkerchief. "I'm sorry, Miss Harris," he said, "but Mrs. Dickens and I are old friends. We published her excellent cookery book, but her daft husband thought she should use a pseudonym. Just printed the last edition, eight years on. Not bad, eh?"

Jo smiled. "A worthy run." She turned to Catherine. "If you don't mind me saying so, that's a strange pen name."

"Isn't it?" said Catherine. "I played Lady Maria in the most awful play, for one of our amateur theatricals."

Dickens! Jo realized. This was the estranged wife of Charles Dickens, the famous author. He'd left Bradbury and Evans because they'd refused to publish his statement on their dissolved marriage in *Punch*. Since then, Mr. Dickens had been slandering her name as a poor wife and mother, even claiming that she was unfit and belonged in an asylum. Jo felt immediate sympathy but tried not to let it show.

Catherine stood and gathered up her bonnet and reticule. "I must be off, Frederick," she said. "You have business to do, and little Edward will be wanting his tea." She turned to Jo with a smile and tapped her on the sleeve. "And you will be wanting to talk to Frederick," she said. She was a tall, broad woman, and Jo found it pleasant to look her in the eye.

"Glad to have met you," Jo said, moving aside. Catherine Dickens' skirts rustled as she left.

"Now, Miss Harris," said Evans as he motioned her to sit down, "you'll be wanting to know what we have for you to draw for us. Reginald keeps track of all that, of course. But we do have a new story I'm following. Have you by any chance heard about the murder of Dr. Morton?"

Jo was surprised. "Why, yes, I have. I know some of the people involved in the investigation."

"Perfect!" said Evans. "What I want to know is, will there be anything we can use? I'm trying to decide between a memoriam for him as a renowned surgeon, or something uplifting about the detecting business. How far along is the investigation, do you know?"

"I don't," said Jo, "but I do know there have been no arrests or public suspicions."

"Well, then, if I'm going to make the printing deadline and still have this be current, we'll need to go with the memoriam. What sort of picture might be best? A seated portrait of him sounds dull. What about a scene in the hospital? I hear he was killed in Old St. Thomas's?"

"His body was found there, yes," Jo said.

"Then that's what I want. Morton performing an important surgery in Old St. Thomas's. I realize it can't truly be staged, but could you get enough material to create such a scene?"

"Of course," she said. "When would you need it?"

Evans consulted his agenda, which lay flat on the desk. "We just had an issue come out two days ago. Our next is November 24th, so . . ." he counted days. "I'd need it by this time next week. Will that do?"

"Yes, I can manage that," said Jo. "Anything else?"

Evans flipped a few pages. "For December, we need some images from the Hunterian Museum. We're doing a feature. Not necessarily a job for a woman, mummies and skulls and that sort of thing, but . . ." he looked up with the question in his twinkly eyes.

"I'm not an anatomist," said Jo, smiling, "but I think you'll be pleased."

"Excellent!" He smiled. "For that article, four or five small images I can scatter throughout the piece."

"At my usual rate?" said Jo.

"Oh, well, you'll have to work all that out with Reginald," said Evans.

"Thank you so much, Mr. Evans," said Jo, rising to shake his hand, "and it was very nice to meet you."

"And you, young woman," said Evans, as he looked around for his spectacles.

"On the shelf behind you," said Jo.

"Oh! Yes! Ha!" Jo heard him chuckling as she left the office.

❦

"I'm not sure that the two cases Morton took over from Woodsmith have anything in common," said Honeycutt, having reviewed the information with Slaughter. It was early in the day, but at least the weather was calm and it had not been difficult to get to the station. The office was cold, however, and the cup of tea wasn't doing its job.

"I see what you mean," said Slaughter as he studied the list of surgical deaths. He had not removed his gloves yet. "One very difficult internal problem, and the other just an infected toe. Perhaps they were a challenge for anesthesia?"

"That's possible. Both were anaesthetized, both with chloroform."

"And both were originally supposed to be Woodsmith's patients."

"That's correct."

Slaughter began pacing behind his desk. "But Woodsmith did not seem particularly angry about it. He complained only after the pattern had emerged over a year."

"True."

"And I don't see the temperament in Woodsmith for that sort of revenge. It seems too petty."

"Agreed."

"Let's focus on the fourteen patients of Morton's. Some died several days after surgery, and a few on the operating table." Slaughter paused in his pacing. "Was there any relationship among these patients?"

"Not according to Matron, sir," said Honeycutt, checking his notes. "After I spoke with her, I went to see the usual dresser, Sam Wetherby, and the secondary dresser, a man named Seamus MacDougal. They confirmed that Morton had delivered the anesthetic personally to all fourteen of the patients shown by his name."

"We need more. Matron must have records on which nurses attended these patients. Perhaps they could tell us something. Did Morton know any of these patients previously? Did they have families who asked after them?"

"I can return to St. Thomas's this morning and ask more questions."

"A good idea. I am very concerned about motive, Sergeant. We cannot assure everyone at the hospital that they are safe unless we know whether this was a personal crime or the action of someone who might kill again. I believe that the placement of the body indicates something personal, but if I'm wrong . . ." He shrugged in frustration.

"And you, sir? Are you off to the theatre?"

"Yes, we must find out whether Cyril knew that Morton was tormenting his sister, Mary Simmons." Slaughter sighed and pulled a piece of paper from his pocket. "The superintendent sent a note early this morning. He's concerned about the amount of the time the investigation is taking. I've been asked to appear in his office on Monday. To explain myself." Slaughter's tone was rueful.

"He must have read the story," said Honeycutt.

"What story?"

"In today's *Morning Post*."

"I never spoke with a reporter from the *Morning Post*. They mostly do stories about foreign affairs and society elites."

"It's about Sir Henry and Lady Featherstone and their admiration of Colonel Rigby and his anti-slavery work in Zanzibar. But it talks about the murder, and mentions it as being on Sir Henry's watch."

"As if he could have done something to prevent it?"

"It doesn't go that far, sir. But it does make us sound incompetent. Shall I have Jones find a copy of the paper?"

Slaughter shook his head. "No, thank you. But this does add some pressure, doesn't it?"

Honeycutt nodded. "I'll spend the day tracking down the fourteen patients who died, their nurses, and their families."

"Yes, see what you can find out about them. I'll need a copy of that list. After I talk to Mr. Price, I'll find Dr. Woodsmith. We have only Sir Henry's assurance that he wasn't bothered much by Morton stealing his patients."

Honeycutt smiled. "You're worried because Dr. Woodsmith seems too good to be true."

"I am," said Slaughter. "He may be just who he seems to be: a talented surgeon with an excellent bedside manner and many happy patients."

"And a lovely wife," added Honeycutt.

"And a lovely wife."

By the time Slaughter arrived at the Surrey Theatre it was late enough in the morning that he was hopeful of finding people about.

Tommy had told him that in the middle of a run, there often wasn't much to do. But the stage door was open as usual, and Cyril was in the scene loft chatting with Agnes and Rex.

"Good morning, Inspector Slaughter!" said Cyril with artificial gaiety. He had bags under his expressive eyes and was pale despite the colorful scarf. "How can we help you today?"

Rex gave a gruff good morning, picked up his hammer, and went over to a large flat he was repairing. Agnes smiled and said, "Who will you be wanting to talk to?"

Slaughter said, "Excuse me for interrupting. I'd like to speak with Mr. Price if I could?"

"Of course, Inspector," Cyril said, flipping his blond hair out of his eye. It fell back immediately. "Is my dressing room all right?"

Slaughter followed him, and Cyril took a seat at his dressing table, motioning to the chaise longue across the room. "Agnes said you're coming to the performance on Friday," said Cyril. "I do hope you enjoy it."

"I'm sure I will," said Slaughter.

"As I recall, you said you read Shakespeare, Inspector?"

"I do, actually," said Slaughter. "I'm not an expert, but I do love his work."

"What's your favorite?" He looked really interested, not as if he were only being polite.

"I think *Hamlet*."

Cyril nodded. "A popular choice. Is it the ghost? Or the indecisiveness of Hamlet about killing his uncle? I assume you're a student of human nature, as a police inspector."

"I do enjoy seeing his thoughts. We don't get to see people's thoughts much in my profession."

"But you'd like to know mine about . . . what, exactly?" Cyril settled back in his chair.

"Well, I have a rather unpleasant question. It's about your sister."

"My sister? You mean Mary?" He looked worried. "Has she something to do with the murder?"

"We don't think so, but you didn't mention her when we asked you about Dr. Morton."

"Is she in some kind of trouble, Inspector?"

"Not now, but apparently she did have some trouble with Dr. Morton. Unwanted advances. Did she tell you about that, Mr. Price?"

Cyril thought for a moment, and Slaughter watched him. It looked like he was concerned, then considering, then making a decision. Maybe seeing people's thoughts wasn't so hard. But were they his thoughts, or those of a character he was playing?

"She did tell me a little," Cyril said slowly. "I offered to talk to Matron, but she didn't want me to."

"Were you angry about Morton doing those things to her?"

Cyril's brows knit together. "Of course I was. How dare that . . . doctor touch my little sister? But she begged me to consider her standing and her reputation. She told me other nurse probationers had been thrown out of the school for less."

Slaughter waited.

"You think I might have hated him enough to kill him." Cyril looked down at his feet. Slaughter glanced down too. Red oriental slippers. Actors were interesting.

"All I can tell you is that I didn't."

He looked up. Honest eyes, thought Slaughter. Or playing at honest eyes.

"I can tell you," said Cyril softly, "that I'm not sorry he's dead. He liked to hurt people, Inspector. Got satisfaction from controlling them."

"I know," said Slaughter, "but killing isn't the answer. Not ever."

The silence lasted a few seconds as the two men looked at each other. Then Cyril flipped back his lock of hair and turned to face the mirror.

"Now, Inspector, you can't honestly believe that! Are you siding with Hamlet? Look what happened to him."

Slaughter spoke to the reflection in the mirror. "He decided to kill, and ended up dying for it. That's what happened."

"True." Cyril began arranging the pots of makeup on the table. "Are there other things you wanted to ask me, Inspector?"

"No, I think I have what I need," said Slaughter, rising.

"Look, Inspector, did you mean what you said about Shakespeare? That you love his work?"

"Yes, I really do," said Slaughter. "All that is human can be found in Shakespeare."

"Do you own any of his works?"

"As many as I can afford," admitted Slaughter.

Cyril glanced at the desk but didn't see what he wanted. "Wait here, Inspector," said Cyril, dashing to the dressing room door. "I'll return directly."

While he was gone, Slaughter looked around him. Two wigs in the corner, on wooden heads. Theatrical programs behind glass on the wall. Costumes, presumably for *Richard III*, on a rack in the corner. The chaise longue he was sitting on was badly worn. He wondered whether it was used for resting or something else.

"I found it, Inspector. I have a copy of *The Rape of Lucrece*. We have tried several times to work it into a play. Thomas Heywood wrote the first script of it, in 1658. But even with its classical setting and its Shakespearean credentials, we can't make it right for the stage. So please, with my compliments?"

Did one take gifts from a suspect? Slaughter thought not. But it was a book.

"May I consider it a loan? I shall return it to you when I've done reading." Cyril opened his mouth to protest, but Slaughter said, "Just in case someone comes along who can dramatize it."

"Very well, Inspector. And I hope to see you on Friday. Enjoy the performance!"

◦⁓◦

Honeycutt left the station intending to go back to the hospital. He was not looking forward to asking more questions of Matron, but there was no avoiding it. Then it occurred to him that he could go to the coroner's office first. Instead of focusing on nurses, he could find the next of kin for the patients who had died after Morton performed surgery on them. He convinced himself that fear of Matron had nothing to do with his decision.

The day was still fine, and the walk to the coroner's office a pleasant mile or so. It was good to stretch his legs after the station, which was large and modern but seemed bereft of comfortable chairs. But as he rounded the corner toward London Bridge, he noticed a large group of people crowding the pavement and edge of the road. Peering over the heads of the crowd, he asked a large man in a tall hat what was happening.

"It's a cart," he said. "One of those damned goods carts run up on the pavement. Trying to avoid another cart, with more behind him. The tangle is blocking everything."

Honeycutt sighed. Traffic was not his area, and he was sure the Borough police would be involved already. Nevertheless, he moved gently through the crowd, murmuring "Police, give way please" until he got to an officer and introduced himself.

"Anything I can do to help?"

"No, sir, no one's hurt. Just the usual jam at the bridge. All the building across the way isn't helping, either."

Honeycutt decided to walk back and take a different path, hearing the grumbling of the public all the way. More routes were clearly needed across the river, he thought. And the carts go any way they want. There should be a system, with traffic flowing in particular patterns, maybe even signals like one has with trains. Modernization, he thought. That's what's needed.

The clerk at the coroner's desk looked harried. He was a small man, with sandy hair. Honeycutt noticed that his cuffs had been turned; they were peeking out of his sleeve covers. The job must not pay much, he thought.

"Excuse me," he said, removing his hat. "I'm Detective Sergeant Honeycutt from Christchurch station."

The clerk looked up wearily. "And how may I help you, Sergeant?"

"I'd like the records of fourteen patients who died at St. Thomas's Hospital within the last year, please."

The clerk sighed and glanced at the clock on the wall. "Do you have the names and dates?"

"I do," said Honeycutt, holding out the list. The clerk looked and gave a little grunt.

"If you could wait out here, sir, or perhaps come back in an hour?"

Honeycutt decided to walk around a bit, avoiding the bridge. First, he went back to St. Thomas's Street and watched the bricklayers and pipe-fitters work on the railway station. Then he turned around and visited Borough Market. Although a market of some kind had been there for centuries, several of the buildings were only about ten years old. More builders were here too, creating the railway viaduct that, by agreement, flew over the top of the market. Honeycutt felt he could literally look up and see the future, the massive viaduct shading the area where fruit and vegetable sellers had their goods laid out in crates, taking orders for all over London. The place had a new and vibrant feel to it.

Honeycutt returned to the coroner's office at twelve o'clock and took a seat in the small lobby, still able to hear the noise from the traffic jam near the bridge. Some of the carts were being redirected down this street, the horses looking like they'd rather have another profession. Inside, a young woman in black sat in the other chair, holding a handkerchief and looking miserable. She noticed him and gave him the look he often received because of his height.

"My condolences," he said.

"Thank you," she said.

The clerk came back carrying a stack of paper packets wrapped with ribbon. "You can look at these here, but I'm afraid you can't take them with you," he said. "I'll bring the others out when you're finished with these."

There was no table, so Honeycutt stood at the counter and opened the packets one at a time, making notes as he went. Address, next of kin, cause of death. The clerk came out with the other stack. Honeycutt stood at the desk for half an hour. Then he decided to have a second look at the two cases that Morton had taken from Woodsmith. He again opened Oscar Morgenstern's packet. The coroner's report was on top. Death due to infection following surgery, exacerbated by the patient's obesity. He was unmarried and had no surviving family. For Nan Deighton, the cause of death was lung congestion caused by adverse reaction to chloroform. The report also noted that the deceased had been in the early stages of pregnancy. That was interesting. Next of kin was Mrs. Sylvia Parker in Clifton Road, St. John's Wood. Honeycutt circled the address in his notes, deciding to make her his first visit.

"Thank you," he said to the clerk, rewrapping the ribbons carefully and handing the packets across the counter. He touched his hat to the mourning woman as he left. St. John's Wood was further away than the hospital, but he wanted to be thorough. If he went there now, it would be late afternoon by the time he returned.

He stopped by the station first, bought a pie from the seller outside, left a message for Slaughter, and caught a cab. Once arrived in Clifton Road, he found Number 14 without difficulty. It was a fairly new suburb, and many of the houses were detached and painted different colors. Steps led up to little porches in front of the doors. Several servants were out doing errands, carrying baskets and greeting each other. He was surprised when the door was opened by a person who could only have been Mrs. Parker herself. She was a large, powerful woman with gray hair done up in a sweeping style. Her dress was gray also, of rich fabric with a brooch shaped like a dragonfly over her breast. She looked a little startled. Honeycutt took a step backward down the porch.

"Mrs. Sylvia Parker? I'm Detective Sergeant Honeycutt from the Metropolitan Police."

"Good afternoon," she said. "I was just getting ready to go out."

"I'm glad I caught you at home. I wonder whether I could have a few words with you about your cousin, Nan Deighton?"

A shadow passed over Mrs. Parker's face. "Of course," she said. "Do come in."

The parlor was light and airy, with very individual furnishings. There were Indian pillows, and a Turkish hookah on a small table. An ornate desk sat in the corner. He saw no servants about.

"Please, sit down," said Mrs. Parker, motioning him to a striped settee and taking a seat in an upholstered chair. A tiger rug lay on the floor between them. "What do you need to know about poor Nan?"

"You may have heard of the death of the surgeon who operated on her—Dr. Morton?"

"Yes, I read about it in *The Times*," she said. "Horrid man."

"You didn't like him?"

"I never met him, but there were rumors. And he killed my Nan."

Honeycutt felt his eyebrows raise. "He operated on her toe, I believe," he said.

"He took advantage of a young probationer who wanted to help," she said curtly. "She volunteered for that surgery, to use the chloroform. He was experimenting." Her face showed conviction.

"Do you think he killed her deliberately?"

"No. Why would he do that? He was just using her, like some animal." Her glance lowered briefly to the tiger rug.

"May I ask what you might have been doing on the morning of his death, Saturday the 18th? And the evening before?"

There was a pause as she stared at him, then she laughed, a big, bold laugh that echoed off the woodwork.

"I could have done it, I suppose," she said. "But I'm afraid I was in Kent, visiting my late husband's sister and her husband." She went to the desk and took out a calling card, handing it to him. "They'll be happy to tell you. I stayed with them for five days. I was there until Monday."

"Thank you," said Honeycutt. "I also have a very delicate question to ask you."

She sat down again.

"The coroner's report. It said she was . . . *enceinte*."

Mrs. Parker stared at him, her face going pale. He could feel a draft along the floor and heard a cat meow in a bedroom upstairs. "I had no idea," she said in a halting voice. "My husband and I had just moved to London a few weeks before she died. Then my poor Frank became ill, so I didn't attend the inquest." She looked down at her hands, which were starting to shake. "That bastard," she said in a low voice.

"Who might you be referring to?" asked Honeycutt gently.

"That young man she was carrying on with. She wrote me about him."

"Would that be Sam Wetherby?"

"She didn't tell me his name, only that she'd met someone." She looked at Honeycutt, and her eyes seemed to be imploring him to understand. "I wasn't her mother, you understand. She'd lost her parents. I paid for her to come here to study, but we weren't close. She wrote me occasionally. It was only after she died I realized I should have moved here sooner, should have tried to be closer to her."

"I'm sorry to bring you such news," he said.

Mrs. Parker nodded, her eyes wide. "She was always such a willful girl, but so kind to everyone. It seemed natural for her to be a nurse. I only wanted what was best for her."

It was very quiet. He couldn't even hear the servants in the street.

"I don't feel much like going out now," she said. "If there's nothing else, Detective Sergeant?"

"No, Mrs. Parker. I apologize for disturbing you. Can I call someone to help you?" He looked around for a bell pull.

"No, there's no one. Thank you. Please see yourself out."

As he left, he heard her start to cry.

After leaving the theatre, Slaughter mused on the ability of actors to deceive. He felt he had no clear view of Cyril Price at all. As he hailed a cab for Harley Street, the line from *Hamlet* came back to him: "a man may smile, and smile, and be a villain." Was Price such a villain? Or was he what he appeared to be, a man of the stage, a man of drama, but a good man? Tommy thought him a good man, and Tommy was an excellent judge of character. But Slaughter sensed there were things hidden about Cyril Price.

The ride was long, and the Inspector began to feel chilled sitting still in the cab. He had brought the copy of Tapper's list with him, reviewing it as best he could with all the bouncing around. It was mid-day, and the way across Waterloo Bridge, though it should have been faster, was not as direct as if the cabbie went through

Westminster, which didn't have tolls. All along Regent Street there were wealthy people shopping, wearing elegant clothing, and purchasing all the products the Empire could offer. They passed All Soul's Church, with the tower all of London thought looked like Manby's fire extinguisher. Regent Circus South was the usual madness of carts and omnibuses going in all directions.

Felix Tapper's list was both depressing and intriguing. Thirty-four deaths, but rarely on the operating table. Most had expired from various forms of blood poisoning, including pyemia, in the hospital during the week or so after their operation. Twenty of those who died had been Woodsmith's patients, although there were fourteen of Morton's, including the two he had taken from Woodsmith. All these patients had suffered through surgery, some with anesthetic and others without, only to die in horrible pain anyway. Three had undergone a second surgery for the limb infected with pyemia, then died.

Slaughter looked out the cab window at the people going about their business in Marylebone. The clean white Georgian houses, the newer terraces, displayed pots of autumn flowers. Many doctors had moved to Harley Street in recent years, and yet the place seemed immune from the sickness and despair in the hospitals. People appeared not to realize how close they were to an accident, an injury, that might make surgery necessary.

Back at Number 64, Slaughter paid the cabman and went into the office. A nurse was in the front room putting packets of paper in the drawer of a large bureau. She was in her fifties, with graying hair, and moved about with a slight limp. She looked up as Slaughter entered.

"May I help you?" she said, not unkindly.

"Yes, please, I'm Detective Inspector Slaughter of the Metropolitan Police. I'd like to see Dr. Woodsmith if he's in?"

"I'm afraid he's in with a patient," she said, "but if you'll have a seat, I will ask if he can see you soon."

Slaughter removed his hat and sat down to wait. The room, he noticed, was quite pleasant. Light came in from the street through lace curtains, the white buildings reflecting even in the gray gloom of late October. There were two vases with flowers, one near the window, and one on the low table in front of him. A copy of the *Illustrated London News* was on the table beside the flowers. He picked it up and flipped through. An item called "Medical Murder Yet Unsolved" caught his eye.

Most readers of our newspaper will recollect the achievements of Dr. Thaddeus Morton, surgeon at St. George's and later St. Thomas's Hospital. His recent unfortunate demise has thus far baffled the police, despite the callousness with which it was carried out. While some have voiced concern that the murderer might still be in the vicinity, Sir Henry Featherstone has assured the public that—

The door to the consulting room opened and a large man came out. He looked rather jolly for someone visiting a doctor, his red nose prominent above expansive gray whiskers. "Well, thank you, Doctor," he was saying, "I shall be here Thursday week at nine o'clock sharp."

Woodsmith was right behind him. "And no eating that morning, Colonel, remember." He put his hand on the colonel's shoulder.

"No breakfast! I understand! Damned inconvenient, what? But no matter. I'll be happy to have it over. So will the missus—ha ha!"

"Good day, Colonel," Woodsmith called as he left. He turned to Slaughter.

"Inspector! How nice to see you. What can I do for you?"

"I'd like a few minutes of your time, Doctor, if you don't mind."

Woodsmith glanced at the nurse.

"Mrs. Luff, would you have Mr. Penrose wait for me when he comes in, please? I shouldn't be long. Should I, Inspector?" he looked at Slaughter.

"Shouldn't be, no, sir."

Woodsmith closed the door to the consulting room behind him. It was a large room, with a desk and chairs across from the door, and a screened area in the corner with a porcelain sink and items Slaughter could not identify laid out on a tray. There was a locked cabinet in the opposite corner. Slaughter took a seat in the chair in front of the desk. Woodsmith, rather than going behind the desk, sat halfway on the edge and looked amiably at Slaughter.

"So, I assume this is about the investigation, rather than a medical matter?" He looked concerned, as if it might be the latter.

"Yes, sir. It's about Dr. Morton. I have a list here I'd like you to look at." He handed it to Woodsmith.

"Well, let's see," Woodsmith said as he looked down the page. "Surgical deaths at St. Thomas's. I understand. These poor patients." He began to read the names. "Oh yes, Mr. Morgenstern. Such a kind man. Horrible injury." He pointed at the page. "What are the stars for?"

"Those are cases that were assigned to you, but Morton took the surgery."

"Ah, yes. I should have realized." He looked a little abashed. "I assume Sir Henry told you I complained about that."

"Why would Morton take some of your patients?" asked Slaughter.

Woodsmith swung his leg over, stood up, and began to pace behind his desk. "Dr. Morton was a supremely confident surgeon, Inspector, with good reason. I believe I told you I sometimes observed his work. All of the cases he took from me, you see, were anesthesia cases, and he believed he was better than I was at those." Woodsmith shrugged. "He may have been right. But after those surgeries, Inspector, I still took responsibility for those patients. I believe that all patients deserve to be treated with dignity and respect."

"I noticed that almost all of these patients died, not from the operation, but from infection after surgery. I take it that's typical?"

Woodsmith nodded. "I'm disappointed to report that it is," he said. "Surgery is still a very difficult business. Anesthesia has made it easier to perform, but it does nothing for the suppuration afterward. In fact, some claim that because anesthesia allows for longer surgeries, there is even more chance for infection later. But we don't know what causes it, yet. It might be the wound itself, whether it's smooth or jagged. It might be the depth into the body. It could be some form of shock. We just don't know."

He paced. "And more, we don't understand suppuration itself. Is the presence of pus a good thing, or a bad thing? Does it precede healing, or prevent it? When there is a great deal of pus, does that indicate the body is pushing the poison out, or that it is beyond repair?"

Slaughter realized he was feeling a little sick.

"Can you explain," he said, clearing his throat, "why more of these deaths are your patients rather than Morton's?"

Woodsmith paused. "No," he said, "no, I can't." He had stopped pacing and was staring down at the carpet.

"Did you discuss this fact with Dr. Morton?"

"No."

There was silence. A horse could be heard walking her cab outside, but that was all.

Woodsmith looked up. "I'm afraid, Inspector, that if you have no more questions, I must continue with my patients. Mr. Penrose, my four o'clock, is surely here by now."

As he walked over to Portland Place to hail a cab, Slaughter hoped that Honeycutt had discovered more information about those who had died. But with so many deaths, with so many surgeries that seemed successful but then turned into morbidity, he was unsure what could be learned. What if this were not a personal crime at all? What if someone were simply furious with surgeons and physicians pretending they knew the answer to human suffering?

∽

"Darling," said Geraldine, "you didn't kill him, did you?"

The Wednesday night audience was usually unruly, so the actors had arrived early to prepare themselves. As the director, Anthony liked the performers to have a brief, inspirational meeting once a week. Although he felt it unnecessary, and at times even intrusive, Cyril had been willing to go along. He led each meeting personally, pulling out quotations as appropriate.

"The Bard said all the world's a stage," he had begun earlier in the evening, standing on a bench from the palace in Scene 3. "And that everyone is merely a player. But what about the players?"

He had looked around. Geraldine and the dozen or so of the company had nodded in sympathy.

"What about the players themselves? Are we not flesh and blood? When you prick us . . ."

The chorus responded, "Do we not bleed?"

"We do bleed," said Cyril, lowering his voice. His chin tipped down dramatically. "We bleed our art. We bleed so that our public may escape a bit, from poverty, and despair, and sheer boredom. We bleed to show them the possibilities of life, of feeling, of humanity. We bleed because we are connected to a glorious heritage. Man has performed since the earliest times, to entertain but also to instruct." He had raised an arm in emphasis. "And here in our extraordinary city, the heart of civilization, where do we instruct? In the pricey seats of Drury Lane, the elegant theatres of Covent Garden?"

The cast had shaken their heads.

"No! We do it here, in the land of warehouses, river docks, and leather tanners. We bleed here, for the bricklayers and the costermongers and the policemen."

"The policemen?" said the actor playing Polonius. "You've gone round the bend." The others laughed.

"Yes, the policemen! The errand boys of justice, the representatives of Portia! Even they come to the theatre to distance themselves from their work, to experience true art. And will we give them their art, all of them? The best that we can do? As those who hold up to a mirror the truth of man's depravity and glory?"

"Yes!" the cast responded, though a few were still grumbling about the police.

Cyril had jumped down off the bench, and the assembly had gone off to get ready. Geraldine had followed him back to his dressing room and closed the door.

"Of course I didn't kill him! What makes you say so, my dear?" He sat down to begin the long process of hair and makeup.

Geraldine took the end of her scarf and trailed it across the back of the chaise, as if her question had been purely casual.

"It's just that I wonder whether you might have been"—she paused—"*closer* to Thaddeus Morton than anyone knows."

He looked up at her in the mirror. He knew Geraldine. She was observant, intelligent, and talented. She could also be maddening. They had never really been friends, although they had worked together successfully for many years. More like colleagues, with all the competition that implied. He chose not to reveal his surprise at her suggestion.

"I cannot imagine what makes you think that." He began pinning back the hair back from his brow. The wig was murder on one's real hair.

"It's true," she said, watching the green fabric trail along, "it did take some imagination. But not much. I was returning past Surrey Gardens one night, in the carriage of a gentleman I would prefer not to name."

She paused.

"You've been in many such carriages, darling," he said.

"I have, darling, I have," Geraldine purred. "And always with such worthy companions. But that night I saw you leaving the Gardens. It was very late. You seemed . . . shall we say, disheveled?" She sidled up to the picture of Edmund Kean. "Was Mr. Kean so inclined, do you think?"

Cyril put the pins down. "My dear, you have so far said nothing interesting, much less implicating. What on the Bard's green globe are you talking about?"

"It was a lovely night, you see. My companion had ordered the carriage to stop just near the gates. He wanted to show me some . . . affection, without the bouncing and jarring of the road. Even in my, shall we say, indecorous position, I was able to see you out the window."

Cyril rolled his eyes at her. Geraldine's appetites were legendary.

"And about a minute later, Morton came out the same gate," she said.

Cyril's hand froze near the pot of rouge.

"Did he also look . . . disheveled?" He tried to keep his voice light.

"No," she said, and turned toward him. "He looked haughty and content, like someone who'd just eaten an entire Christmas goose. His look was one of utter satisfaction."

Cyril said nothing.

"So, I wondered," she continued, "whether you might have been the one who killed him?"

Cyril began to apply the rouge. A bit to cheeks, a bit to chin. Geraldine moved closer, putting her lovely hands, her famous hands, on his shoulders.

"Don't worry," she said, "I shan't tell anyone. The man was a monster. He even tried to . . . compromise me. I was just curious."

Cyril patted her hands, removed them from his shoulders, then rose to face her.

"If I had killed Thaddeus Morton," he said, "I certainly wouldn't tell you. Or anyone. And my dear," he kissed her cheek gently, "I've seen what you do to men who try to compromise you."

⁓

John placed Sir Henry gently on the seat of the carriage, tucking the Scottish wool blanket around his legs. Hannah had been invited to come to the board meeting, but she declined. She knew that several of the members did not appreciate having a woman there, and the situation was tense enough without adding to it. She had kissed her husband goodbye, handed him his papers and wished him luck, then gone upstairs to read *Lady Audley's Secret*.

Sir Henry was glad she hadn't come. It was quite cold, and he needed to think about the best way to handle the situation. The board, he knew, would demand explanations and information.

Surrey Gardens was dark and chilly, although there were several people about. Medical students accompanied each other to their lodgings, arguing about the day's lesson in anatomy. A young couple strolled out the gate, likely one of the porters and a nurse. Probationers were not allowed to leave the property without an appropriate chaperone, but nurses were independent. Porters and nurses had similar hours, and there had been several romances at Old St. Thomas's. One couple had married quite happily, and even invited Sir Henry to the wedding. He had gracefully declined, not wanting to put any pressure on them to impress him. Goodness knows they weren't paid enough for a big wedding, and some men insisted their wives leave their position after marriage. Sir Henry admired the groom enormously when he heard he had not done so, and both porter and nurse were still employed, now at Surrey Gardens.

John wheeled Sir Henry in the side door in order to avoid the front steps. Most of the board members were already there. Sir Henry preferred to arrive a few minutes late, after everyone was seated. It both added to his authority and prevented the embarrassment of people talking down to him. He wheeled around the room as the others chatted, greeting each member personally, asking after families and such, before they began.

The meeting was called to order. The secretary read the minutes from the last meeting, which had taken place in August. The first item on the agenda pertained to finance. The secretary read out the income and expenditures of the hospital itself, then that of the Nightingale School and the medical school, which had separate budgets. The numbers were trending downward. There had been a small decline in the number of patients, and a decline in the amount of donations. In addition, several candidates for the schools had withdrawn their applications in the previous week. Sir Henry strove to look as amiable as possible.

Mr. Stone, a barrister, was the first to speak. "Gentlemen, I am confident that I am not alone in thinking that our current situation is the result of the unfortunate demise of Dr. Morton," he said. Heads nodded around the table. "Potential patients, donors, and candidates are, to put it simply, afraid to come to Surrey Gardens."

"Agreed," said Mr. Farrington, the editor. "They think there's a killer on the loose. I can't say as I blame them!"

Mr. Critchlow, who sold scientific equipment, chimed in. "But surely the death of Dr. Morton was the result of some personal altercation? Why should anyone else be afraid?"

Heads turned toward Sir Henry.

"There is no cause for concern," said Sir Henry, smoothly. "It's only been nine days since the death of Dr. Morton, much too short a time to explain any changes in numbers. The police believe it was personal, and we have no reason to think otherwise."

"But chloroform, damn it!" swore Mr. Allen, who ran a shipping company. "He was killed with chloroform. That makes people afraid of anesthesia, just when we've had such success with it for surgery."

"It certainly doesn't help that the press has reported this in a way that increases worry rather than decreases it," grumbled Mr. Critchlow, glaring at Mr. Farrington.

"My papers have only reported the truth! The police seem to have no idea what to do. There are no results yet from their investigation, or even a list of suspected murderers. No one has been arrested. What else are we to report?"

"I don't think we can do anything about the police investigation," said Mr. Allen.

"I have done my best," said Sir Henry, "to persuade the detectives involved to move as quickly as possible."

"It could have been some criminal off the street," said Mr. Critchlow.

"With his body left sitting up in the old operating theatre?" said Mr. Perkins. He managed a collection of pie vendors and rarely spoke at meetings.

"He's got a point, damn it," said Mr. Allen. "It wasn't a criminal off the street. They don't carry chloroform."

"More do than you think," said Mr. Farrington. "Just last month, we were looking into a story of criminals using chloroform to make their victims insensible before robbing them. Some even use it on parlor-maids to burglarize a house."

"Use it on parlor-maids to make them more pliable," murmured Mr. Perkins, and was ignored.

"How do we even know that people are staying away because of the murder?" proposed Mr. Allen. "What about death rates, or how long people have to stay in the hospital?"

"Our survival and recovery rates for amputation," said Sir Henry, "are actually substantially better than they were at Old St. Thomas's. There has been talk about why. The Nightingale contingent credits the improvements in ventilation, but there is also the greater use of disinfectants."

"Sir Henry," said Mr. Critchlow, "is it your impression that as soon as the killer is found, the patrons and patients will return?"

"Yes indeed, gentlemen. I am quite convinced that our setbacks are temporary."

"But Sir Henry," said Mr. Farrington, "the issue is money. Even if our benefactors return at a later date, the money we've lost is gone forever. It's been a fortnight. Another week at these levels, and we will exhaust the hospital's funds in . . ." He looked over at the secretary, who was scribbling on a pad.

"Twelve days," said the secretary.

The board gasped.

"Twelve days, damn it!" said Mr. Allen. "Twelve days! The culprit must be found, Sir Henry. We didn't spend last year raising additional funds to move the hospital only to have the whole venture collapse at our feet!"

As the agenda moved on to other subjects, Sir Henry struggled to maintain his composure. The hospital was his life now. He had completely forgotten his musings about retirement. For the remainder of the meeting, he concentrated as best he could on the remaining topics. He supported a new lock on the door to the probationer's room, voted against a measure to house porters on hospital property, and agreed to additional authority for the Ladies' Committee to raise funds.

John bundled him into the carriage for the chilly ride home.

"John, it's bad enough that the coachman has to sit out in the cold," said Sir Henry. "Ride in here with me, will you?"

The carriage clattered along Kennington Road, then turned toward the Vauxhall Bridge. What on earth was Inspector Slaughter doing? Why was the investigation taking so long?

"John, you met Inspector Slaughter. Does he impress you as a competent policeman?"

"He does indeed," replied John. "Very dedicated."

"But we have no answer regarding who murdered Dr. Morton."

"True. But I can't imagine this is an easy task. Inspector Slaughter seemed to me to be a thinker, rather than one who makes swift conclusions. He's methodical."

Sir Henry sighed. "I suppose so. But in this case, even a hasty arrest might be helpful."

John looked surprised. "Am I to assume that the board is worried about money?"

Sir Henry smiled. "When isn't the board worried about money? But yes, we have fewer patients, fewer patrons, and fewer students applying, all because the murder hasn't been solved."

"But you wouldn't want an innocent man arrested, would you?" said John.

"No, John. I suppose I wouldn't."

⚬⚬

Honeycutt did not have time to visit the hospital after interviewing Sylvia Parker, so he had instead journeyed back to the station to report to Slaughter.

"There seems no need to return to the hospital, if death records are at the coroner's office anyway," said Slaughter.

"I agree, sir. My notes are fairly extensive. I began with the next of kin for Nan Deighton, since I had time and she was in St. John's Wood." Slaughter listened as Honeycutt told him about the interview.

"Then the next step would be to visit other next of kin?" asked Slaughter. "How many are there?"

"If we take the first named person off each report, it's twelve. But only nine live in London, or they did when the coroner's report was filed."

"I suppose that's what you'll be doing the next few days," said Slaughter, concealing his annoyance. "Our efforts are being reported as insufficient, according to the press. We should be thorough."

That night Slaughter decided to take home all the notes. It was quite chilly, and he felt he'd be more productive in his study, wearing his slippers and listening to Ellie tidy up the kitchen. While he hated to admit it, he was stung by what he'd read in the magazine. He was also worried about the Superintendent's visit on Monday. That was several days away. If he had no result by then, or at least an arrest, he might be in disgrace, or even reprimanded.

He was no stranger to being under pressure, but he'd found that rushing the process of analysis was not a good way to get results. He had seen his superiors buckle under the demands of those above them. His own mentor, Detective Inspector Douglas Martin, had arrested a baronet. All the evidence indicated that the baronet had stolen a diamond bracelet while at the house of Lady Aston. But the evidence was based on testimony from a man who, as it turned out, was the actual thief. The old Superintendent, who was publicly embarrassed, had reprimanded Martin in front of his sergeant and several constables. In the crime of murder, making unfounded accusations was even more serious. In this case, the killer seemed to have completed his job and was unlikely to make a mistake that would expose him. Or her. So it was all about probing, getting people to reveal not only their thoughts, but their feelings, about the victim. That took time.

Slaughter pulled his coat more firmly around him, struggling with the box of papers against the evening breeze. The walk home from the station wasn't long, but he was chilled by the time he arrived. Ellie met him at the door with a cup of broth.

"Let's get you in and warm," she said, taking the box. "Tommy saw you coming from the upstairs window. Your slippers are where you left them. Drink this, and I'll have dinner ready shortly."

"Has Tommy gone to the theatre already?" he asked as he hung up his coat and took off his shoes.

"Not yet," she said, smiling. "He'll go after dinner. We're having chicken and mushroom pie."

"And I love chicken and mushroom pie!" said Tommy, bounding down the stairs two at a time. "Say, what's in the box?"

"All the papers for the case," said Slaughter. "I'll work from home tonight."

"Oh! Can I see before I have to go?"

"Not yet. No chicken and mushroom pie on my papers, please!" Slaughter ruffled Tommy's hair as they went into the kitchen.

"It's not ready yet," said Ellie, checking the oven. "You're early. Go on into the study and get out from under my feet, if you please."

"Then I suppose you may," said Slaughter to Tommy, who followed him into the study and flopped down in the wing chair.

"What have we got, Inspector?"

"The usual," sighed Slaughter. "Too many suspects, not enough truth."

"How can I help?" asked Tommy. He took Slaughter's empty pipe off the desk and put it in his mouth, pretending to smoke.

Slaughter began taking papers out of the box, then noticed the book Cyril Price had given him. He had swept it into the box with the other papers on his desk at the station.

"Here," he said, "read this."

Tommy glanced at the title and looked toward the kitchen, lowering his voice. "I don't think Mrs. Slaughter will care for this. *The Rape of Lucrece*. Is it about a real rape?"

"I'm not sure. It's a poem, by Shakespeare. Mr. Price said it's been too difficult to make into a play."

"Maybe I can do it!"

"Maybe you can," said Slaughter absently, looking through the papers. Coroner's report, testimony notes, articles from newspapers. He got out a piece of paper from the desk drawer and sat down. A map, he thought. I need to map out everyone, where they were at the time, what they've said.

Ten minutes later Tommy looked up from the book. "This is hard to understand," he said, "but I think this man Sextus is going after another soldier's wife. He's gone to see her and tells her how wonderful her husband is, but it says here he's 'Pawning his honor to obtain his lust.'"

"Any murders?" said Slaughter, continuing his mapping.

"Well, one of his kinsmen killed someone at the beginning. I think that's just to show this Sextus is from a bad family."

A few more minutes passed.

"He kept trying to talk himself out of doing it, but he did it. He raped Lucrece." Tommy put the book down and frowned.

Slaughter's map had several circles: one for the Surrey Gardens, one for the theatre, one for Old St. Thomas's. He'd also drawn a plan of Old St. Thomas's, with an "x" for Morton's body.

"Inspector," said Tommy. "Why would a man do that to a woman?"

Slaughter stopped drawing. Even at twelve, Tommy had been on the streets and knew about men and women.

"Some men think that women are like objects for them to use," he said. "As if women don't own themselves."

"You mean they think women are like slaves?"

"In a sense, yes. And some men need to prove their power by harming them. Didn't you hear of men like that before?"

Tommy thought a moment. "There was a man who helped run the workhouse," he said. "They said he used to hit women because he enjoyed it. People said he killed his own woman, hitting her too hard."

"It's the same sort of thing," said Slaughter, "and rape is a particularly brutal way of asserting that kind of power. What happens to Lucrece?"

Tommy skimmed ahead. "Looks like she tells her husband and the other men what happened, then kills herself."

Slaughter grimaced. "Looks like I gave you quite the cheery tale. Not very appropriate. I'm sorry."

Tommy laughed. "You couldn't tell from the title?"

"I wasn't thinking," said Slaughter.

Tommy stood and put the book down on the desk. "What are you doing?" he asked, looking down at the desk. By this time Slaughter had added another page to continue the map.

"I'm writing down everything we know about the case, according to the place where things happened, and the time."

"So, what have you got?"

"It appears that Dr. Morton was at Surrey Gardens as usual on Friday, the 17th of October. According to the coroner, he died Saturday, late morning or early afternoon. He died of chloroform overdose, but we have no evidence of anesthesia use at the scene, so the killer would have both brought it with him or her, and taken it away afterward. The body was set upright using a wooden board. There are plenty of wooden boards around, since the old hospital is closed and they're boarding things up. Dr. Morton had a ticket in his pocket to a gala at the theatre on the 28th of August. He was apparently blackmailing a number of people, including Geraldine Orson . . ."

"For drugs," Tommy added.

" . . . and Hannah Featherstone."

"For being an actress."

And for her affair with Cyril, thought Slaughter, but let that go. Tommy worked with these people.

"So, our biggest suspects are Geraldine Orson and Lady Featherstone?" said Tommy.

"They should be, except that someone else could have done it to protect them."

"John!" said Tommy. "He's big and strong, strong enough to lift Sir Henry. If he was trying to defend Lady Featherstone, he could have done it."

"Right. So, there's three suspects already."

"Plus everyone hated Dr. Morton," Tommy reminded him.

"Then there's Dr. Woodsmith. Dr. Morton took several of his cases."

"Ooh, yes. Sam said that happened sometimes."

"Then there's Sam, who is good enough to be a doctor but isn't one. And the several nurse probationers who were pestered by Morton, who liked to annoy young women. He brought Mary Simmons to tears, and she's Cyril Price's sister."

Tommy's eyes widened in surprise. "Oh!"

"And Matron, who defends the nurse probationers. And Felix Tapper, who provided opium to Geraldine and knows everything that goes on in the hospital. And . . ."

Ellie popped her head in. "Dinner's ready," she said. "Better hurry so Tommy can leave."

11

"Which do you think is more important, Sergeant," Slaughter asked, "a surgeon's manner, the way he makes a patient feel safe, or his technical skill?"

Thursday had dawned bright and sunny, so they were sitting in front of the station.

"I'd prefer technical skill, myself," said Honeycutt. "I'm not sure I'd want someone who was very kind but didn't know what he was doing."

"But that's not true of everyone," said Slaughter. "And how would you know whether the surgeon knew what he was doing? A person who exudes confidence, who reassures you that you'll be fine—that might be the doctor you prefer. He seems to know what he's about."

Honeycutt thought a moment.

"But aren't surgeons more like mechanics, sir? I mean, they're highly trained and everything. But their job is to repair the body. Surely their knowledge of anatomy is more important than friendliness."

"I had a case a few months ago," said Slaughter. "A very old woman was one of the witnesses. We had to interview her in her bedroom, with her doctor in attendance. She was quite wealthy. During the interview, she asked the doctor to leave. She began talking to me about how much she disliked him. Her old doctor had recently retired, after caring for her and her family for many years. This new man was quite young, and she thought he was incompetent. He didn't listen, she complained, to anything she said about her ailments. Instead, he'd use his stethoscope, listen to her breathe, and tell her that any concerns she had about bronchitis were unfounded. He'd heard nothing through his scope. The problem, she said, was that newfangled contraptions were replacing compassion and the willingness to listen to what the patient said."

"But surely the young doctor would know the latest techniques?"

"I'm sure he did. But she didn't want the latest techniques. She wanted to be heard."

They sat a while in the sun, thinking about the case. Perhaps, thought Honeycutt, this was yet another area where Slaughter felt the old ways were best. Honeycutt would rather have a modern doctor with a stethoscope and the latest information than someone who would allow him to diagnose his own illness. And, having heard so much about surgery, he'd much rather live in an age where anesthesia was available, even with the risk of infection.

The inspector interrupted his thoughts. "Let's go back in. I'd like to review, again, where everyone was on Saturday the 18th."

Despite the sunshine, when they went inside, their cheeks were pink with cold. Jones went to fetch cups of tea.

Slaughter fished a piece of paper out of the box, which he had brought back with him that morning.

"I mapped out everyone involved in the case," he told Honeycutt as he laid the paper down on the desk between them. "And I've tried to mark where everyone was at the time of murder. Could we compare with your notes?"

"Of course," said Honeycutt, taking his notebook out of his pocket.

Jones came in with tea, frowning. His mustache drooped in despair.

"I'm sorry, sir," he said. "I couldn't find matching cups this morning."

"Quite all right, Jones. I wonder if you can help us with some strategizing?"

"Of course, sir!" said Jones, snapping to attention. He looked down at the desk. "Is this what you have?"

"First, we have Cyril Price."

"The actor."

"Yes. He says he was in and out of the theatre, which seems odd for a Saturday morning after a performance. Might want to follow up on that."

"Good idea, sir," said Jones. Honeycutt made a notation in his book.

"Next would be Geraldine Orson."

"One of the women being blackmailed by Dr. Morton, sir?" asked Jones.

"Yes, over her use of drugs."

"Powerful motive, sir."

"According to my interview, she was sleeping, alone in the house," said Honeycutt. Jones glowered. Honeycutt shrugged in return.

"Then we have Dr. Woodsmith. My notes say he and his wife were home together all morning," said Slaughter.

Jones put his finger on the side of his nose and nodded knowingly.

"Sam Wetherby?" Slaughter looked at Honeycutt, who paged through his notes.

"In the surgery room, tidying up."

"Suspicious, sir, I'd say," said Jones. "Does he have a motive?"

"Only that he disliked Morton, same as everyone."

"Hmm."

"On to Felix Tapper. He was at the hospital doing inventory and cited Matron as his witness."

"I couldn't help but notice, sir," said Honeycutt, "that Tapper and Matron seem to have some sort of relationship."

Slaughter raised his eyebrows. "In your estimation, would they lie to the police?"

"Not likely, sir, in my estimation. There also would have been others around the hospital if we want their alibi confirmed."

Slaughter consulted his map. "And Mary Simmons."

"The one who wants to be a nurse?" asked Jones.

"Yes, and who was abused by Dr. Morton. You talked with her, Honeycutt."

"She was attending a class at the hospital at the time."

"No getting around that, sir," said Jones, stroking his mustache.

"And last," said Slaughter, "or so it seems, would be Lady Featherstone, or her husband, or their manservant. Sir Henry said he and his wife were home. Damn."

Jones looked surprised. Slaughter rarely swore.

"I didn't ask Mr. Addo his whereabouts on the morning of the murder."

"We never interviewed him formally, sir," said Honeycutt.

"Well, there's an oversight," said Jones.

"It is indeed. All right, apart from that omission, Jones, what do you make of it?"

Jones looked down at the paper, then up at the ceiling.

"I'd say you've got two separate pools, if you like, of suspects. Each," he raised his finger, "in a different type of theatre. You have the doctors and nurses and students, all in the hospital near the surgical theatre, and actors and such at the Surrey Theatre. You've got a lot of suspects, but no witnesses to the crime. And it seems like everyone disliked the victim."

Jones began pacing in the small space by the office door.

"There also seems to be a lot of connections, a lot of relationships. I think, if you don't mind me saying so, that the clue is in those relationships. Hate for Dr. Morton might come out of love for someone else. Or fear that something would happen to someone else." He stopped.

"That's very astute, Jones," said Slaughter. "Thank you."

He turned to Honeycutt. "Sergeant, please go and determine whether John Addo has an alibi for Saturday morning before visiting more next of kin. Jones and I will go back to the coroner's office and search through the files you discovered to look for more relationships. And then I am due at home to prepare for a night at the theatre. Perhaps *Richard III* can shed some light on all this."

The afternoon at the coroner's office with Jones did not prove fruitful. Among Morton's deceased patients, there was no particular pattern to their family relationships, and no surnames that overlapped with anyone at the hospital or the theatre. Few family members had attended the inquests, of which there had only been half a dozen anyway.

"Nothing to prevent a grieving relative coming in to town to kill him," said Jones quietly, as they were looking at the papers.

"That's true. But notice that most of these relatives are quite elderly."

"How can you tell?" asked Jones.

"Their relation to the deceased. Grandmother to a young patient, father to a man in his fifties."

"Would such people be able to come and stay to look after someone for two weeks or more as they died of sepsis?" asked Jones. He'd looked up the word "sepsis" and felt proud he could use it.

"St. Thomas's specializes in treating the poor," said Slaughter, "It seems unlikely. Let's make sure we have all the relatives' names for these fourteen."

∾

Tommy had rushed home from the gasworks so he could eat before going to the theatre. He knew he'd be late to help at the performance tonight, since he would accompany Inspector and Mrs. Slaughter to the play, riding in a real cab. Cyril had told him it was all right for him to miss the usual pre-performance lunacy.

"No hot dinner tonight," Ellie said when he got in the door. "I've got cold meat and fresh bread and cheese, and some apples. We don't want to be late."

"Fine with me," said Tommy. "I love cold supper." He went upstairs to wash. He loved any kind of food, thought Ellie.

As they sat down to eat, Slaughter arrived.

"I'll go upstairs to change, or should I eat first?" he asked, taking off his shoes. He was trying to be matter-of-fact, as if going to a theatre was a usual thing, but he had to admit to himself it was rather exciting. He and Ellie hadn't been to a performance in quite a while. And it was *Richard III*.

"Have your dinner," called Ellie from the kitchen. "It's cold meats, so I won't have much washing up and we can get there in good time."

Slaughter came into the kitchen and joined them at the table.

"How was everyone's day today?" he asked.

"Good!" said Tommy. "There was a bit of cleanup work at the gasworks, but they said I could leave early. Oh!" he said, fishing a piece of paper out of his pocket. "I almost forgot. Reggie gave this to me for you, from the station."

Slaughter read the note and sighed.

"What's it say, then?" asked Ellie, concerned.

"It's from Honeycutt. John Addo was with Sir Henry at home Saturday morning. As for the next of kin of Morton's patients, he interviewed three more, but they all said they felt Dr. Morton did all he could. Of course, so many people die of infection at the hospital. And they do it a week or two later, so maybe the families don't associate the death with the surgeon."

"So that means you still have no good suspects?" asked Tommy, grabbing a second slice of bread.

"It means we're having trouble finding anyone with a grudge against Dr. Morton heavy enough to actually kill him." He shook his head.

"I'm so sorry, Cubby," said Ellie. "And with the pressure you're getting to finish it, too. I do wish people would be patient. It's not as if the murderer is just going to jump out of the woodwork and shout, 'Here I am!'"

Slaughter mustered a small smile. "True," he said. "And how was your day?" he asked her, enjoying his sandwich of meat and bread.

"I worked with Jo a bit on the flyers for John Addo's talk next week. Then we went to the printer's, but he's asking too much for adding the drawing. So we had him make us a sample, and we'll take it round to other printers."

"Sounds like a good idea," said Tommy, his mouth full.

"Finish chewing, then talk. Then I got home in time to finish the bread. Oh! I just remembered." Ellie got up and hurried into the study. "Oh dear," they heard her say as she returned to the kitchen with a paper in her hand.

"Jo forgot the sample. And she's the one going to chat with other printers tomorrow. Well, she'll just have to come by and get it," Ellie shrugged. "Tommy, would you mind—"

"Taking a note in the morning," they said together. "Yes, I'd be happy to, Mrs. S."

They finished their dinner. Tommy cleaned his shoes while Slaughter and Ellie changed into evening dress. Even if Tommy had owned something for wearing in the evening, he didn't need it since he was working backstage. But he was excited about the cab.

They walked together to Blackfriars Road and easily found a cab to hail. Tommy looked up at the driver.

"Can I sit up there with him?" he asked Slaughter.

"Why don't you ask him?"

Tommy was a slight-framed boy, so the driver agreed. Slaughter and Ellie couldn't hear the conversation from inside the cab, but they knew Tommy must be talking excitedly to the cabbie as they drove along.

"We'll need a little more of a tip for the driver, I think," said Slaughter.

Having arrived and paid the cabbie, Slaughter and Ellie stood in the queue for the tickets as Tommy disappeared around the side of the theatre. The audience was milling about on the pavement. Some had brought a pie or sandwich, having come from work. A few had red earth on their boots, or grubby collars. Some of the women had on their best hats with feathers. A wily publican had set up a cask in front of the shop next door, and people were buying beer. A Lambeth constable walked by, nodding to the better dressed of those waiting for the theatre doors to open.

As Slaughter was handed their tickets, the house manager, a large, intimidating woman, came out of the main door onto the pavement. She greeted customers as they entered, showing their tickets.

"Careful as you go, sir," she said to a man with a cane going up the step.

"Here, you can't bring that beer into the theatre. Arnie!" she yelled to the publican. "Come get everyone's cups!"

"Watch your hat," she said to a woman going through the doorway right in front of Slaughter and Ellie. They heard her mumble "trollop" as they passed and went into the lobby.

The lobby was carpeted, with posters from previous performances on the walls. There were some fanciful drawings portraying the Royal Circus, which had been housed in the building in the last years of the previous century. They approached one of the inner doors. People were pushing and shoving, jovial in their efforts to enter the stalls. "May I assist you in finding your seat, sir?" said a young woman who seemed to appear out of nowhere. Slaughter handed her the tickets.

"Down the main aisle, on the left," she pointed.

The seats had an excellent view of the stage. Friends were greeting each other in the pit until the stagehands began going through the house, lowering the lamps. Then everyone took a seat, still with much talking, until the curtain rose on Cyril Price, standing center stage. The crowd burst into applause.

His blond locks were hidden, the dark wig making him look completely different. His body was bent rather than tall and proud. Instead of his normally bold expression, his face looked sinister, and he leaned forward as if telling the audience a secret. There was a hush.

> "Now is the winter of our discontent
> Made glorious summer by this sun of York;
> And all the clouds that lour'd upon our house
> In the deep bosom of the ocean buried."

As Richard's evil became increasingly known throughout the play, the audience began to hiss when he appeared on stage. During the fourth act, there were growls and murmurs at the foreshadowing of the death of Lady Anne. As Richard recapped all the people he had murdered, the audience became louder in their hatred of the character. This seemed to energize the actor, and by the time he desperately proclaimed, "My kingdom for a horse!" several men in the audience were on their feet shaking their fists. Several of the women were in tears when the play concluded.

As they were walking up the aisle to the exit, Tommy came bouncing in the lobby door to greet them.

"What did you think?" he said. "He's very good, isn't he?"

"Yes, indeed," said Slaughter. He looked over at Ellie.

"That poor Lady Anne," she said. "Why on earth did she agree to marry him? And then she seemed to take her own impending death so calmly." She shook her head sadly.

"Miss Orson's good too, isn't she?"

"Oh, yes," said Ellie as she led the way out onto the pavement. "I believed her utterly."

"Do you want to go backstage to meet everyone?" said Tommy. "Or do we need to get home? Cyril said I could go home now if I want."

"I've met everyone already," said Slaughter, "but Ellie?"

"Oh, no thank you," said Ellie. "I much prefer the characters to remain in my mind just as I saw them."

❧

Sam had decided to accompany Jo to Old St. Thomas's when she told him about the assignment. She'd come by the hospital that afternoon to ask him what exactly the hospital's surgeons wore so her drawings would be accurate for Mr. Evans.

"I still have my key to the old hospital," he offered. "I could help, if you don't mind waiting till after work."

"I'd be happy for your company," said Jo.

Jo had spent the morning at the boarding house. She had been washing her other dress in the laundry sink downstairs, when Mrs. Bagley had come in.

"There you are, Miss Harris. I was looking for you. Wanted to ask you a question."

Mrs. Bagley was in her fifties, a formidable woman who had run the boarding house for over two decades. But she was a creative manager, roping in her lodgers to help run the place in return for reduced rent. Bridget, for example, was often called upon to do some baking. But it was Jo's skills she needed now.

"You know that Miss Davies is getting married and will move out in a fortnight. I want the right kind of woman to take her place. Someone who'll pitch in."

"Will you be running an advertisement?" asked Jo. "That's how I found you."

"Yes, but I also want a bigger sign in the parlor window, facing the street" she said. "Can you do a drawing of something that would attract the right sort of lodger?"

Jo thought a moment. "Like a portrait of a young woman?"

"That would be fine," said Mrs. Bagley. "I just want something that will catch the eye. Make her a respectable young woman. I'll give you two shillings off the rent for it."

The deal had been made, and Jo had added creating the drawing to her housekeeping duties that morning. She hadn't been able to get to the hospital till afternoon.

"Not a problem," said Sam when she found him in the prep room. "I can leave here at three o'clock, as soon as I finish setting things out for the surgeries tomorrow. But you said something about surgeon's clothes?"

"Yes," said Jo. "What do they wear during surgery?"

"They wear these coats," he said, walking over to the pegs.

"But they look just like ordinary street coats," said Jo. She looked closer. "Only more disgusting. Is this what you told me about?"

"Yes, exactly. Some of the doctors think the dried blood is a badge of honor. Some don't think about it at all."

Jo looked over at him with a grimace. Sam shrugged. "It's horrible, but I've told you what I would do about it, if I could."

"I'm not putting that in my drawing," she said. "It would be too difficult to do anyway, with the coats so dark. And I don't think the editor wants anything gruesome. Which one is Morton's?"

"This one." Sam pointed. "The filthiest, naturally."

"And the dressers wear what you're wearing?"

"Yes, although some wear an apron also. Do you want to see one?" He went over to a bench and leaned over to get an apron. As he did so, something fell out of his pocket and landed on the floor with a clang.

Jo leaned down to fetch it. "What's this, Sam?" She picked it up and saw it was the ouroboros, the pin he'd given Nan. Jo was confused, and saddened by memories. "How do you have this? I thought you told me it was lost when she died."

"It was. But I found it later, here at the hospital." He gently took it from her and returned it to his pocket.

He put the apron in front of his waist to show her. "Here's how the apron's worn."

She rose and wiped her eyes. "I see. Thanks, Sam. This helps a lot. I need to go find some medical students to see what they wear, too."

"Go out this door, then off to the left toward the medical school rooms. You'll see plenty. You can also get some tea, if you like, while waiting for me to finish my work."

Jo walked out on the grounds. It was gray and cloudy, although it hadn't rained when she'd traveled down on the omnibus. Most of the students walking about outside had their overcoats on. She wondered whether she would be allowed in the classrooms, but assumed a woman would not be welcome. Instead, she wandered the corridors of the medical school, making mental notes of what people were wearing. Standard collars, slightly looser coats. Probably so they have greater use of their arms, she thought. Most had notebooks in a pocket—she could see their outlines through the cloth. Quite a few had their hair cut a little longer than the style. She wondered where they had it cut.

One of the students caught her eye and introduced himself.

"I'm Teddy Moore, a student here," he said. He was tall and handsome, with a childish face and dark curly hair. His eyebrow was raised in question.

"Hello," said Jo, reaching out to shake his hand. "I'm Jo Harris, artist for *Once a Week*. I'm making a drawing of Dr. Morton in the surgery at the old hospital, for a feature."

"You seemed to be looking at everyone's clothes." His eyes twinkled.

"I was," she said, giving him a direct look. "I should show medical students in the seats, shouldn't I?"

"You should," he said. "In fact, I have attended a few of Dr. Morton's surgeries. Can I be of any help?"

The look in his eyes indicated he was offering the sort of help in which she had no interest.

"No, thank you." She thought a moment. "Oh, I'm sorry, yes. May I see your notebook?"

"Of course," he smiled, taking it out of his pocket. She noted its style, and that it was covered in thin leather, with a strap.

"Thank you."

"May I accompany you to wherever you are going?"

"No, thank you," said Jo. "Surely you have a lecture to attend or something?"

"I suppose so," he said, a question in his eyes. He did have lovely eyes, and he knew it.

"Then goodbye. And thank you again." Jo turned and walked steadily toward the nursing school wing, to find the tea room.

While Jo was talking to medical students, Sam finished his work and went to get his coat. It was such a shame, he thought. Jo was like a sister to him, but she had seen the pin. There was nothing for it. She was an intelligent woman. A few hours' thought and she would know what he had done. He had no regrets about Dr. Morton. The beast had killed his poor Nan. He'd sensed that at the time, even without knowing, while the other doctors were busy shaking their heads over the vagaries of anesthesia. When Sam discovered that she had been with child, he'd planned his revenge: kill Morton with his own ill-used chloroform. Sam sighed and reached for a bottle of it now, putting it in his pocket with a carefully folded cloth. It would happen in the same place, the operating theatre where he had mounted Dr. Morton so he could gaze eternally upon his own handiwork. Morton's arena of death. At least his last victim would feel no pain.

Sam found Jo in the tea room at three o'clock. He had his coat and hat on and was ready to go.

"I've brought my key. We'll have to get a cab," he said as they walked up New Street to Kennington Road. "I'll pay."

"Oh no, Sam."

"Do let me play the gentleman, Jo. It's been a long time."

Jo understood. She hailed a cab.

They arrived at Old St. Thomas's in half an hour. The traffic had been heavy at that time of the afternoon, and the sky was turning gray.

"We should hurry, or I'll lose the light," said Jo as Sam turned the key in the tower door.

"It's all right," said Sam as they crossed the garret. "Even at the end of the day, the glass ceiling lets in lots of light. Come this way so you're at the bottom, where they wheeled the patients in."

He was right about the light. The operating theatre was still bright. Jo looked around to decide where she should sit. "I think perhaps here," she said, going up a few steps into the seats. "I'll do it from the perspective of a medical student. Want to pretend to be Morton?"

Sam took his place where the surgeon would be, tipping his profile toward the back center row with a supercilious expression.

"Now, Sam," said Jo, "don't be silly."

❧

As Slaughter entered the station Friday morning, a young woman was waiting for him in the lobby.

"Inspector Slaughter?" she rose as he entered, "I'm a reporter for the *Daily News*. I'm hoping you have time to answer some questions."

She was an ample person, with a maroon dress and her hat somewhat askew on her head. Slaughter looked around and saw Jones in the corridor. He raised an eyebrow, but Jones just shrugged.

"The *Daily News*?" said Slaughter. "An admirable paper. Your stand on the American Civil War has been clear for some time."

"Yes, Inspector. We are a liberal paper but dedicated to the northern cause in America. Very pleased to know you read my work."

"Your work?"

"Yes, I write most of the pieces on the American Civil War and anti-slavery."

Slaughter frowned. "I seem to recall they are signed with a man's name."

The woman sighed. "Yes, that's Thomas Walker, our editor. But I've written most of them myself. I'm Elizabeth Stendahl. "

"That's excellent," said Slaughter. "Well done. What can I help you with?"

"I'm writing a story on the murder of Thaddeus Morton."

Slaughter sighed. "Miss Stendahl . . ." She held up a hand in protest.

"I understand you are under a great deal of pressure to solve this murder quickly," she said, "and I want to tell your side of the story."

"My side?"

"I am interested in the process of detection. If you could detail some of your methods for our readers, they might sympathize with the new detectives in the Metropolitan Police. Most readers think you are just overpaid constables. They want to hear about how you do what you do."

Slaughter thought for a moment. Publicity that showed they were working hard might be a good idea, if the public thought they were doing too little.

"Please," said Slaughter, gesturing toward his office. He noticed that Jones did not jump in to offer tea.

Miss Stendahl sat down and flipped open her notebook.

"I'd like to ask, Inspector . . ."

"Detective Inspector," said Slaughter. Might as well get it right in print.

"Detective Inspector," she said, making a note. "What process do you use to determine the culprit of a murder?"

"We're quite methodical here," said Slaughter. "We observe the scene, note anything interesting about the victim, examine the coroner's report."

"Then you talk to suspects?"

"Not immediately. First, it's important to find out as much as we can about the victim, and the circumstances of the crime. The people he knew, anyone who might have had a motive."

"And how do you discover who might have had a motive?"

"It's more a process of uncovering, really. People who knew the victim might talk about other people too. The victim may be a completely innocent person, or he may have made himself unpleasant to others. Most people have at least one person who dislikes them, so that can give clues to the victim's personality. Then one can start considering what qualities the murderer might possess."

"That all sounds very psychological," said Miss Stendahl. "Is there no action, no excitement?"

"Unless the murderer does something, like attack another victim or commit another crime, it's not very exciting. It's more a matter of being thorough in the investigation. It takes time." Slaughter hoped he was making a point that readers might understand. For a moment, he felt like he was trying to convince the Superintendent rather than a reporter.

"What about physical evidence?"

He thought about the ticket in Morton's pocket, and the missing pin from Miss Simmons' uniform. "Yes, but there isn't always very much physical evidence."

"Would you say it is more like putting together a puzzle?"

"It is indeed. Just so. And you don't always have all the pieces."

"How do you go about it once you have some information?"

"Every detective does it differently. I am particularly fond of mapping things out on paper: locations, relationships between people, lists of habits."

"Would you consider it a creative process?"

"In my case, yes, but it's not artistic. However, because I read quite a bit, I often find that themes from my reading come into play, particularly themes about evil, and love, and revenge."

Miss Stendahl took a note.

"What sorts of things do you read?" she asked.

Slaughter didn't want to mention *The Rape of Lucrece* specifically, so he just said, "Shakespeare. Milton. Greek philosophy."

"So, a detective should be educated, then?"

"I think it's useful. Human activity is understandable, if only in that most things have happened before. And the great themes of human existence are explored most thoroughly in books."

Miss Stendahl stopped writing and looked up. "That's the perfect way to end my piece," she said, rising to shake his hand. "I know I've taken up time you need to work on the case. Thank you so much for letting me interview you."

"You're welcome, Miss Stendahl. I look forward to reading your piece."

"Mr. Walker's piece." She smirked, and adjusted her hat.

"Yes, of course," said Slaughter.

Jones came sidling up as he stood in the corridor. "I already had to ask two of them to come back later," he said ruefully.

"Two of who?" asked Slaughter.

"Reporters. You told me you were going back to Morton's place before lunch, so I told them to come back around two."

Slaughter thought for a moment. "I think," he said, "in that case I'll be working from home this afternoon."

"Understood, sir," said Jones, tapping the side of his nose. Slaughter began packing up his notes.

∽

"That's odd," said Ellie. It was afternoon, and the study was bright and cozy. The light was always good this time of day, so Ellie was doing her sewing. It was nice to have Cuthbert working at home, although he was concentrating on his work.

"What's odd?" Slaughter said absently, laying out his notes on the desk.

"Jo should have been here by now. She has to go see the printers, and I'm sure they'll all be closed by five. I wonder should I send Tommy to her boarding house with the papers now?"

"You can't," said Slaughter, looking up. "He's at Covent Garden with flyers. But they're doing another gala at the theatre tonight, so he'll be home this evening."

"Oh, yes. I forgot. Well, that will be nice," said Ellie, and returned to her sewing. A few minutes passed, the clock ticking on the mantle, and then, "It's very odd that Jo hasn't come by."

"What was Jo doing today, did she say?" Slaughter asked, as he made a note from a file.

"She said she was going down to the hospital to look at what the surgeons and dressers wear for surgery, for some drawing she's doing. Sam Wetherby was going to help her."

For his part, Slaughter had spent mid-day at Dr. Morton's house in Rutland Gate. He had returned there after going through the names that Honeycutt had given him. It had been inconvenient to go first to the agency to get the key, but he had found the papers easily in the musty stillness of Morton's study. He'd gathered together Morton's personal papers on the patients who'd died, to compare them to his notes from the coroner's office. There wasn't much.

Suddenly he rose from his chair.

"Honeycutt," he said firmly. "I must talk to Honeycutt."

"Now?" said Ellie. "Will he be at the station?"

"No, I told him he could go to the bank, then pay his rent, so he could avoid the reporters too. He lives in Brunswick Street. It's not far." He was putting on his shoes, grabbing his coat, and checking his pockets for change. He turned to Ellie, a worried expression on his usually placid face.

"Look," said Slaughter, "I've got to see Honeycutt, and then I may be out for some time." He was gathering a few pages and stuffing them in the pockets of his overcoat.

"I understand," said Ellie. "A policeman must go where he must. But Cubby?"

"Yes?" He was obviously in a hurry.

"Be careful, dear."

He gave her a quick kiss and left.

The walk to Honeycutt's boarding house was cold, but it wasn't raining and he was able to make good time on foot. The lamp lighters were starting to light the street lamps, although it wasn't dark yet. Slaughter found the boarding house in Brunswick Street easily. As he went up the steps, a young man was coming out.

"Hello. I'm Detective Inspector Slaughter. Do you know in which room Sergeant Honeycutt resides?"

"Sergeant . . . ? Oh! You mean Mark. Yes, upstairs then to the right, number seven."

The lobby was small, with red carpet and a healthy aspidistra in the corner. Slaughter didn't notice. He took the stairs two at a time.

"Sergeant," he said when Honeycutt opened the door to his knock, "I'm sorry to disturb you when I said you could go home. But I must check this with you." He pulled the papers out and waved them.

"Of course, sir. Come in," he gestured to a table in the middle of the room. Slaughter laid out the pages.

"Do you have your notes from interviewing Mrs. Parker?"

Honeycutt's coat was hanging from a chair. He pulled out his notebook and flipped through it.

"Yes, sir, right here." He handed the notes to Slaughter.

Slaughter looked through.

"Yes! That's it. It's all to do with Nan Deighton."

"The nurse probationer who died on the operating table?"

"Yes. She had an infected toe, and Woodsmith was supposed to operate. Morton took it over, as we know he sometimes did. But an infected toe is hardly a place to showcase one's skill. And then she died, not of infection but of anesthesia that Morton administered himself. What if he did it on purpose?"

"You mean Dr. Morton killed Nan Deighton? Why would he do that?"

"She was expecting," Slaughter said, taking out the notes from the coroner's office. "So, we know she had a fellow. And Mrs. Parker is the one who knew that. But this was like *The Rape of Lucrece*. And then there was the pin."

"The pin, sir?" Honeycutt was completely confused.

"You told me that Mary Simmons had a pin, but it was stolen. I think the pin was the one I saw in Jo's notebook, the one that belonged to Nan. Morton took the pin off of Nan when she had her surgery. He gave it to Mary Simmons, his newest conquest."

"Then who stole it from Mary?"

"The person who figured out that Morton killed Nan Deighton, and then killed Morton to avenge her death. The one who knew about anesthesia, and Morton's habits. Somehow, he lured the surgeon to the old hospital, and that's where we must go now, at once." He gathered up the papers.

"Why, sir?" said Honeycutt as he put on his overcoat.

"Because Jo Harris is in danger."

Slaughter headed out the door. Honeycutt began to follow, then turned back, quickly unlocked the trunk, and quietly slipped the gun into his pocket.

∾

The cab clattered up Blackfriars Road, then entered the warren of streets eastward toward St. Thomas's. The sky was still light gray, and people were passing each other with their afternoon shopping. When the cab came out on Borough High Street, the traffic blocked the road.

Slaughter leaned out to cry up at the cabbie, "Can you go another way? We must get there quickly!"

"Ain't no other way, guv'n'r," said the cabbie. "It's Friday, innit? It's always like this."

"On foot," snapped Slaughter to Honeycutt, who jumped out of the cab and paid the driver. They ran across Borough High Street and up to St. Thomas's Street. At the corner, Slaughter looked to the right, then straight ahead. Which way would he take her? Up the tower, or in the back from the alley? Better to take a different route.

"Up this way," he said to Honeycutt. They ran up to the main entrance. The gate was closed and padlocked with a chain.

"Should we get in through the alley, sir?"

"It's our only choice," said Slaughter. They rounded the corner to encounter some builders coming down the road on their way to the High Street, talking and laughing. They passed the tower and turned into the alley.

They ran across the courtyard, then Slaughter put up a hand. "Quietly," he said. "The door to the operating theatre is quite close to the courtyard."

He had hoped the door was still unlocked, and it was. But relief had to wait. He could hear muffled voices in the theatre.

He waved Honeycutt up to the garret. "You go up to the back of the seats," he whispered. "That way you might come in behind them. I'll come in the patient entrance below, but not just yet. Pull his attention toward you, away from this door." Honeycutt nodded and disappeared into the darkening garret.

Slaughter waited by the ward doors.

Honeycutt pulled his gun and carefully opened the upper door used by the medical students. As soon as he caught sight of Wetherby below in the theatre, he pointed his weapon at him. Jo was lying supine on the wooden table. Sam was holding a cloth over her face, and with his other hand held a bottle of liquid over the cloth. Even in the fading light, Honeycutt could see he was carefully pouring drops onto the cloth. There was a sticky sweet smell to the room.

"Stop or I'll shoot," said Honeycutt.

Sam looked up and peered at him, and then the gun.

"Just a few more drops," said Sam, as if in his sleep. He looked sad and tired.

Honeycutt cocked the gun. The lower door slammed open. Before Wetherby could turn fully around, Slaughter hit him over the head with a piece of lumber. Sam slumped to the floor, the bottle of chloroform shattering. The smell was overpowering. Slaughter grabbed the cloth from Jo's face, then turned back and opened both ward doors wide.

Honeycutt ran down the steps and jumped easily over the low wall separating the student area from the operating floor. He reached Jo and put his ear to her chest. She was still breathing, slowly. He grabbed her sketchbook from the rim of the seating area and fanned her face. After half a minute, he checked her breathing again.

"Better, sir. I think she'll come round if we get her some air."

"Good. Please put Mr. Wetherby in handcuffs first, in case he also comes round. Then let's carry Miss Harris out into the courtyard."

They sat next to Jo on the grass as she started to stir. Slaughter glanced sharply at Honeycutt.

"A gun, Sergeant?"

Honeycutt looked abashed. "I might have had to shoot him if you hadn't hit him over the head," he said. "He wouldn't stop administering the drops."

Slaughter wanted to upbraid the young man, tell him that guns were not needed in this country. That there was no excuse for bringing such a weapon. But he certainly hadn't issued an order to that effect, and it had clearly been the American's instinctive response to incipient danger.

"Sometimes the old-fashioned ways are best," he said instead.

12

"He had a gun?" asked Tommy, fascinated. He kept his voice low, since Jo was resting in the study. Slaughter had returned home with her while Honeycutt had taken a hand-cuffed Sam Wetherby to the station. Tommy had returned from Covent Garden about the same time.

"Yes, he did. I assume he brought it with him from America."

Ellie came into the kitchen. "Let's be quiet now," she said. "I think she's sleeping."

"She should be, if Sam used chloroform," said Tommy. "Is she breathing all right?"

"Yes, I think so," said Ellie. She brought over the leftover meat and bread to the table. "Now what's all this about guns?"

"The Inspector says Sergeant Honeycutt had one. Pointed it right at Sam!"

"He did, but it wasn't needed. I hit Wetherby with a piece of wood." Slaughter sipped his whiskey and took a bite of ham. He had to admit he was quite tired.

"But how did you know it was Sam?" Tommy's eyes were wide.

"A few things came together this afternoon while I was working on some of the medical records."

"So, you solved it just through thinking?"

"A lot of it through thinking, yes."

Tommy nodded, his expression serious. "That's why I want a tutor," he said. Slaughter smiled at him.

"Ellie?" Jo's weak voice could be heard from the study. They all went in to see how she was faring. Slaughter lit a lamp.

"How are you, Miss Harris?"

"I think I'm all right. Just a little weak." Then she started to shake her head mournfully. "How could Sam have done it? He's such a good man."

"Good men can have deep feelings," said Slaughter. "His were for Nan Deighton, I think."

Jo began to weep. For Sam. For Nan. And she couldn't share all of her feelings. Tommy fetched her a clean handkerchief.

"Thank you. Would he actually have killed me?"

"It certainly looked that way, Miss Harris. Did you threaten him in some way?"

"I can't imagine how, if I did," she said, her forehead knitting.

"Might you somehow have discovered that he killed Dr. Morton?"

"I don't know. I was thinking about it as we got to Old St. Thomas's. The pin. How did Sam get the pin? But I hadn't yet made the connection."

"What pin?" asked Tommy.

"The one he gave to Nan. He dropped it earlier, at the hospital. It was cheap metal, but quite distinctive. I drew a picture of it, a snake eating its own tail. You saw my drawing, Inspector."

Slaughter nodded. "I did indeed. You can find a vastly inferior sketch of it there on my map."

"So what happened to it?" asked Jo.

"Morton gave it to Mary Simmons, a nurse probationer. Sam stole it back from the nurse probationers' room."

"But how did Morton get it from Nan in the first place?"

Slaughter glanced over at Ellie. So did Tommy. Then Slaughter spoke gently to Jo.

"We think Dr. Morton forced Nan and got her with child. She could have told Sam, or Matron, and ruined his career. He couldn't afford another dismissal like what happened at St. George's Hospital. Nan's toe infection gave Dr. Morton the perfect opportunity to eliminate the whole problem, by using more chloroform than was necessary. So many patients die, he thought no one would notice. Then, since she was dead, he took the pin to give to his next paramour."

Jo looked shocked, frozen like a statue. Tommy ran to get her some brandy. She took a sip, then looked squarely at Slaughter.

"You're saying Sam figured it out. That Morton had gotten Nan with child then killed her?"

"I believe so."

"I had no idea. Nan never said a thing." Jo's voice sounded small and sad.

"I think you'd better get some rest," said Ellie. "Tommy, please go and make up the bedroom upstairs." She almost said "your bedroom," but thought better of it.

Once they'd helped Jo to bed and Ellie began tidying and closing down the house, Tommy followed Slaughter into the study.

"I'm glad it wasn't Cyril. Or Miss Orson," Tommy said.

"Cyril! I almost forgot. I need to return his book. It turned out to be a great help."

"Because it was about a rape?"

"Yes. It's been going through my mind. How men take advantage of women and act as though they own them. Morton did that regularly, but I didn't realize how far he would go."

Slaughter lowered the lamp.

"We found out a lot of things we shouldn't have," said Tommy, shaking his head.

"What do you mean?"

"About Nan, and Miss Orson's medicine, and Cyril, for a start."

"You know about Cyril?" Slaughter knew that Tommy was an awfully worldly twelve years old, but the sexual proclivities of men . . .

"Everyone in the theatre world knows about Cyril," Tommy shrugged. "And you found out Lady Featherstone was an actress once. I'm not sure people want all these things known."

"When there's a murder," said Slaughter, "many things are revealed that people wish weren't known."

They walked into the kitchen, and Tommy sat down with a thud, putting his head in his hands. He looked miserable.

"But poor Sam. They'll hang him, won't they? He was teaching me all about medicine."

Slaughter wanted to point out that Sam had killed Morton, that he was a murderer. That you don't go around murdering people, even when they killed someone you love. That it was the role of the law to punish those who tried to act as their own judge and executioner. That without the law, and its enforcement, humanity would degrade to its basest form.

Instead, he squeezed Tommy's shoulder and said, "I'm so sorry, Tommy."

∽

Bridget had prepared scones especially for the talk at the Women's Reform Club. They looked so delicious that several attendees had tried to help themselves before the talk had even begun.

Ellie stood aside with John Addo, who looked cool and comfortable.

"Thank you so much for agreeing to speak with us tonight," she said.

"You are more than welcome. It will be good to get more support for abolitionist causes."

"Is there anything you need before I introduce you?"

John Addo shook his head and took a breath. "I am ready."

As Ellie mounted the stage and began her introduction, Jo said in a low voice to Tommy, "It's nice to see so many people here." The lad agreed.

Tommy had more time in the evenings now that *Richard III* had closed. He'd spent some of it at the penny gaffs near Covent Garden, naturally. But when Ellie had told him about the speech, he thought he'd come along to help. And even though it had been almost a fortnight since her attempted murder, he wanted to look after Jo.

The two of them had helped arrange the chairs and made sure the small speaker's stage was swept, with the lectern in place and a glass of water handy. Then they'd collected donations at the door.

Ellie finished her introduction and sat down in the front row, next to Slaughter. As John Addo stood, an expectant hush fell over the attendees. He had a stillness about him, a majesty that made one want to look at him and listen to what he said. A powerful presence, thought Slaughter. He'd be good on the stage.

But for now, the stage was for telling his own story. Addo was aware that in addition to friends and well-wishers, owners of various publications were present. Thomas Walker was there from the *Daily Mail*, and Frederick Evans from *Once a Week*. Even *The Times* had sent a reporter.

"I must agree with the American Frederick Douglass, who visited London more than fifteen years ago. Some of you may have attended his speech then, at Finsbury Chapel. He said that slavery is such a strong evil that it takes many nations to root it out. Great Britain was accustomed to benefit from this trade in human flesh, but in recent years has rejected the practice as inhumane. Nonetheless, slavery continues, despite its being outlawed here and in British colonies. And beyond British control, it continues in its most egregious form in America."

John then told the story of being taken as a child on the Gold Coast and how he was rescued by Henry Featherstone. He talked about the daring feats of the West African Squadron. He told of many slaves being returned to the coast of Africa, and how they had remained slaves to the local traders instead of being shipped to America. How he had served Sir Henry and been able to come with him to London.

Many in the audience were moved by John Addo's story. They thought of their own sons and what it would be like if they were taken into slavery. And those who might have doubted Addo's ability to become an Englishman were quickly disabused of that notion. With his education and Sir Henry's support, he had a fulfilling life, he said, even if some might think he had simply traded being a slave for being a servant. The prejudices of his audience, about race, about class, about servitude, were disturbed by the presence of this man.

Tommy nodded in agreement throughout the speech. It was wrong, he thought, to think you could own someone. Wrong to control someone else's life. He thought about Sergeant Honeycutt, whose family had owned slaves. Did it matter if you were nice to your slaves? Yes, but it was still slavery. John Addo had mentioned Frederick Douglass's belief that cruelty was necessary to perpetuate slavery. Without cruel treatment, slaves would gain hope and would rebel. With even a little kindness, they would think of themselves as free. As everyone should be, thought Tommy.

After the speech, club members had moved through the crowd. Money was donated to the American Anti-Slavery Society. Reporters came up to John Addo and asked questions. Ellie could not help but be pleased at the enthusiastic reception of the speaker and the money being raised. But she was still concerned about Jo.

The four of them got into a cab afterward so that Jo could be taken to her boarding house in Shoe Lane before Slaughter, Ellie, and Tommy headed further on to Southwark.

"Are you quite all right?" asked Ellie.

"Yes," said Jo. "And I want to thank all three of you for caring for me during this time. You've all been true friends." She smiled at Tommy especially, who sat up tall.

"You just let us know if you need anything," said Tommy.

Jo left the cab and walked up the steps to the boarding house. The lamp was on low in the parlor. Bridget had returned earlier and was already in her room. Jo could see no light under her door.

She changed into her night clothes, washed her face in the basin, and pulled out the box from under her bed. She again found the picture she'd drawn of Nan.

"I'm sorry, Nan," she said. "I'm sorry that Sam is now in gaol, and will likely go to prison, or worse. He loved you so, Nan. As much as I did. So much that he killed someone, the man who murdered you and your child. I cannot fault him for it, although I know I should."

She poured herself a small glass of port, as she always did before bed. She held up the glass to Nan's picture.

"You've been avenged, Nan. That's got to mean something."

❧

"Have you found a tutor?" Honeycutt asked Tommy at the dinner table. He had begun coming every Sunday. Ellie had insisted.

Tommy had a mouth full of roast mutton but nodded eagerly.

Ellie said, "Cubby found a student who's studying for his London University examinations."

"His name is Samson Light," said Tommy, swallowing. "Isn't that funny? I'll go up to Bloomsbury Mondays and Thursdays to learn from him."

"He'll need to come here if he wants me to feed him," said Ellie.

"What degree is he studying for?" Honeycutt accepted another helping of potatoes from Ellie.

"Biology," said Tommy. "It will be good for studying medicine, later."

"Mr. Light already matriculated, then returned to London for the intermediate examination," explained Slaughter. "He's staying here for his Bachelor's exam, so he's trying to earn his keep. I'm delighted to have found someone associated with the University."

"Cubby likes that they allow anyone to take the examinations, no matter where they've studied," said Ellie.

"So, you can study elsewhere, or even on your own, and still get a degree?" asked Honeycutt.

"Exactly," said Slaughter. "That writer Dickens has called it 'The People's University.'"

"What an excellent idea," said Honeycutt. "Sounds almost American in its democratic intent."

Ellie laughed. "And now Tommy has Cubby running all over town buying books."

"I can't imagine he had to ask twice," said Honeycutt. Now that their first big case was over, he knew that much of Slaughter's spare time was spent reading or shopping for second-hand books.

There was a pause in the conversation as Ellie refilled their drinks, then went into the pantry to fetch dessert.

"Did you go to the sentencing on Thursday?" asked Tommy, quietly. Honeycutt glanced at Slaughter. He didn't know whether this was an appropriate topic, but naturally Tommy had been much affected by Sam's arrest.

"No, I had to follow up on the case of the missing dog," said Honeycutt, hoping to distract him.

Tommy didn't change subjects. "Will he hang?"

Honeycutt looked up, but Ellie was still in the pantry. Slaughter sipped his glass of water.

"I'm afraid so. He killed Dr. Morton, even if in many other ways he was a good man."

"Was it Lord Chief Baron Pollock doing the judging? Jo showed me his picture. He looked very stern."

"No, I don't think so. Oh! Now look at that," said Honeycutt. Ellie had brought in a jam pudding, which she'd baked that afternoon. "That looks delicious, Mrs. Slaughter." This was certainly better than another lonely night at the boarding house. Tastier, too.

When Honeycutt had left for home and Ellie had gone up to bed, Slaughter sat alone in the study and thought about Sam Wetherby and the turn of the criminal mind. Dr. Morton, of course, would not be missed by anyone who had known him personally. But he was missed by those who were in need of his skill. Slaughter wondered whether that mattered, whether the death of an important person, one who had contributed to the advancement of society, was somehow more tragic.

In the classical sense, he thought it was. A tragedy was not merely a sad story. A tragedy, he had taught Tommy, was the story of someone's fall as a result of their overweening pride. Their demise must somehow be the result of their own failings. In the case of ordinary people, this was rarely the case. But some murder victims, like Morton, possessed pride at this classical level. An ancient Greek would have recognized Morton's arrogance, and not only as an able and experienced surgeon. His treatment of people showed his disdain for others. He had possessed an overly strong sense of his own superiority. He could well have caused more pain than he had cured.

Slaughter had to admit he had trouble seeing Sam Wetherby as a criminal, even though he had committed a horrific crime. He reached over to the nearest stack of books, picked up Marcus Aurelius' *Meditations*, and began to read.

Historical Notes

Most of the action in this novel takes place in 1862, a time of great change in English life. A few real-life characters take part in the story.

Mrs. Sarah Wardroper was the first superintendent of the Nightingale School for nurses, having been appointed by Florence Nightingale herself. According to Miss Nightingale: "Her power of organization and of administration, her courage and her discrimination in character were remarkable. She was straightforward, true, upright; she was decided ... Her force of character was extraordinary; her word was law."

Eliza Cook was a poet, born the daughter of a brasier in Southwark. She championed the Chartist cause and rights for women and workers. She was likely lovers with American actress Charlotte Cushman. The poem "A Love Song" appears in *Melaia and Other Poems*, her second published collection, in 1838.

Ebenezer Farrington's *Penny Illustrated Paper* was noted for its fine illustrations despite its cheap price, which was thanks to the use of the new Ingram Rotary Machine to create the engravings.

Elizabeth Garrett, later Elizabeth Garrett Anderson, after much studying and many refusals for medical school, entered the Worshipful Society of Apothecaries after being refused for examination at the University of London. Having obtained her licentiate status, she opened her own practice. She would found the New Hospital for Women and Children in 1872.

Dr. William Guy was a statistician who held a Bachelor's in medicine from Cambridge and was professor of forensic medicine at Kings College. From 1859-1869 he was the Medical Superintendent for Millbank Prison where he emphasized hygiene and diet for prisoner health.

John Locke was Liberal Member of Parliament for Southwark, although to my knowledge he did not open the new hospital.

Sarah Parker Redmon was a free black abolitionist from Massachusetts who came to England to study at University. She gave a speech at the International Congress of Charities, Correction, and Philanthropy, which was held at the International Exhibition in the summer of 1862.

Although the Women's Reform Club was invented, there were many societies of philanthropic women in London engaged in similar causes, including abolitionism, women's health, and female suffrage. Some resided in Red Lion Square.

There is no record of a Ladies' Committee for St. Thomas's Hospital before 1880, but most hospitals and charities had something similar.

The Surrey Theatre during this era transitioned from a circus/variety program to one of melodrama to cater to Southwark working-class audiences.

Nan's toenail surgery was inspired by the true case of Hannah Greene, one of the first patients to die of chloroform anesthesia. In January of 1848, fifteen-year-old Hannah had her toenail removed, a few months after a similar surgery where ether was used. She died within minutes of inhaling the chloroform, leading to investigations about safety and dosage.

The 1862 International Exhibition in Kensington took place on the site of what is now the Science Museum and Natural History Museum. Although not appreciated at the level of the Great Exhibition of 1851 at the Crystal Palace, it was a marvelous collection of culture and technology, and brought to London many visitors from around the world.

St. Thomas's Hospital's herb garret and operating theatre have been preserved in the Old Operating Theatre in Southwark. The operating theatre was rediscovered in 1956 after being boarded up since the move in 1862.

The Royal Surrey Gardens was a park, amusement, and zoo from 1837 until it was closed in 1862. The site was thus available to St. Thomas's Hospital during the construction of the new hospital, now alongside the Thames in Lambeth, across from the Houses of Parliament. Its construction had to wait until the completion of the Albert Embankment in 1869.

There is some controversy about whether Surrey Gardens was a healthier or less healthy location for the hospital. According to the St. Thomas's Hospital report of 1867, fatalities from amputation were lower at the new location. There were complaints, however, of poor ventilation, lack of heating, and lack of water closets. Today's St. Thomas's Hospital, the original building, was built to a design very much in keeping with Miss Nightingale's recommendations.

A note on naming and spelling: St. Thomas's Hospital and St. Thomas's Street are the historic spellings used in most Victorian documents, so they have been retained. Blackfriars Road may be found on some Victorian maps as Great Surrey Street, although the name was changed as early as 1829.

Bibliography

Agha, Riaz and Maliha Agha. "A history of Guy's, King's and St. Thomas' hospitals from 1649 to 2009: 360 Years of innovation in science and surgery." *International Journal of Surgery* 9, no. 5 (2011): 414-427.

Barash, Paul B., ed. *Clinical Anesthesia*. Lippincott Williams & Wilkins, 2009.

"Blackfriars Bridge and Blackfriars Road." In *Survey of London: Volume 22, Bankside (The Parishes of St. Saviour and Christchurch Southwark)*, edited by Howard Roberts and Walter H Godfrey. London: London County Council, 1950.

Bowers, Robert Woodger. *Sketches of Southwark old and new*. London: William Wesley and Son, 1905

The British Almanac of the Society for the Diffusion of Useful Knowledge. London: Knight and Co., 1862.

Chadwick, Jane E. *Bradbury and Evans: An Inky Tale*, 2016. https://www.aninkytale.co.uk

Cook, G.C. and A.J. Webb. "Reactions from the medical and nursing professions to Nightingale's 'reform(s)" of nurse training in the late 19th century." *Postgraduate Medical Journal* 78 (2002):118-123.

Cooke, Simon. "Periodicals of the mid-Victorian period: the physical properties of illustrated magazines." *The Victorian Web*, 2014. https://victorianweb.org/periodicals/cooke.html.

The Diaries of Hannah Cullwick, Victorian Maidervant. Liz Stanley, ed. London: Virago Press, 1984.

Dickens, Catherine Thomson. *What shall we have for dinner? By lady Maria Clutterbuck*. United Kingdom: n.p., 1852.

Douglass, Frederick. "Reception Speech. At Finsbury Chapel, Moorfields, England, May 12, 1846 & Dr Campbell's Reply." *My Bondage and My Freedom*. Lit2Go Edition, 1855.

Engineering Timelines: The Bridges of London. http://www.engineering-timelines.com/why/bridgesOfLondon/bridgesLondon_08.asp.

Evelyn Tables. Royal College of Surgeons of England, 1646. http://surgicat.rcseng.ac.uk/Details/collect/10201

Fares for hackney carriages, and distances within a circle of four miles radius from Charing Cross, measured by authority of the Commissioner of Police. With an abstract of the laws relating to the fares, hiring of hackney carriages, and misconduct of drivers. Published by authority of the Commissioner of Metropolitan Police by C. Knight, 1866. At Hathi Trust.

Fitzharris, Lindsay. *The Butchering Art: Joseph Lister's Quest to Transform the Grisly World of Victorian Medicine*. New York: Scientific America / Farrar, Straus and Giroux, 2017.

Flanders, Judith. *The Victorian House*. London: Harper Perennial, 2003.

Ford, Martin. "Gangs of Baltimore." *Humanities* 29, no. 3 (May/June 2008).

Graves, Charles. *The Story of St. Thomas's 1106-1947*. London: Faber and Faber, 1947.

Griffin, Rachael. "Detective Policing and the State in Nineteenth-century England: The Detective Department of the London Metropolitan Police, 1842-1878" (2015). Electronic Thesis and Dissertation Repository, 3427.

Griffin, Richard. "Letter: Poor-Law Medical Reform". *British Medical Journal*, May 24, 1862.

Heywood, Thomas. *The Rape of Lucrece*, Edited by Bailey, Chris, ed. 1638 text.

Hudson, Derek. *Munby, Man of Two Worlds: The Life and Diaries of Arthur J. Munby 1828-1910*. J. Murray, 1972.

The Illustrated London News, volume 41, 1862.

The International Exhibition of 1862 : the illustrated catalogue of the Industrial Department, 1862, Internet Archive.

Journal of the Royal Institute of British Architects. United Kingdom: The Institute, 1903.

Kelly's Post Office Guide to London in 1862, Visitor's Handbook to the Metropolis, and Companion to the Directory. London: Kelly & Co., 1862.

Kidd, Charles. *On chloroform in midwifery practice*. University of Glasgow, 1864. Wellcome Collection.

Knight, Paul R. and Douglas R. Bacon; "An Unexplained Death: Hannah Greener and Chloroform". *Anesthesiology* 96 (2002): 1250–1253.

London and Its Environs: A Practical Guide to the Metropolis and Its Vicinity. Edinburgh: Adam & Charles Black, 1862.

London Meeting, *National Association for the Promotion of Social Science* (England), 1862.

Loudon, I. "Why are (male) surgeons still addressed as Mr?." *BMJ* (Clinical research ed.) 321, no. 7276 (2000): 1589-91.

Marin, George Whitney, *Verdi in America: Oberto Through Rigoletto*. New York: University of Rochester Press, 2011.

Matnon, Jo. *Elizabeth Garrett Anderson*. New York: E. P. Dutton & Co., Inc., 1965.

Mayhew, Henry. *London Labour and the London Poor*. London: George Woodfall and Son, 1851.

McDonald, Lynn. *Florence Nightingale: A Reference Guide to Her Life and Works*. United States: Rowman & Littlefield Publishers, 2019.

McInnes, E. M. *St. Thomas' Hospital*. 2nd Enlarged Edition. London: Special Trustees for St. Thomas' Hospital, 1990.

Medical Act, 1850. Retrieved from https://www.legislation.gov.uk/ukpga/Vict/21-22/90/contents/enacted.

Old St Thomas' Hospital, *A-Z of Herbs: A Historical Compendium, The Old Operating Theatre Museum and Garret*, 2020. Retrieved from https://oldoperatingtheatre.com/old-st-thomas-hospital-a-z-of-herbs-a-historical-compendium/.

The Proceedings of the Old Bailey, 1674-1913. Accessed at https://www.oldbaileyonline.org/.

Remond, Sarah Parker." The Negroes in the United States." January 1, 1862. Iowa State University, Archives of Women's Political Communication.

Ritchie, J. Ewing. *The Night Side of London*. London: William Tweedie, 1858.

Robinson, Victor. *Victory Over Pain: A History of Anesthesia*. New York: Henry Schuman, 1946.

Routledge's Popular Guide to London and Its Suburbs, with original illustrations and map. London: Routledge, Warne, & Routledge, 1862.

Russell, William. *Autobiography of a London Detective, by "Waters"*. New York: Dick & Fitzgerald, c1864. At Hathi Trust.

"St Thomas' Hospital", in *Survey of London: Volume 23, Lambeth: South Bank and Vauxhall*, Howard Roberts and Walter H Godfrey, eds. London, 1951.

Snow, John. "On the fatal cases of inhalation of chloroform." *Edinburgh Medical and Surgical Journal* (1 July 1849): 75-87.

Snow, Stephanie. *Blessed Days of Anaesthesia*. Second edition. Oxford: Oxford University Press, 2008.

Snow, Stephanie. *Operations Without Pain: The Practice and Science of Anaesthesia in Victorian Britain*. Hampshire: Palgrave Macmillan, 2006.

"The University of London: The University," in *A History of the County of Middlesex: Volume 1, Physique, Archaeology, Domesday, Ecclesiastical Organization, the Jews, Religious Houses, Education of Working Classes To 1870, Private Education From Sixteenth Century*, ed. J. S. Cockburn, H. P. F. King and K. G. T. McDonnell (London: Victoria County History, 1969).

The World's Guide to London in 1862, by Day and by Night. London: Darton & Hodge, 186